Hard Luck Story

Hard Luck Story

Richard Haley

ROBERT HALE · LONDON

ISBN 978-0-7198-1082-4

Robert Hale Limited
Clerkenwell House
Clerkenwell Green
London EC1R 0HT

www.halebooks.com

For Mary with love

Typeset in 10½/14½pt New Century Schoolbook
by Derek Doyle & Associates, Shaw Heath
Printed in the UK by the Berforts Group

ONE

He left the off-licence with his bottles clinking in a plastic bag. It had been a nuisance having to come out so late but he was out of vodka and he badly needed a drink. He'd had a long hard day and hadn't finished dinner till nine. He knew that if he didn't have a couple of drinks he'd not sleep. Not that he'd get more than three or four hours' sleep anyway, with the things he had on his mind.

The little shop was on the main road and he'd not been able to park there because of the yellow lines. He walked a few yards along the road and then turned left on to the quiet back street where he'd left his car. On the point of pressing the key fob to unlock the doors a hand grasped his shoulder. Someone said softly, 'Just before you get in these posh wheels, pal, we need to spend a few minutes with you, OK?'

Mellors froze, his heart pounding, his mouth suddenly dry. 'Who . . . who are you?' he said hoarsely.

'No one you need to know, pal.'

The hand grasping Mellors's shoulder felt like a vice, but he managed to half turn his head to see that there were two stocky men standing behind him, both wearing balaclavas. The second man said, 'You can make this nice and easy for yourself, Mellors, or you can make it very hard.'

The first man chuckled. 'Even nice and easy won't be all that easy, pal, but it'll be a bloody sight better than very hard, believe it.'

Mellors was shaking so badly he could barely control his voice. 'What . . . what do you, what do you *want* from me? I'll give you all the money I have on me—'

'We know you've got plenty of folding, pal, but it's not about smackeroonies. We're here because orders have come down from the big boss. We don't know who he is but I reckon you do.'

Mellors felt as if his guts were filling with iced water. 'I'll . . . I'll go and see him . . . see what's on his mind.'

'I've been told that what's on his mind, pal, is you not doing what you're told. The big boss gets very twitchy, so I hear, when folk won't take orders.'

'I'll go and see him,' Mellors repeated. 'If he's upset I'll talk it all through with him.'

'Too late, pal. They tell me the big boss doesn't go in for too much talking. They tell me his way is to give orders that he likes to see carried out PDQ, know what I'm saying?'

'The big boss might think we're doing too much talking as it is, Switch,' the second man warned.

'You're right, Danny. This guy's a right one for the chat.'

'I'll do it!' Mellors cried. 'All right, I didn't want to do it but I will. Just don't knock me about.'

The man called Switch removed the bag quite gently from Mellors's trembling hand and laid it carefully on the ground at the side of the car. 'The problem is, Mellors, you didn't do whatever it is you haven't done when the big boss *wanted* it done. And this is so you don't make the same mistake again, right.' He then gave Mellors a blow in the belly with a fist that felt as hard as a brick.

Screaming with pain, Mellors doubled over, hands clutching himself where he'd taken the blow. The man called Danny now seized him by the shoulders and forced him to the ground, laying him at right angles to the car. Mellors glanced round desperately; there had to be someone in one of those terraced houses who could see him being attacked. But it was dark and late and if anyone had seen anything it looked as if they weren't prepared to do anything about it.

The men began to give Mellors a kicking. They were experts. It quickly became clear they'd been told to leave his head untouched and to be careful not to break anything. They kicked his buttocks and his thighs, his back and his upper arms. They wore only track shoes but to Mellors they felt like boots; he'd never known such carefully calculated pain. The kicking abruptly ceased afer a couple of minutes, by which time he'd drawn into himself as tightly as possible. His breath was coming in short ragged bursts and his face was drenched in tears.

'OK, that's it, pal,' Switch grunted. 'You want my advice, the next time the big boss wants something done, don't argue the toss, just do it, know what I'm saying? No hard feelings, me and Danny, we're just paid muscle. We have to do what we're told, same as you.' He picked up the plastic bag, which held the vodka. 'What do you want me to do with your bottles? Tell you what, I'll plonk them on the passenger seat, right. You'll need a stiff one when you get home, course you will. All the best, pal. Let's hope we don't have to meet like this again, eh.'

The men went silently off along the dark street and a short time later, from his cocoon of pain, Mellors heard an engine fire. He very slowly got himself to his feet, wincing and yelping, and began to ease himself, very carefully, into his Jaguar. He took one of the bottles of vodka, opened it and took a gulp. He'd have taken several more but he couldn't risk losing his licence on top of everything else. He sat for a good ten minutes until he could trust his aching limbs to drive safely. Fortunately, it was an automatic so he only needed one leg to cope with the controls as he drove slowly home.

She lived in Bingley. Bingley was part of the Bradford metropolitan area but it wasn't exactly a district. It kept the atmosphere of what it had once been; a village situated some miles outside Bradford on the road that ran north to the Dales. The Mellors's house was a very large detached, stone-built and gabled and standing in a quiet avenue on the side of a hill. The front garden was well tended, with close-cut lawns and seasonal flowers in the beds. It looked as if Mellors was nicely placed; Bingley houses weren't cheap. Crane sighed. There'd have to be a bit of money about for Mellors's wife to be able to afford a PI.

Crane didn't like domestics and these days he was in a position to pick and choose, but he still found it difficult to turn work, any work, away when he thought of his arduous early days doing private cases. He rang the front door bell. The door was opened promptly. She'd probably been looking out for him. In a nervous state, maybe, as women in this situation usually were. 'Mr Crane? Do come in. What a big strong man you look to be.' She gave a little giggle and led him along a hall and into a front room. It was large and square and gave further proof that the Mellors were comfortably off: floral tie-back curtains, Persian-patterned hearth rug, a stone fireplace with an ornate laquered screen, a modern three-piece suite, an elegant drinks table against a back wall, Impressionist prints in gold frames. Crane had been in so many family rooms in his lengthy career that he could take in and evaluate decor at a glance.

'Please sit down, Mr Crane. Or can I call you Frank?'

'Please do.'

'I'm Josie.'

'How can I help you, Josie?'

'As I said on the phone, husband trouble.'

'You think he might be having an affair?'

'I'm damn sure he is, the bastard.' She gave another giggle. It might have been a nervous reaction but she came over as completely self-possessed.

'What makes you so sure?'

'I do hope you're shock-proof,' she said, smiling widely.

'With the work I do I have to be.'

'The bastard's an S&M freak.'

'How do you know?'

'Because I'm the one who belts his arse with a cane till he can

8

hardly sit down.' She giggled yet again.

Crane had come across many examples of human oddity in his time but S&M was a first. He wondered if Josie, too, had a taste for the cane on what looked to be, as he'd followed her into the room, a shapely and attractive bottom. 'I have to confess that I indulge as well,' she told him, as if guessing what he was thinking, 'but he goes easy on me. Nothing like the whacking I give him. It makes the sex mind-blowing, even if Tony has to sit down *very* carefully for the next day or two.'

Crane smiled. She wore jeans and a sleeveless cotton top in pale blue and it was disturbingly easy to imagine her slender body naked, cane expertly wielded. She had very fair hair, almost blonde, and very sleek, which she wore long. It seemed almost dated, like that of an actress in one of the old black and white films, yet it suited her perfectly. The impression of glamour was enhanced by the things she could do with her eyes. She watched Crane now in a sort of demure yet knowing way, as if inviting him to envy the pleasure she took in her unusual sex life. Her other features went with the eyes: full lips, well-shaped nose, defined cheekbones. She had a curious little-girl type of voice. It seemed quite natural but gave a faintly unnerving effect of a child living in an adult sexy body.

'I think I have shocked you after all, haven't I?' she said.

He shook his head. 'It's not something I've come across before, to be honest, but I have *read* about Ken Tynan and Ian Fleming. Is the S&M connected to your husband's possible affair?'

'He went out just over a week ago, saying we'd run out of voddy. He was gone quite a long time. When he got back we had a couple of drinks. I could see he was sitting carefully. I knew what that meant, I've had a *lot* of experience. But it was nothing to do with me; we'd not had a cane session for at least three months. In fact, he seemed to be going off it. With little Josie, anyway.'

She picked up a handbag that lay on a side table. 'When we went to bed he got into his pyjamas while I was in the en-suite.

9

When we got into bed I tried to get him excited but he said he'd had a long day and was too tired. He fell asleep very quickly, he must have taken a tablet. I still had my bedside lamp on and I pulled down his pyjama pants a little. His arse was black and blue. I took a photo with the instamatic.' She opened the handbag and passed Crane some prints. It really was a very badly bruised bottom. 'So he had been playing away, you see. A nice S&M session and some first-class rumpy-pumpy that should have been mine.'

She flashed him that demure but knowing grin and gave her habitual giggle. Crane looked again at the photo. There was something odd about it – apart from the oddness of anyone wanting to seek out such pain in the first place. 'These marks don't look like the strokes of a cane,' he said in a musing tone.

'Tony makes do,' she said. 'We were once on holiday and he'd forgotten to pack his cane. But he had a tripod with him, you know one of those things you stick a camera on, so I belted him with that. Brought up the same kind of bruises. I suppose he had to make do with his girlfriend, seeing as she probably wouldn't have a cane about her.'

He studied the photo a third time. If Tony Mellors had had his bottom beaten the beater had made an extremely thorough job of it. There was no definition to the strokes; each buttock looked to be covered by one great bruise. Whatever implement had been used could it really have produced such damage? And who could have inflicted it? Could any woman have been talked so readily into wreaking such pain? A prostitute might have done it, of course, if the price had been right.

'Look, Josie, there can't be too many women who want to get involved in S&M sessions, and this is one hell of a beating. It could be he hired a call girl to do it.'

She shook her head firmly. 'Not Tony. He's not a prostitute man. And not one to get involved, either. I watch him too carefully for that. One night stands, well, no problem there. We've got what you call an open marriage. But getting his backside belted, that's going too far. That's just for us, our thing, and if he's started wanting it elsewhere that's bad news. And in any case, how would a tom have the expertise to tan his bum like I do?'

It was a valid point. With such refined skills available in-house why fork out for a call girl? It looked as if it had to be a girlfriend who cared enough about him to give him his heart's desire of a really enjoyable thrashing.

Crane turned over the top photo of the two or three he was holding, expecting to find more of the same. Instead he found the next one to be a print of Josie. She was naked and the photo was taken from behind with the focus on her bottom. It was a very fine bottom. If bottoms had been graded like hotels it would have gone straight into the five-star bracket. A slender waist gave on to buttocks that looked to be satiny but firm and perfectly rounded.

'Oh, silly me!' she broke out. 'That must have got in by mistake. We did some before and after snaps one night, you know, before and after the cane. I suppose you'll want to see the after one now, won't you, you naughty man?'

'No.' He handed the photos back to her. 'I prefer the view without the cane marks.' He glanced at his watch. 'I have to move on, Josie. If you want to engage me I'll run through my charges.' He did so but she barely seemed to listen, her eyes never leaving his with a lingering smile. She was indifferent to the bottom line and shrugged. 'He'll be paying, Frank, I'll make sure of that.'

'If I do find that he is having an affair what do you intend to do about it? Had you thought about that?'

'I'd kill him,' she giggled.

He smiled. He'd heard similar words before, several times. 'I could murder the swine, the way I've helped his business and brought up his kids.' Women could be very bitter, understandably, as they were usually the ones picking up the pieces, but he'd never known any of them to find a husband being unfaithful as amusing as Josie did. But then, he'd never known

11

anyone like Josie before.

'What's Tony's job, Josie?'

'He works for the council. Planning department. He's gone a long way and done very well. Can't fault the lad for hard work. That's how we met. I was working for some solicitors as a PA. They'd send me off to do those document searches cheaply that they charge the client top whack for. Tony was working his way through the departments at the time.'

'Can you give me a rundown on his working day?'

'Not easy. He moves around a lot. He's involved in the big development schemes, you know, where they pull bits of the city down and re-build. He spends a lot of time with builders; we've both been to some nice dinners builders give when they're lobbying for a new scheme.'

'Perhaps one morning I'll park along the drive and shadow his car.'

She looked sceptical. 'Wouldn't it be better to see where he goes in the evening when he's supposed to be working late?'

'If Tony *is* being unfaithful, he could be fitting in a rendezvous during the working day. I once shadowed a man to Baildon Moor at lunchtime. I caught him having leg-over and chips in the back of his company car.'

She gave a little shriek of laughter and tossed her long sleek hair. 'Leg-over and chips! I like it. It sounds a lot of fun. Are you a leg-over and chips man, Frank?'

'The work I do is so demanding, I'm sometimes lucky if I can find time for lunch at all.'

'What a pity! I can't get over how big and strong you look. Your feet must pop out at the bottom of the duvet.'

'I've . . . got a bed a little longer than normal.'

'Makes me wonder what else might pop out from under the duvet.'

There was no answer to that, not if he didn't want to encourage her. He knew when he was getting the come-on, especially when it was written on the wall in block capitals. The

Mellors had an open marriage and blind eyes were turned to one-night stands as long as they didn't turn into anything serious and affect proprietorial rights over swishing canes and stinging bottoms.

But Crane made it a general rule not to get involved with clients in these sorts of situations. It could become complicated and it was best to keep it professional.

'He leaves the house at eight, Frank. I just hope for his sake he's not taking you to Baildon Moor on a daily basis.'

He detected a genuine note of menace in that jokey, little-girl voice and though she came across as a fun-loving scatterbrain he sensed there was a lot riding on keeping Mellors free of involvement. She appeared not to work and looked to enjoy a lavish lifestyle. If things went wrong and Mellors cleared off he guessed Josie would drive a hard bargain in a divorce settlement: the house, an allowance, half the investments and pension rights. He said, 'Have you got a photo of Tony I could have?'

'I can find one,' she said, grinning. 'That picture of his arse won't get you very far, will it?' She went off to another room, wiggling that alluring bottom with great skill, and returned with a seven-by-four-inch photograph taken in clear light of Mellors standing by a Jaguar. The man came as something of a surprise. He had very ordinary looks, with thinning brown hair and plain features. He gave Crane an indefinable impression of being a man who *would* work in the public sector, not exactly a jobsworth but someone who sought security, a clear working structure and a pension based on final salary. It was near impossible to picture him giving Josie the cane.

'This will do fine,' he said. 'I can keep it?'

'That might be best, before I'm tempted to throw darts at it.'

'I'll be on my way then, Josie. I'll get back to you if and when I've anything to report.'

'Oh, don't rush off! How about a coffee? Let's get to know each other a little.'

That demure but sexy look was working overtime. 'I'm sorry, but I have another appointment in fifteen minutes.'

'Next time you come you must leave an hour free. I'll pay, of course.'

'I doubt I'd have anything to report that would take an hour.'

'I'm quite sure we'd be able to fill the time.'

Maybe, he thought, as he got in his car, just maybe. She really was very attractive and if the one-night stand rule applied it was unlikely to get complicated. And it wasn't going to be easy to get that picture of her soft pearly bottom out of his mind. He smiled and waved to her as she stood at the door. He guessed that, as the Mellors had an open marriage, he'd always have an open invitation to Josie's open thighs.

They moved steadily along the footpath. It was sunny and there was a breeze and it gave Melanie a feeling of well-being. The moor always did, especially when she was with Damien.

They drew abreast of the Cow and Calf rocks and could see in the distance the rooftops of Burley Woodhead. They stood by the landmark for some time in silence, both, it seemed, exulting in the light and the wind and the sky's blue dome.

'I used to see myself hiking across Ilkley Moor with you when I needed a break from swotting,' he said.

'You can't have had too many breaks from swotting, not to get a double top.'

'It was a fluke. I had the luck to hit on the right areas to concentrate on.'

'Well, you can call it a fluke, but I call it slogging hard work by one very bright guy.'

He gave a wry grin. 'I had absolutely no distractions. No worries of any kind. All it needed was for me to sit down with the text books.'

'Oh, come on, Demmy—'

'I feel a bit . . . kind of guilty, Mel. The others will have all this debt to face when they leave uni. It'll be essential to take part-time work in the holidays to bring a few bob in. If they want to get married they'll have to find a chunk of money as a down payment on a house and take on a big mortgage. I've had none of that. Dad's covered all my tuition fees. He bought Mollie and Peter a house when they got married and he's going to buy us one when we settle down. And he bought me that motor on the road down there. It just seemed the very least I could do was work hard for a decent degree.'

They began to walk along the track again that sloped down to join the road skirting the moor. Melanie said, 'We can't choose the conditions we're born into. How many young men with your background would have worked as hard as you've done?'

He nodded, the wind ruffling his auburn hair, but he still looked slightly ill at ease. Melanie knew, if she was honest with herself, that it was a source of some relief to her that they wouldn't need to face life together with a burden of debt. She, too, was at university and she'd not graduate until next year, but she'd fallen for Damien before ever knowing how wealthy his background was. And she knew how conscious of it he was. She'd known him long enough now to know how genuinely he cared about people who came from modest backgrounds and had to face all the financial problems he'd been spared. She said, 'Will you try for an internship?'

'I'd love to. Dad could fix it, natch, he knows so many people. But lately I've begun to think I should go into some kind of business. Banking, building, the retail trade, whatever. Just to get a feel for what the business world is really like. You read of so many MPs who go straight from uni into an internship doing research and then straight into politics. I'd like to have a hands-on grasp of the private sector before I tried for a seat myself. I could work for the Party in my spare time.'

Down on the road they could see Damien's maroon sports car parked in a layby. Melanie thought every day how lucky she'd been to meet Damien, who never took his background for granted, and to be so happy with him. Life was now so full of

15

promise with money enough for them both to fulfil their potential. She knew there'd be a debit side, which would mean having a husband who'd be working such long hours, especially if he was successful in becoming an MP. But all that was a long time in the future. In the meantime they could simply revel in being young and having fun.

'Demmy, what does your father actually do?'

'That's the sixty-four-thousand-euro question,' he said with a twisted grin. 'I really wish I knew. He works from an office in a modern block in Well Street and spends long hours in it. It seems to be something to do with pulling old buildings down and putting new buildings up, but he's not actually a builder. Just seems to organize things and set up deals. He knows all the builders and has a lot to do with the town planning department. He also has some obscure connection to importing and exporting goods. But how he actually *makes* all that money is beyond me. I've asked him about it many times but he has a knack of talking about it that seems to leave you knowing less than when you started.

She nodded. Brendon Docherty was a lovely man but he did tend to fill the air with cheerful sounds that never seemed to have much at the centre. She remembered the few casual questions she'd put to him herself that after a few minutes of jovial chat had told her nothing. Nothing, anyway, that could be pinned down. He never gave an impression of being deliberately evasive and Melanie wondered if the secretiveness was something to do with the delicate and complex deals he probably worked on and had now become second nature. Well, it took all sorts and what she did know was that he had a genuine affection for her and that she was getting to be very fond of him.

Damien said, 'When do you start at the crisp factory?'

'Next Monday, I'm afraid.'

'We'll make the most of this week, then.'

She might have a boyfriend from a wealthy family but they'd not be married or living together for at least another year and in

the meantime she needed to earn some money to cover her
student expenses. She knew Damien would have helped her if
she'd asked, but she hadn't asked and she knew he respected her
independence.

She said, 'You'll be working for the Party, I suppose.'

He nodded. 'Stuffing envelopes, helping with the bring and
buys, running errands. One of those general dogsbodies without
which the Party couldn't survive.'

He walked a little ahead of her on a narrow part of the track.
He was tall and broad and lean. She wondered if the senior Party
members had sensed they could have a winner one day in him. A
first-class degree, clean looks, outgoing, a hard worker,
dedicated, sound background. Surely when he'd served his time
knocking on doors and gaining business experience and
maturing into his mid to late twenties, he would be eased into a
safe seat. And if he got into the Commons, with his brain and
capacity for hard work, where would it end? It was all so
exciting.

Crane shadowed Tony Mellors from his home to his office. The
extensive planning department was no longer housed in the
town hall itself, though Mellors appeared to have a desk there or
possibly an office, which seemed to indicate the seniority of his
position. Mellors parked his car in one of the handful of
contracted spaces in the multi-storey adjoining the Norfolk
Gardens Hotel. The car was a Jaguar XF. Crane was already
wondering how a council official, even at a senior level, could run
to a motor that from memory he could put a number on just
slightly south of forty thousand pounds. Then there was the
Bingley house, which had to be in the four to five hundred K
bracket, with, in the drive, Josie's gleaming new automatic Clio.

Crane also parked in the multi-storey and studied Mellors as
he walked from his car to the stairway. He wore a dark-grey
worsted suit with a fine pinstripe, a pale-blue cotton shirt and a
dark-red silk tie. His black shoes were of leather and looked as if

they'd be as comfortable as a pair of slippers. Crane could price the rig-out at many hundreds of pounds.

But he had to remind himself that he'd not been set on to scrutinize Mellors's life-style; his instructions were simply to *cherchez la femme*. But he couldn't help wondering how a man in Mellors's position could afford such a comfortable existence. Having seen him into the town hall he'd passed on to other work until lunchtime when he'd come back to see if he was able to check where Mellors went for lunch. At twenty to one, Mellors emerged from the town hall's main entrance. He was with a woman and Crane, strolling casually on the opposite side of the road, gave a faint smile. He wondered if this meant he'd *retrouvé la femme*. The pair walked the short distance across the town centre to a pub at the bottom of Hustlergate. Crane idled outside for a few minutes then drifted in casually himself. The pair were sitting on a banquette at a small table. Mellors had before him what looked to be a Scotch and soda while the woman sipped an orange juice. Crane eased himself on to a stool at the bar, which was angled in a way that gave him a sidelong view of the couple. He ordered a tuna salad and a half of lager and he studied Mellors and the woman with what appeared to be cursory glances as he turned the pages of the *Daily Mail*.

The woman wore a dark jacket and trousers with an ivory cotton shirt that had a pleated stand collar. She had short brown. well-tended hair. She was not unattractive but she had plain looks and her appearance could only be described as homely, though she did have quite a good figure from what he could judge beneath the office clothes.

To Crane's mind the situation was unusual. Men cheating on their wives tended to go for lookers, women who had hair that cascaded and noses that wrinkled very prettily. And Mellors had an attractive wife, a wife who was keen on sex and would thrash his backside to order. Had this woman acquired that kind of mastery of the cane? He found it difficult to imagine. The bruises on Mellors's bottom that Josie had photographed had very much given the impression of a botch job. A beating that had certainly not shown the kind of precision that could be obtained with a cane. Perhaps, as Josie had said, Mellors's girlfriend had had to make do and mend, letting fly with any suitable object that came to hand, a broom handle, a folded fishing-rod, a loose chair leg.

That's if this woman *was* the girlfriend. Maybe she was simply an office colleague, someone he worked with and treated to a pub lunch now and then. Both Mellors and the woman looked to be exactly what they were; council officers who were totally reliable and highly regarded in the sort of secure, dull environment the public sector tended to provide.

Behind his paper Crane pulled a wry face. He was instinctively pigeon-holing them. But this same Mellors had his bizarre sexual arrangements and a very lavish life-style. How did these things gel with the nondescript looks, the thinning hair, the unimpressive frame, the public sector production line?

Talking quietly, the couple ate their scampi dishes. Then they sat for a further ten minutes before getting up to go. On their way back they parted, the woman to return to the town hall, Mellors to retrieve his car. He then drove the short distance up Manchester Road to Tennyson House, which contained the planning department. Crane supposed Mellors would spend the rest of the day here and if that was the case he himself could return later to check on where he went after work.

But, though Mellors parked at Tennyson House, he didn't leave the car. As Crane watched from a visitor's parking spot, a young woman came out of the office complex with a thick file, which she fed in through Mellors's car window with a smile. Mellors then drove off directly, apparently in a tight timeframe. Crane had had a cancelled appointment and so had a little time to spare. He decided to shadow Mellors a bit longer to see what he did next.

What he did next was strange. He drove on a route that took him along Manningham Lane and beyond the park to a district called Frizinghall. Here he turned left on to a side road. It was a cul-de-sac as woodland cut it off at the top. Crane continued on the main road for a short distance, parked in another side road, then walked quickly back to the road Mellors had taken. Mellors's Jaguar was parked outside a large terraced house. Moving more slowly now as if just taking a stroll Crane walked along the road on the opposite side to where Mellors had parked.

Mellors was standing just outside the door of the house. There was an elderly woman at the door and as Crane drifted past he saw her hand him a brown-paper parcel. She was smiling and Mellors looked to be thanking her effusively. Crane passed on and walked into the wood a short distance along an earth track. Glancing behind him he saw Mellors getting back into his car. When he'd rejoined the main road, Crane returned to where he'd parked his own car. He'd not now be able to get back on to Mellors's tail, but he hadn't in any case got any time left to devote to the man. He would continue to check him out over lunchtimes and early evenings. There was an outside chance that the woman he'd spent this lunchtime with could be the woman in question, unlikely as it seemed.

Crane was puzzled. Why would Mellors be picking up a parcel himself? Wasn't it one of those menial tasks he could have off-loaded on to a junior? There was also something about the old lady handing the parcel to Mellors that rang a distant and uncertain bell in his memory. A bell that had a decidedly sinister chime.

TWO

Melanie stood on the production line watching the potato crisps flow slowly past her. Her job was to remove any that had come from a blemished vegetable, so that the crisps that were bagged up further along were all perfect. It was mind-numbing work but the money was decent and she'd been told she'd be transferring to the office next week. The work would include filing, checking invoices and answering the phone. That wouldn't provide much mental stimulus either but it would be a vast improvement on seeking out dodgy crisps.

She wondered what Damien would be doing today. Something to do with Party activities, no doubt. They were having a bring-and-buy sale at the end of the holiday season and she guessed he would be calling on Party members to ask if there were any items they'd care to contribute. She gave a little smile. He had such charm, such an engaging manner, that she was sure he'd come back with a full boot.

As the crisps moved steadily past her she could daydream with the unengaged part of her mind about being on the moor on that fine sunny day last week. She wondered if one day they'd walk up there with their own children and pass on to them the pleasure they'd always got from that great open sweep of land.

She glanced at the clock. This was the sort of work in which five minutes seemed like half an hour. But after this year she'd not be doing these kinds of jobs any more. Next year she'd

21

graduate and when she left uni she and Damien would live together, first in rented accommodation until they'd found exactly the kind of house they wanted. She'd been so incredibly lucky. They'd not need to go through that slog of working up from a poky starter home. Because of Mr Docherty's generosity they'd be able to move directly into a house large enough to have spare bedrooms for guests or for when children came along.

She wondered if she was beginning to take it for granted, the comfortable existence she could look forward to with Damien. But she shouldn't forget that before she'd met him she'd totally accepted that she'd have the same sort of future as her friends: fees to be paid, deposits to be found, being thirty at the earliest before she could think of children. Well, there'd be none of that now and she was beginning to be affected by Damien's slight sense of guilt that she'd have none of those problems. And, again like Damien, she felt there'd be a payback time. She was determined to make herself an ambitious and forward-looking teacher, keen to give to society the benefit of her hard work and the skills she'd develop along the way.

It still seemed too easy, though, when she'd never have to worry about the size of the gas bill.

At lunchtime, taking off their overalls, Melanie and Becky walked down the road to the local pub in their jeans and T-shirts. Becky was a woman of about her own age who'd shown Melanie how to go about the work on the production line. As they ate their sandwiches and sipped soft drinks, Melanie said, 'I suppose I'm standing in for someone who's on holiday.'

Becky drew down the corners of her mouth. 'You can bet Linda *wishes* she was on holiday. . . .'

Melanie gave her a questioning glance as the other woman finished her Coke. She watched Melanie for a short time in silence. 'Linda's getting over being duffed up,' she said. She put a finger to her lips. 'Not a dicky-bird back at the works, Mel, she's cracked on to Ronnie she's had a fall in the shower.'

'I'll not say a word to anyone, but . . . duffed up. . . ?'

'It's the reptile who minds her.' Becky watched her in another silence. 'She's on the game in her spare time. Needs the money to see to her debts. She got into debt because she took a loan from the wrong bloke. The boyfriend's a wrong'un as well, wants most of the money she makes from her tricks and is in with a lot of other wrong'uns. He gave her a belting something chronic over the weekend.'

'Oh, Becky, how *awful*!'

Becky smiled sourly. 'It'll be an eye-opener for you, how the other half lives, coming from a nice home down Crow Tree.'

'I'm from a very ordinary background. I do know these things happen and I really am very sorry about Linda.'

'No, you're in a different carry-on to ours at the crisp place. I bet you're at the university, aren't you? But you've no edge, I'll say that for you.'

Melanie smiled, glad she could be considered to have no edge. She genuinely liked Becky, who'd been friendly and outgoing from the start in her rough and ready way. She had untidy blonde hair, which needed attention at the roots, and though pretty had the sort of *jolie-laide* looks that went with her youthful vigour and were unlikely to last. She was working overtime so that she and her plumber boyfriend could scrape together a down-payment for a small house, like most of the young people in the country who were lucky enough to actually be in work. 'We'll need to be there five years before I dare let myself get knocked up,' she'd said in resignation. 'Ma had already had two kids before she was my age.'

'It's such a difficult time we're going through,' Melanie said, feeling the inevitable prick of guilt. 'The recession and inflation and all the prices going up.'

'Tell me about it. You'll know you're born when you pack it in at the university. You'll have to pay the money back for being there, won't you?'

Melanie nodded, putting on a rueful face. She didn't want to give Becky the slightest impression of the debt-free future she could look forward to.

'I do hope Linda is better soon. Some men are just dreadful. She should go to the police.'

'The bogies'll just see it as a domestic and might get round to doing something about it a week on Monday. She'd not go near the bogies anyway. She knows what she'd get then would put her in the A and E.'

'Oh, Becky, I can't bear to think about it.'

'Hello.'

'It's me, Jason, Frank Crane.'

'How're you doing, guv?'

'I'm fine. It's about a bloke called Tony Mellors. I'd like you to look into his background. The usual stuff: salary, savings, mortgage, etc. He works in the council planning department and if you could get some kind of a fix on what he actually does it would be a big help.'

'Got his hand caught in the till?'

'He'd have his work cut out. But he does seem to be living a bit high on the hog unless he's got private means. Home's a big place in Bingley.' Crane gave him the address.

'Leave it with me, guv. I'll get back in forty-eight.'

'Just while you're on, Jase, the bloke's wife thinks he's having it off elsewhere. That's what I've been hired to find out. Well, I may have found the bit on the side, but there are other things about him that are looking a bit odd, apart from the expensive lifestyle. Yesterday I caught him calling on an old lady who handed him a brown-paper parcel. I couldn't see why he'd not sent a messenger to pick it up if it was something to do with the department, but if the parcel was his and had been misdirected why hadn't the old lass got the Post Office to sort it out? It rang some kind of bell I can't quite put my finger on.'

Jason was silent for a few seconds. 'I guess I know what rang the bell, guv. We're talking fifteen, twenty years back when there was that business of drugs being sent through the post. Some of

24

our Asian friends were getting heroin and cocaine in smallish quantities concealed in innocent-looking packets, such as cylindrical magazine containers, that kind of thing. It was a nice earner for a while but the police nailed it in the end and it all went quiet.'

'Ah, I remember. I was in the CID at the time, though I wasn't involved. It would have been canteen gossip. But how does this relate to little old ladies?'

'There was another angle to postal scams. Drugs were being smuggled from Afghanistan through countries that didn't tend to have checks as tight as ours in the UK. Then the drugs would be parcelled up in Belgium, say, or Holland and the parcel sent to innocent old ladies who'd been specially targetted. Now, on this side, a gang member would approach the old lady and tell her she'd be getting a parcel that was really intended for him. His colleague on the Continent had rung him to say the parcel was on its way but it turned out he'd managed to get the right number on the parcel but the wrong road. The number and road tallied with the old lady's address. So would she just accept the parcel and the gang member would pick it up. No need to waste time with the mail people.'

'Clever. The gang people would all keep their noses clean. If the police had had a tip-off and were tracking parcels all they'd end up with would be a bewildered old lady who did the flowers at church.'

'That's about the size of it. And with the parcels destined for respectable addresses there wasn't too much tracking, anyway. It was a pretty safe earner and cheap to run. I last heard of it many years ago, but maybe it's making a comeback.'

'The thing is, Jase,' Crane said slowly, 'I can't believe this Mellors bloke could possibly be into anything like drugs, not a respectable council official.'

'Could have an innocent explanation. But if he's living a bit top-side. . . .'

'The work I do I could believe most things of anyone, even

council officials. But drugs, I can't buy it. Apart from anything else, if this particular scam was sorted years ago why would it take off again now?'

'The really big drugs money is made by the barons up Liverpool way. But you need to lay out a lot of money up front. And if a deal goes pear-shaped you're down a very big fistful of smackeroonies. But the parcel scam, well, it might be low level but it's a whole lot safer and cheaper to operate and you can keep your anonymity. Could be a nice earner for a cautious type.'

'OK, Jase, you've given me a lot to think about.'

'But I reckon you're probably right, guv. You don't think in terms of H and crack with a jobsworth. I'll get back to you.'

Crane put down his phone. Maggie looked at him over her VDU. 'Frank, if the lady engaged you to see if he's being a naughty boy where does Jason come into it? Even if the chap *is* up to something.'

'You know me, Maggie, once a CID man it's never out of your system. I'll not be able to pass on Jason's costs, but if there's something dodgy going on I can put Terry in the picture. He's done me plenty of good turns, God knows.'

He began to run it past her, the parts of the phone call she'd not been able to hear. Jason was known to them as The Man with No Surname, as all that Crane had for him was a mobile number. He'd never even seen him; he'd come recommended by word of mouth. Jason was an expert at getting together personal details on just about everyone: unlisted phone numbers, bank details, share holdings, property, cash in off-shore accounts. It was time-consuming work, though Crane knew how to do it. But it was cost-effective to give it to Jason, who was totally reliable and appeared to do little else. It wouldn't, though, be cost-effective in this particular case.

Maggie said, 'I can never remember a council official being caught as a drugs runner.'

Maggie had also worked in the police force, as a PA to a senior officer. She was now retired and did a few hours a week looking after Crane's invoices and diary.

Crane nodded. 'No job for a jobsworth, as Jason said himself. There must be some innocent reason why Mellors was picking up a parcel from an old lady but I'd like to know for sure. . . .'

They'd driven out to the Anchor just beyond Gargrave on a warm cloudy evening and now sat over drinks while waiting for their meal.

'How are things at the crisp factory?'

'Even more mind-numbing than I could have imagined it was going to be,' she sighed. 'It's so nice to be able to get away and put on something summery.' She glanced down at her yellow cotton spot dress.

'It's a very nice dress. I remember it from last year.'

'I'm glad you like it because I'll be digging it out again *next* year.'

He smiled, nodded. She knew he'd have bought her a dress if she'd given the slightest impression it would be nice to have a new one, but she also knew how much he respected her determination to stay independent until they were married.

She put a hand over his at the small table. 'We're so lucky. We have such a nice life. One of the girls at the factory is looking after me. She thinks I'm from another planet because I live on Crow Tree. I keep telling her I'm perfectly ordinary but she'll not have it. Says I haven't a clue how so many at the factory live. I suppose she's right. You and me, we read the broadsheets and we know how very difficult it is for some: losing their jobs, having their houses repo-ed, having to live on sink estates, poor schools. But we don't know it from the inside. Becky told me about a friend of hers who's on the game and whose boyfriend knocks her about. She's in a lot of debt because she took a loan from a loan-shark, who's probably charging five hundred per cent interest. It really upset me.'

'You're right,' Damien said, 'we know these things happen but none of it happens to us. It would be nice if we could help this girl.'

She sighed. 'Help Linda and half the factory would be queuing up.'

'I know. I suppose that's why I want to be an MP one day. I once read something that sticks in my mind. It's from Luke: "Unto whomsoever much is given, of him shall be much required." Well, I know it'll be an uphill struggle but I really would like to help in trying to improve society. It would be nice to think that one day kids like Linda might have a fighting chance.'

As their meals were put before them Damien said, 'She should go to the police, Mel, the girl who's being knocked about.'

'I said the same but they're very cynical about the police not being keen to get involved.'

'The trouble is, once the police *do* get involved, the woman and the bloke have often patched things up. It's a pity a spot of rough justice couldn't be applied, someone who'd give the boyfriend a belting so he'd know what it feels like.'

'That's a great idea! When Linda comes back I'll tell her that if ever her boyfriend duffs her up again I'll send you round to duff *him* up. . . .'

Crane had obtained the woman's name from the voting register. He gave her a disarming smile. 'I'm from the Royal Mail, Mrs Tempest, and I've had an advice that a parcel may have been misdirected to your address.' He held up the photocard of his driving licence but she barely gave it a glance.

'But he's *taken* it now, the other gentleman. It was his lady friend's name on the parcel, do you see, only the sender had got the wrong road on the address. They'd been in touch on the phone and that's how this gentleman knew they'd got the wrong road.'

'I quite understand,' Crane said reassuringly. 'Just so long as the parcel got into the right hands. Would you know the gentleman's name, the one who called for it, just for the record?'

'Faraday, was it, Fennell? I wrote it down on the phone pad.

Just a moment.' She stepped briefly back into the hall, then reappeared. 'It was Fielding,' she told him. 'Mr J.W. Fielding.'

'Thank you, Mrs Tempest, that's all I need to know. But with the parcel being reported as having gone astray I needed to check it out.'

'I do hope I did the right thing.' A look of anxiety crossed her wrinkled features. 'I suppose I should have told the postman. But with Mr Farnley saying it would save time and trouble. . . . And he was such a nice man. The sort of person you could trust with your savings.'

Crane gave her another warm smile. 'Well, we'd prefer it to be sorted out by the Post Office, madam, but if it's got to the correct destination that's really all that matters. I'll leave you in peace now and many thanks for your help.'

Crane walked back to his car, smiling faintly. Mrs Tempest had been selected very skilfully. Helpful and willing but on the vague side. It hadn't occured to her to wonder how the Post Office would have known a parcel had gone astray in the first place, of the thousands that were in transit at any one time. Yes, she'd been chosen well.

He got into his car but sat for a few minutes before driving off. So Tony Mellors had become J.W. Fielding for the purpose of picking up a parcel that had been cleverly targetted at a vague old lady. Could Jason possibly have touched on the truth here, that it had been a relatively safe way of getting drugs into the country? But Mellors? A senior official in the council? How could a man like him possibly be involved in those kinds of shadowy goings-on?

'He was such a nice man,' she'd said. 'The sort of person you could trust your savings with.'

Those words were to stick in his mind.

The three young women, Melanie, Becky and Linda, sat over their drinks and sandwiches in the little pub down the road from the crisp factory. Linda had dark red hair, which had been expertly cut in a short style. She was pretty and her features had the sort of balance that was sought after in fashion models. She also had a good figure, firm breasted and narrow waisted, and the casual clothes she wore, Melanie could tell, had not been cheap: a printed peach-coloured blouse over stone trousers in stretch cotton. But her mouth and the left side of her face were swollen, and the skin round one of her eyes was discoloured by a healing bruise. She was back on the production line and Melanie had now been transferred to the office. She'd heard Linda telling the other women about the pretend fall in the shower. They'd looked concerned but sceptical, as this was probably not the first time Linda had come to work in a damaged condition.

Melanie said, 'You really should report it, Linda. At the very least he should have been warned that this must never happen again.'

'Exactly what I said, Mel. Let him get away with it and there'll be no stopping him, know what I'm saying? If you just take it he'll get worse. Don't forget Dulcie, she was in the factory once a month with a face like a bag of spanners.'

'I don't want the bogies in, Becky. You know what they're like about domestics.'

She'd spoken with reluctance. She'd eaten barely a mouthful of her sandwich. Melanie sensed she felt constrained in front of her, gave an impression that Melanie wasn't 'one of them', who'd worked in the factory since leaving school.

'You've got to get it stopped, Lin, he could ruin your looks big time.'

Linda said, 'Let's talk about something else. I gave him a lot of mouth, that's what got him going.'

'Well, I think you want your head looking at. I think you're mad.' She snapped her glass down irritably on the table.

'I gave him the mouth. Now let's please talk about something else.'

Melanie glanced at her. It was difficult to picture this quiet young woman being aggressive. Sitting here, one hand grasped in the other, she just came over as very vulnerable and very unhappy.

The basic pattern of Tony Mellors's days continued to be part of the morning spent in the town hall and most of the afternoon devoted to the planning department premises in Manchester Road. Most days he had lunch in the same pub with the homely looking woman that Crane had overheard being called Heather. But Mellors frequently drove out to different parts of the metropolitan area where, clipboard in hand, he made copious notes about various buildings, many of which had once been custom-built for the old textile industry: dye-houses, combing sheds and woollen mills that were now rented by IT operations, mail order and discount warehousing. Crane guessed that Mellors was examining premises that were part of the city's long-range plans for re-development. He'd probably be a qualifed surveyor with a good idea of what the various buildings would cost for the council to buy and demolish.

However busy he was he always seemed able to find time for a pub lunch with Heather. Yet Crane couldn't convince himself there was an affair going on. He saw them very much as good friends, brought into companionship by spending so much time working together. He'd not found them in any situation where sex could be involved. Mellors frequently went home late, but only because he worked over in his town hall office. Heather often worked late, too, but Crane doubted there'd be any opportunities in the town hall itself for Heather to remove what he could only imagine would be rather decorous underwear.

No, he was near certain Mellors wasn't involved with another woman. The bruises on his bottom in Josie's photo must have been a one-off, a call girl willing to go the distance for the right fistful of tenners. But it still came back to why go to a call girl when sexy Josie was more than willing to tan his backside.

He couldn't get it together. But there was now getting to be rather a lot about Mellors he couldn't get together: the old lady and the parcel, a way of life that surely couldn't be funded by what Mellors earned working for the council.

He knew he should go and see Josie and tell her her suspicions were unfounded. He'd given the case a good deal of attention for over a week. He'd have to accept that if he took himself off the case it would mean continuing his surveillance of Mellors unpaid. But the old CID instinct was here to stay and he felt compelled now to know exactly what the man was up to.

In the late afternoon, after work, Melanie took Becky and Linda home in her mother's elderly Yaris. She dropped Becky off at her family's home in Heights Lane, then drove Linda to where she lived in a flat in Conway House, on the edge of a council estate called Willow Park.

Becky chattered busily on as Melanie drove with the preoccupied care of one who'd not long had her licence, but Linda had been very subdued, quieter even than she'd been at lunchtime. She made no move to get out of the car when Melanie drew to a halt outside the flats. Melanie gave her a questioning glance.

'It's . . . not . . easy, Mel,' Linda said in a low voice.

'Your boyfriend. . . ?'

'If I ever went near the police he really would spoil my looks.'

'The police wouldn't let him, Linda. There'd be an order set against him forbidding him to go anywhere near you. That's . . . if you want to break away from him.'

Linda became silent, gazing through the windscreen with unfocused eyes, looking to be not far from tears. Melanie felt a wave of compassion for this small, pretty woman whose near flawless features beneath the bruises would be her most valued possession. 'He can be so nice sometimes,' she said in a wavering tone. 'And he's so good-looking. Nice clothes, big motor. He'll often take me for a meal when I'm not—'

She broke off and watched Melanie in another silence. 'I . . I suppose Becky told you. I'm on the game. Alfie makes the arrangements, makes sure I'm safe . . . all that.'

'And keeps the money?' Melanie couldn't stop herself saying.

'It's to pay off the debts.'

'What's that got to do with Alfie?' she said gently.

Linda shrugged in a hopeless gesture. 'He . . . he just looks after the money. He's sorting things out. He gives me pocket money, wants me to dress nicely and have my hair seen to.'

'But . . . but surely the people who lent you the money would come to you for payment?'

'Alfie knows who they are. He sorts it all out.'

'Was the person who lent you this money a loan-shark?'

Linda nodded, blinking back tears she couldn't restrain. 'It was only a grand. I'd got behind with the bills and the credit cards. But then the loan went up to two grand with the interest and I don't know where it is now.'

'And that's when Alfie took over?'

'I . . . I met him at Seventh Heaven. He was so friendly and nice. Still is, now and then.'

Melanie sighed. It was so difficult. She'd had friends who'd been made unhappy by manipulative men yet couldn't break away from a compulsive relationship, however much misery it caused. She'd stopped trying to encourage breaks and cooling-off periods when she'd reluctantly had to accept that what was wanted wasn't realistic advice but simply tea and sympathy.

'What does Alfie *do*, Linda?'

She brushed her wet cheeks with the back of a hand. 'I'm . . . I'm not sure. He sort of comes and goes.'

'He doesn't go to an office? Dress to do manual work?'

She shook her head, fell silent again. After a time she said, 'He's . . . he's into things. . . .'

Melanie nodded sadly. She'd already had her own suspicions about Alfie. Good-looking, a club charmer, highly skilled at talking attractive kids into high-end prostitution and just happened to know men who lent money with nothing in writing and astronomical interest rates. And what else? There'd be many

ways of turning a crooked pound to a man like Alfie. She put a hand over one of Linda's. 'I'm very sorry,' she said, 'sorry you've been knocked about and find yourself in this situation. It would have to be your decision to get yourself out of it, but if you want any help or just want to talk about it, do let me know.'

'It does help, being able to talk about it,' Linda said, forcing a smile. 'Becky's a good mate but she's too bossy: do this, do that, tell him to get lost. But you, you seem to understand where I'm at.'

'Could you not talk to your mother?'

'She's been divorced twice. Couldn't wait to see the back of me. Haven't seen my real dad in seven years. Couldn't even tell you where he *is*.'

'Frank Crane.'

'Jason, guv.'

'Go ahead, Jase.'

'Your Tony Mellors. His council salary's about seventy grand. He owns the Bingley house outright and he owns a place on the coast just beyond Sandsend. Didn't just buy it, had it built. That cost him three-fifty grand and it's worth near half a mil now. He has money in off-shores, thirty grand here, forty there and so on.'

'Jase, you've never brought me any duff info but I'm finding this very hard to get together. How does he do that out of his salary?'

'He doesn't, guv, is the short answer.'

'Could he have inherited?'

'I checked his folks out just in case. Very modest background.'

'I checked on that parcel he picked up from the old lady, by the way. It worked exactly as you said: the misdirection, would the old lass hang on to it for him and so on. And he gives himself a false moniker.'

'Looks like the old methods work best.'

'Can it *possibly* be drugs?'

'The parcel scam's a carbon copy of the way it used to be done back in the nineties.'

'Well, the houses and the motors and the off-shore loot must come from somewhere.'

'If it is drugs there are bound to be more people than Mellors involved. In fact it seems kind of odd him doing the leg-work. I'd have thought it would be some kind of middle man. And middle men don't normally touch that kind of money.'

'Any ideas what else he might be into?'

'I reckon he could be in line one day for top banana in the planning department.'

'I've been shadowing him. He spends a fair amount of time checking out old properties.'

'That the council's aiming to put purchase orders on?'

'Could be.'

'That could open a *lot* of doors to a man of a bent disposition.'

'Scams with tendering?'

'Not only that but certain blokes might just get wind of which properties may be coming on to the schedule for replacement and buy them up. The original owners would probably be keen to get shot at any decent price and would sell without much hassle. And let's say the crook who buys them knows every dodge to screw the best price from a council keen to meet scheduling deadlines. And what if your friend Tony Mellors has something to do with *buying* the properties for the council?

'And then, like you say, there's the tendering from builders who've been known to get their heads together and rig the tenders. So the lowest tender gets the contract but even then the builders make a tidy profit that's well over the odds.'

'But crooked deals like that, Jase, the council will have safeguards.'

'And what if the man supervising the safeguards is a bent jobsworth?'

'Look, Jase, you're right, if Mellors *is* involved in that kind of crooked stuff he couldn't be doing it all on his own.'

'If he is a bad lot he's got to be working with someone else or for someone else.'

Crane was silent for a short time. 'OK, Jase,' he said, 'Once again you've given me a lot to think about. Many thanks and what do I owe you?'

'Six hours, usual rate. If you could drop it in at The Delvers in Heaton, early doors. It'll be a bird called Tina. Curly hair, big knockers.'

Grinning, Crane put down the phone. That was how The Man with No Surname always operated. Cash in a brown envelope, which almost certainly bypassed the HMRC, and handed to one of his many girlfriends, always attractive if slightly rough-looking. He filled Maggie in on the parts of the discussion she'd not heard.

'It's not looking too good for Mr Tony Mellors, is it?' she said.

'It hands me a big problem. His wife thinks there's another woman involved but what's a hundred times worse is Mellors having to go inside one of these days, have any ill-gotten gains impounded and losing a well-paid job.'

THREE

Crane pulled into the drive of Ash Mount, the big house on the hillside in Bingley where the Mellors lived their mortgage-free lives. The front door was drawn wide as he approached, with Josie framed in the opening and wearing a beaming smile of welcome. Fair hair falling sleekly to her shoulders, her eyes held that demure yet inviting look he remembered so well from before.

'Nice day for it,' she said obscurely. 'Do come in, Frank.'

She led him into the spacious room with the floral curtains, the long stone fireplace and the richly patterned Persian rug. She turned to face him then suddenly squeezed the top of his right thigh. 'Ooh!' she cried in her little-girl voice, 'is that a mobile vibrating in your pocket or are you just pleased to see me?'

Crane had to smile at yet another variation on the original Mae West quip. 'Maybe it's because you're playing so hard to get,' he said, but Josie didn't do irony.

'Frankie, how could you *possibly* believe I'd play hard to get with a big strong man like you? Sit there, that'll make a nice start,' she said, pointing to a long sofa.

Crane's words had simply slipped out and he wished now they hadn't. He'd have preferred to sit in an armchair as he knew what sitting on the sofa was likely to lead to. She instantly plonked herself next to him, sitting so close that their thighs touched and body heat began temptingly exchanging itself through their summer clothes. She was wearing a pale-green cotton shirt over ivory-coloured linen trousers and the three top buttons had been left undone to reveal a fine display of cleavage.

'This is fun,' she said, putting a hand on his leg and leaving it there. 'Shall we have a drink?'

'Please don't go to any trouble with coffee.'

'I'm not talking *coffee*, Frankie. Gin, Scotch, voddy?'

'I tend to steer clear of alcohol during the day with the limit being so low. Look, Josie, about your husband. I've shadowed him for a week and I can find no evidence of any kind of another woman.'

'What about those bruises on his bum, Frankie? You can't get those do-it-yourself. It's not like playing with your John Thomas.'

'I can only think it really was a one-off session with a prostitute.'

'I told you before he'd not go *near* anyone on the game. He'd be terrified he might come away HIV positive. He's one careful bloke.'

It was a fair point. Crane had to accept that for all the lavish lifestyle, Mellors had the look of a man who took obsessive care of himself. He said, 'Maybe there was no actual sex involved.'

'Look, sweetheart, great sex is the whole bloody *point* of having your backside belted.'

'Well, whatever, but I really couldn't trace any other woman. But he does see quite a lot of a woman from the office. He buys her lunch most days. She seems rather self-effacing and has very ordinary looks—'

'Heather Durkin,' she broke in. 'His PA. He keeps her sweetened because she looks after him so well. Works over when he has a rush on, all that. You'd have to pay him to sleep with Heather – top whack.' She began to laugh derisively.

Crane shrugged. 'Well, Heather's the only woman in his life away from home.'

Josie ran a hand down her long glossy hair then put her head

closer to his. He caught a slight smell of alcohol. It was only three
o'clock but maybe she'd had a glass or two of wine with her
lunch. She looked to live a pleasant idle existence and this easy
life could only be funded by the wads of money Mellors seemed
able to lay his hands on.

'Give it another week or two shadowing the beggar, Frankie,'
she said, her little-girl voice soft and breathy. 'It really wouldn't
do for him to get serious. If he's getting his arse seen to
elsewhere I need to nip it in the bud PDQ.'

Even through the murmured words he felt he detected a steely
note. It looked as if she had a lot riding on Mellors and if he
walked out he took the lifestyle with him. He also wondered if
she knew that a possible divorce settlement would only be based
on his official earnings. It would give her a reasonable living but
she'd have to whistle for the opulent one she enjoyed now.

'I don't know that I can help you any more, Josie.'

'Oh, you really can't give up just yet, Frankie. He didn't get an
arse like that on him sitting on wet grass. If he's had it once with
his fancy piece he'll be going back for more sooner or later. You've
got to carry on the good work.'

He thought, why not, even though she'd be wasting her
money? He was positive the other woman didn't exist but that
almost obsessive urge had grown in him to know if the innocent-
looking Mellors really could be a drugs runner and a corrupt
official.

'All right, Josie, I'll give it another week or two if you're so sure
he really is having an affair.'

'That's it, Frankie, you be a good boy.' She put a hand on his
thigh again where it seemed to gently quiver.

'Josie, is Tony a qualified quantity surveyor?' he said casually.

'Why do you ask, love?'

'It often helps to know these details. If there *is* another woman
she might be making a move on him because she can see how
well qualified and successful he is.'

'He came almost top in the country in his finals. He only needs to *look* at a building to tell you to the pound what it cost to put up.'

'Really? And it looks as if he's already doing very well in his job. This lovely house, a Jaguar for him, a Clio for you.'

'Just between the two of us, what he makes in his salary doesn't really cover the life we lead.' She tapped the side of her nose. 'He has his own little scams. He doesn't talk about them and I don't ask, but the position he has and the people he knows – builders and suppliers and so forth – well it's not surprising if a few smackeroonies find their way to his back pocket, is it?'

Not surprising, Crane supposed, to someone like Josie, whose morals were looking to be all of a piece: non-existent. He grinned. 'No, he works so hard I'm sure he deserves to make a bit on the side.'

'Too right.'

He now knew that she knew that Mellors's salary wouldn't cover the life they led, but he wondered if she had any real idea of the extent they lived beyond it: the property he owned, the money in off-shores, the expensive holidays he was sure she'd insist they indulged in.

'It's so *hot* today, Frankie,' she said, with a little pout. 'I just feel the need to take off all my clothes and cool down a little. Doesn't it make you feel you want to take off *your* clothes?'

'I do often strip to the waist at home when it's as hot as this, yes.'

She clasped his arm. 'Those *hands*! So strong-looking. When I'm in bed I can't stop thinking of how it must feel to have you running them all over my body, every tiny bit of it: my feet . . . and my legs . . . and the insides of my thighs . . . and my bottom . . . and my little—'

'I'm getting the general picture, Josie,' he said, smiling. With her little-girl voice she sounded like a child counting her dolly-mixtures. 'Thanks for the compliment. I'm afraid I'll have to go now.' He struggled to lever himself up from where he was firmly clamped between the arm of the sofa and her thigh, which

seemed to be generating the heat of a newly filled hot-water
bottle.

'Oh, *Frankie*! Give yourself a break. Why don't we throw our
clothes in a corner and have a lovely lie down on top of the
duvet?' She undid another button of her shirt by way of
encouragement.

He really was tempted but it was supposed to be a working
relationship and he had a strong sense it might lead to problems
he could do without. But it was with a genuine reluctance that
he said, 'I really must go, Josie. I've got such a lot of work on at
present.'

'Oh, Frankie,' she said, her breathy voice at its most
imploring. 'I've been looking forward so much to seeing you
again. Surely you can find half an hour to relax that lean body of
yours.'

'I really am very sorry, but my next appointment's in twenty
minutes.' He freed himself with a final heave and got to his feet.

She, too, got up and put both hands to his face. 'Come again
soon, Frankie, *very* soon. And spend an hour at the very least.
Promise. . . .'

'I'll do the best I can. Must rush.'

'Big kiss.'

He put his lips to hers, trying not to dwell on all the parts of
her body she was keen for him to fondle. Her delicate scent filled
his head. She wore just the blouse and the trousers, two
garments that could be hurled into a corner in a matter of
seconds, to reveal what he knew would be an incredibly attractive
body. She instinctively began rubbing her abdomen against his
and it was almost too much for him, but he had to hold the
thought that a delightful session on top of Josie's duvet might
eventually come at a very high cost, even if it was an open
marriage.

Prising her hands from around his waist with some difficulty
he said, 'I'll be in touch.'

'Very soon?'

'The minute there's anything to report.'

'No, no, just *come*. Give yourself an afternoon off. And in the meantime I want you to think of all the delightful things we can do together. Give me a ring, anytime, and we'll go over all the details. It'll make it easier for me while I'm waiting.'

He got into his car and slid open the automatic windows to release the heat build-up. Josie quickly put her hands through the opening and caught him in yet another lengthy kiss. With a feeling of relief he got the car rolling at last. He wondered if, apart from being a near-nymphomaniac, she was entirely right in the head. Even so, the enticing half hour he'd had with her had been well spent. He'd had it confirmed that Mellors was a highly skilled quantity surveyor who knew everything there was to know about building costs. The hard part was going to be trying to pin down who was pulling Mellors's strings. Jason was right, it wouldn't be possible for him to defraud the council without co-operation – someone who could be considerably more crooked than Mellors.

Melanie had taken Linda home again in her mother's car and they sat for a while before Linda went off to her flat. Her face was healed now.

'You're such a pretty girl, Linda. Please don't give him another reason to spoil your looks.'

'He's been OK just lately. As long . . . As long as I do what I'm told.'

Melanie sighed. And have sex with who she was ordered to have sex with. At top prices, she guessed, because of her looks and her shapely body. She'd be making Alfie a lot of money with that body.

'These . . . men you go with, if you *have* to do it you should get more from it than pocket money.'

Linda passed a hand over her dark red hair. 'He's not too bad, Mel, he lets me keep the money I make at the factory.'

'Well I should jolly well think so!'

42

'There's all the money I owe against the loan, remember. I don't need to worry about that any more. Alfie's got it sussed. And he makes sure there's never any trouble with the punters, know what I'm saying?'

'These punters, they're reasonably decent types?'

She nodded. 'Well-off guys. Business folk, mainly, whose wives have a lot of headaches.' She gave a small wry smile.

It was as Melanie had thought. The sort of men who could think in terms of a hundred pounds plus for time with a woman as young and attractive as Linda. She said, 'Can you not leave Alfie?'

Linda shook her head, eyes moist. 'I'll only be able to live my own life when Alfie takes up with someone else. He'll clear off one day but I'll still have to . . . you know, put out.'

'But the money you owe will be long paid off. In fact I'm pretty sure it'll have been paid off already.'

'Nothing's ever paid off in Alfie's game,' she said in a low voice.

'Alfie's *game*. I don't quite understand.'

'They're all sort of . . . connected. Like the men in those gangster films. The money I make goes to Alfie and everything Alfie gets from his girls, a slice goes to someone else.'

'Who is this someone else?'

'He tells me nothing. I just sometimes hear him muttering on his mobile when he thinks I'm in the bathroom. Mel, I wish to Christ I'd never gone to Seventh Heaven that night. My life was my own then, just like what yours is. I saw you going down Allerton Road at the weekend with ever such a nice looking bloke in a sports car. You looked dead happy.'

Melanie felt herself reddening. It was guilt, guilt because she couldn't have had a better life and Linda a worse. 'I've been very, very lucky, Linda. My boyfriend's a really decent type. I just wish you could have met someone like him. If only you'd not borrowed money from the loan shark. They'd have lent you money at the factory, you know, to tide you over with the bills and deducted it from your wage's at an amount you could afford.'

'I didn't know that. I thought they might let me go if they knew I was in debt. If I didn't have the factory I don't know what I'd do. Me and the girls,' she said sadly, 'they're all I've got.'

Melanie could barely begin to imagine what it was like not to even own your own life. A mother who didn't want to know, a missing father, no one to advise her when she got into debt or care about the company she kept.

'Look, Linda, I'll talk it over with Damien, my boyfriend. He might be able to think of a way to get you out of the mess you're in. He's very clever and he genuinely cares about people. He wants to be a politician one day.'

'No, no, Mel,' Linda broke out, seeming almost to shrink into herself. 'Please don't say nothing to no one, *please*. I just tell you these things because I know I can trust you. But not a word to no one else. You don't mess with this lot, Mel, not if you don't want a faceful of acid.'

Melanie felt as if someone had touched the nape of her neck with ice. 'Acid!'

'It's what they did to Cilla. She was threatening to go to the bogies, tell them what went on. Two blokes came past on a motorbike and threw acid at her.'

'Oh, *Linda*!' Melanie felt breathless with shock.

'They took her to hospital and the hospital got the police in.'

'Did they . . . did they get who did it?'

'She knows who it was, too right, but told them she'd no idea. Didn't want no more acid.'

'Linda, it makes me feel ill.'

Linda was now visibly shaking. 'Well, that's how they keep a lid on things. None of us ever dare go near any bogies.'

Melanie sat in an appalled silence. She just wanted to take Linda home with her, where there was a loving mother and father. People who fed her nourishing meals and gave her sound advice about her future and played classical CDs after dinner on Sunday. The things Linda had told her had made her realize, as nothing else, just how sheltered her life had been. She took hold of Linda's tembling hands. 'I'll talk it through with Damien. No, no, hear me out! I'll not even *mention* your name or where we met. I'll just ask him if there's anything we can do to help that won't put you in any danger. We'll do what we can, Linda, I promise.'

'There's nothing you can do, Mel,' she said with a half-sob. 'There's nothing anyone can do.'

'Hello.'

'It's Joe, boss.'

'You're on a landline?'

'Never ring on anything else.'

But the boss always asked, obsessively concerned that anything said didn't go off into the ether to be picked up by the wrong ears.

'What is it, Joe?'

'It's about Mellors.'

'How's that stuff going he picked up from the old girl?'

'Like hot cakes. Very high quality gear.'

'It's worth the outlay to get the best. OK, Mellors?'

'This next drop you're fixing, he doesn't want to do that one either. I thought the kicking would sort him out but he's still grizzling on. Says he shouldn't be involved with drugs, he's got enough on with the other stuff. Says he's going to see you.'

'OK, Joe, leave it with me. I'll sort it.'

'Look, boss, maybe we should give this next one to Heppy or Walter.'

'No, it has to be Mellors and I'll tell you why. There's no one in this city who looks more respectable than he does. Getting the guy on board was one of the best moves I ever made. Old ladies would trust him with their false teeth when they see him standing there in his pinstripes and his nice tie and an XF against the kerb.'

'Well, he's giving me a lot of earache. Don't know what's got into the guy. It's not just the gear he doesn't want to pick up; he's started bitching about the other stuff too. Says he's worried about being exposed and the job's hard enough without the risks he has to take. I told him, the risks he has to take are what he's bloody *paid* for.'

'And paid very well. He drives round in the Jag and he's got the place on the coast and has that nutty nympho wife of his living a life of luxury. And the money in off-shores. He must have doubled what I pay him with the stock market winners I put him on to.'

'So why's he pissed off, boss?'

'I don't suppose the kicking helped. I thought long and hard before I told you to go ahead. But he has to know who's boss and he has to do what he's told, just like the rest of you. OK, Joe, I hear what you're telling me and I'll have it out with him. Maybe I can find him a sweetener to make up for the kicking. He's essential to our operation but I don't let him know that. There'll not be too many who can price a building like Mellors.'

'Look, boss, like you told me, I had Mellors shadowed for a while to make sure he was doing what you were paying him for. I put Billy Needham on to it, best shadow we've got. Mellors never knew he was being watched. Trouble is, Billy tells me there was some other geezer eyeballing him as well.'

'Was he *sure*?'

'Positive. This other bloke, there were times when he goes wherever Mellors goes: the pub at lunchtime, getting the parcel from the old kid, checking out the buildings you're aiming to buy.'

'Does he now?' The man Joe only ever called boss had been put in a state of great agitation, though Joe would never know this, as with Joe and the others he always gave an unwavering impression of being in total control of every situation, however alarming.

'I assume Billy took the number of this guy's wheels?'

'You bet. We'll have no problem tying a name and address to it.'

'Do that, Joe, and get back to me,' he said, in the same calm tone he said everything. 'Could he be a plain-clothes man?'

'Billy thinks there's a good chance. Says he has that CID look.'

'Give it top priority, Joe, and get back to me soonest.'

'Will do.'

Tanglewood House had a dining room with an enviable outlook over a patio and a lengthy lawn at the bottom of which were carefully pruned forest trees. The sun was just sinking through foliage and the sounds of muted birdsong came through open windows.

'Ah, but you're a bonny girl, Mel. He's a lucky one, that son of mine, to have found you. You do my old eyes a power of good.'

She smiled. 'I think I'm lucky, too, Brendon. And less of the old eyes. You don't look anything like your age.'

'Will you listen to that, Tessa. Doesn't the girl know all the right things to say to make a chap feel just great?'

'Will you stop flirting with your son's girlfriend and pour the wine.'

Mrs Docherty was passing backwards and forwards from the kitchen and now put down the plates with the starter of angels on horseback. An odour of roasting duckling followed her. Brendon poured chilled Chablis and there'd probably be an excellent Bordeaux with the main course. But there was no ostentatious display of the wealth the Dochertys possessed. Tessa did all her own cooking and only had a cleaner once a week to help with the big house. She'd not worn as well as Brendon but was still attractive, if on the plumpish side, with rounded features and bushy blonde hair that always seemed slightly out of control. As so often at mealtimes, she had the preoccupied air of a woman concentrating on getting the dinner exactly right, with its complicated starter and a sauce that needed careful attention.

'Sit down next to me, Mel,' Brendon told her. 'The young fellow will have you the rest of the evening. Will you be taking another drop of sherry?'

'No thanks, Brendon. One of your large Tio Pepes is more than enough on an empty stomach.'

'Sure, but doesn't it make your eyes sparkle.'

He'd flirted with her from the first day Damien had brought her home. She knew she attracted him physically. She didn't mind. It made a nice change. The two or three boys she'd gone out with in the past had tended to have pleasant but preoccupied men as fathers, men who'd not caught her name and called her Meg or Milly. Brendon had been different, a vital and attractive man, who made no attempt to hide his reactions. He was of middle height but broad and strongly built. He had thick, dark hair that waved like Damien's and blunt features that added to a dominating appearance. But he had a warm, enveloping smile that gave an impression you were getting his total attention, unlike those vague fathers who'd not been able to get her name right. It must have been a great come-on to women in his single days, if not now, but he seemed completely devoted to his chubby wife.

'A long time before I met Tessa, Mel,' he'd once told her, 'I went out with a girl who looked a lot like you. Dark wavy hair and cheekbones. She went on to university and I never saw her again. I was sad at the time but. . . .'

So that must be why he found her attractive, because of someone he'd not quite got over. She said, 'I'm sure Tessa made up for her.'

'Oh, sure, there was no one else for me once I met Tessa.'

They were all seated at the table now and Tessa said, 'For what we are about to receive may the Lord make us truly thankful.'

They all crossed themselves, including Melanie, though she wasn't a Catholic. She was indeed very thankful for the perfectly prepared oysters in the tiny bacon wrappers and the steely white wine, having eaten nothing since a distant lunchtime sandwich. She said, 'I've never had such a delicious starter, Tessa. It must be difficult to make.'

'I'm glad you like it, dear. I decided we must have something a little special to welcome you back from Manchester.'

'Sure, Mel,' Brendon said, with the Irish inflection he tended to use at home, 'Tessa's mother could cook for England, to be sure. When I found out the daughter was as good as the mother that was the day I proposed.'

Tessa said, 'And I thought it was because a gin and tonic made *my* eyes sparkle.'

Brendon laughed heartily as Damien winked at Melanie across the table, where he sat next to his mother. He'd told her some time ago that Tessa had none of Brendon's drive and ambition. She'd found all the fulfilment she needed in her home and children. It was as if men like Brendon sensed that a relationship wasn't big enough for two outsized egos, that it was perhaps with a feeling of relief that they could leave the pressure of their long successful days behind and come back to a peaceful and orderly house run by a woman whose aspirations went no further than the children's happiness, the house and garden and her husband's well-being. Yet Brendon had once hankered for a girl who'd been bright enough to study for a degree. Who'd had a look of Melanie, who was also studying for a degree and had ambitions of her own. She was beginning to pick up on hints of complexities in the man's nature that he concealed behind the bonhomie and the cheerful laughter.

He poured red wine into her second glass as the plates of succulent duckling were placed before them. 'How are things at the crisp factory, Mel? I hope they've managed to find you a pair of designer dungarees.'

She giggled. 'No, I've been promoted to the office now where I can wear decent clothes. I'm having to cope with really demanding tasks like filing and checking timesheets and telling a persistent chap called Norbert Kittle that I'm afraid Mr Squires will be out all afternoon. Mr Squires, of course, is sitting two yards from me.'

Brendon's laughter broke out again as he spooned vegetables

solicitously on to her plate. 'Ah, sure,' he said, 'I could be doing with the likes of you in my own office for giving time-wasters the welly.'

'But you're a one-man band, aren't you, in that mysterious office where you do those mysterious things that are so convoluted you can't begin to explain them in a way simple layfolk like me can understand.'

She knew it was the wine that had egged her on to say these things and for a second or so his expression became oddly guarded and edgy. Then he began to laugh again. 'Sure, darling, my work is as difficult to do as 'tis to explain, when you're dealing with people who import and export goods and services. I spend a lot of my time involved in winks and nudges and whispers in ears. Same with designers and builders; you're speaking a sort of shorthand jargon that's near impossible to pin down.'

'But—'

'I do anything that'll earn me an honest sov, Mel. If I was to explain the full range of what I do you'd be here till midnight and so bored you'd have nodded off. Now don't bother your pretty head about the things I do to scratch a living.'

'Well, yes, I can see it must be a *big* struggle to make ends meet.'

Once more his laughter broke out and Damien winked at her again. Brendon was behaving true to form in the veil he skilfully drew over the sort of work he really did during his long days in his office. She wondered if the habit of telling the business people he dealt with only the barest minimum of what they needed to know had become so ingrained in him that it had carried over into his private life. What did percolate through to her behind his cheerful manner was somehow an impression of the hard man he could actually be in his business dealings. But she supposed you didn't get to be as wealthy as Brendon, coming as he had from a poor background, unless you had a very tough streak.

'Have you made any friends at the crisp factory, Mel?' Tessa asked, as they sat for a time over the wine before she brought in the dessert and the coffee.

'Yes, I met two nice girls on the production line before I transferred to the office. We go for a pub lunch most days.'

'Is one of them the girl who got knocked about?' Damien asked.

'Yes, her boyfriend takes his fists to her. Frightful.'

'Heavens above!' Tessa said. 'He wants locking up.'

'Just what I said, Tessa, but she doesn't want to involve the police. He just seems to have this hold over her.'

'I'd like to get my hands on the swine,' Brendon growled, his right hand bunching into a fist on the table. 'Let him know what it's like to be on the receiving end.'

Briefly, Brendon's face had a stony look that made Melanie wonder if there'd been times in his past when he really had settled matters with his fists.

Later, Damien and Melanie went for a stroll round the Tanglewood reservoirs, a local beauty spot, and then called in at the pub, The Reservoir, to round off the evening. Melanie said, 'Your dad looked so angry about Linda being hurt I decided I'd better not mention something that was even worse. Linda has a friend called Cilla who had acid thrown in her face because she was threatening to go to the police. I think it was something she'd learnt about some dodgy activities her boyfriend was involved in.'

'My God! That must be the girl who was in the evening paper not long ago.'

'She knows who did it but daren't tell the police because she's terrified of what might happen.'

'What goes on, Mel? One girl used as a punchbag and another who has acid thrown at her.'

'Absolutely between the two of us, Demmy, Linda says it's a kind of gang. They trap the girls in some way then groom them as call girls. The men take the money and the girls get loose change. But that's only a small part of it. She's sure it's some kind of organized crime.'

'Poor kids.'

'They daren't go near the police and she says they have no real life. And these are their best years, when they should be enjoying life: clubbing, partying, meeting decent blokes. Trouble is, these charmers go to the clubs, too, and *pretend* to be decent blokes, then sift out the prettiest kids, give them a good time for a few weeks then get some kind of hold over them and turn them into prostitutes.'

'There's so much that goes on that we don't know about. You think you know your own city pretty well, but . . .' Damien broke off with a shrug.

'I'd not have known anything like this went on if I'd not gone temping at the crisp factory. I've told Linda I'd talk it over with you and promised it would go no further.'

Damien drank a little of his glass of lager. He fell silent as the cheerful talk and laughter and the soft music from the speaker system went on around them. He looked to be thinking hard. He was concerned about the plight of the factory girls almost as if he'd met them himself. The caring instinct seemed bred in the bone and one day she was certain, he'd make the right kind of MP. He said, 'Can they not get away from these men?'

'Not till they're past their best, pulling the punters.'

'Not long ago, you said if we helped sort out one girl in the factory where would it end. Well, I'm aiming for a political career and politics, apart from it being the art of the possible, tends to be about broad-brush techniques; MPs haven't the time to get too involved in the minutiae. But these kids are like two bristles on the brush and I just feel I can't walk on by.'

'But what could we *do* if they're watched like hawks?'

He ran a hand through his hair, nodded. 'I can see it would be no good if they tried to make a move to another part of the city. But what if they went to another *city*?'

She thought about this. 'The trouble is they're just naïve

young kids. It would be so difficult for them to move to another town and try to make a new start among strangers. They're living a ghastly existence but it's all the stability they've got.'

'Look,' he said, 'I'm thinking of Leicester, a hundred miles down the road. I've got a good friend from uni who lives there. He could give me the location of a decent district where the girls could share a flat and look for work. We could pick them up in the estate car when the men weren't around, ferry them down the M1 and get them into decent accommodation. They'd be cut off from everything here but they'd have each other and it would give them a chance to make a new life.'

'But would you be prepared to do that? It could be expensive as I'm sure neither will have much money.'

'Mel, there's no point in me *having* a few bob if I can't use some of it on things like this. If I ever make it as an MP this is the sort of thing I'd be keen to help clear up. If it is organized crime it won't just be call girls and loan-sharking, there'll be the full range of activity: drugs, illegal immigrants, stolen Mercs, internet fraud and so on.'

'Demmy, it's so good of you, it really is.' She put a hand over his. 'I'll talk it over with them. I daresay they'll think it's too much of a step for them to take, but when I tell them it's going to be the only way they'll get their lives back I'm sure it'll make them think. Do you know, there's no other man I've ever known who'd be prepared to do what you're willing to do.'

'It's the way I've been brought up, I suppose. Mum and Dad always there for us, teaching by example. It left me feeling I owed society a debt.'

She nodded. 'Your dad really is a very impressive man. I get a strong feeling of hidden depths behind the show he always puts on.'

'Hidden depths? Dad? No way, absolutely no way. With Dad what you see is definitely what you get.'

The wine at dinner had made Melanie thirsty and she now sipped lemonade. 'Oh, come *on*, what does he really do in his office to be so wealthy? And he really seems to work entirely on his own. Why hasn't he gone into bigger premises and extended?'

Damien smiled, shrugged. 'I don't suppose I've ever asked myself things like that. All my life he's just spent long days in that office and you get so you take it for granted. He has a thing about not wanting to talk about his work and I respect that. But it's not really unusual, you know, the way he does work. A lot of people work solo and do well: IT specialists, people who've developed a niche business, head hunters, financial advisers.'

'But he's got to be so rich.'

'That's because he's so good at what he does, whatever that is,' Damien said, chuckling. 'It's what we've grown up with, Mollie and me, so the secretiveness just seems quite normal.'

She could understand that. You did tend to take your parents' occupations for granted and were quite incurious about how they spent their working lives. But she was seeing Damien's family as an outsider and to her there seemed to be things about Brendon that made him appear iceberg-like, to keep the bigger part of himself below the surface.

'Has he ever had an affair?'

He looked shocked. 'An *affair*? Whatever makes you say that?'

'He's a very attractive man. Attractive men sometimes have affairs.'

'Dad's always been totally devoted to Mum. He's either working or at home. And he might work late but he always *gets* home.' He grinned. 'All that chat-up he feeds you, he's like that with all the women who come to the house. They all get the flirty end of his tongue.'

But Melanie knew there was a lot more than the standard chat-up in the way Brendon found it hard to take his eyes from her, eyes that were full of what she could only see as a kind of longing. She wasn't a beauty but she had better than average looks and a good figure and she'd certainly been around long enough to tell when she was being fancied rotten.

She nodded. 'I'm sure you're right. I daresay it does no harm in his business dealings to give the wives that embracing smile and the honeyed words.'

Damien said, changing the subject, 'I need to pick you up tomorrow when you've finished your stint at the factory.'

'Why do you need to pick me up?'

He didn't speak for a short time. 'Mel, we've decided we want to live together when you've finished at Manchester. But I've never actually said, "Will you marry me?". Well I'm saying it now and if the answer's yes I'm going to take you to town tomorrow and buy you the engagement ring of your choice.'

'Oh, Demmy, how *wonderful*! You know the answer's been yes ever since our first night out.'

'Shall I kneel down?'

'Normally that would be an absolute requirement but in a bar parlour with all these women. . . . If they saw you on one knee it would only depress them about what they'd had to make do with from the bottom of the bran tub.'

'And you don't need to think it over for a few days?'

'Of course, but please don't let it stop you buying the ring. If I decide against it I can always wear it on a chain round my neck.'

He took her hand. 'OK then, Fattorini's here we come.'

'Oh, Demmy!' She kissed him on the cheek. 'I'll not sleep tonight. And tomorrow I'll be doing a demanding job in a daze; all those important timesheets and invoices and protecting Mr Squires from any possible contact with Mr Norbert Kittle. . . .'

Later, as Damien walked her home, she felt as if her feet weren't touching the ground. She loved him so much and she was so happy. Happy and lucky.

Crane kept on his surveillance of Mellors, but learnt nothing more. Mellors didn't do anything else that seemed unusual and his trips away from the office were to make notes about more properties. He didn't give the slightest indication he was seeing another woman and Crane was still convinced the belting he'd taken on his backside had been the work of a willing, well-paid harlot. It was very frustrating but he stayed hopeful that sooner or later he'd have some clear idea what Mellors was really up to.

On Saturday afternoon his car phone rang. 'Frank Crane.'

'*Hello*, big boy.' It was Josie, speaking in that breathy little-girl voice that made his neck hair tingle.

'Hello, Josie. Still nothing to report.'

'It's not about that, Frankie. I'm inviting you to a do. This evening.'

'A do?'

'One of Tony's business chums. Lovely place near the Tanglewood reservoirs. Smackeroonies coming out of his ears and marvellous food and drink.'

'If it's one of Tony's contacts why aren't you going with Tony?'

'He's had a migraine. That kind of headache where you get flashing lights in your eyes, you feel as sick as a parrot, your head thinks it's been used as a football and—'

'I know what a migraine is, Josie.'

'He'll be laid aside for the rest of the day. He just wouldn't be up to the sort of do Brendon puts on.'

'I'd be a total stranger. The man won't want to see me when he's expecting Tony.'

'Oh, Brendon won't mind. He'll have plenty on his plate. There'll be at least fifty people there.'

'Not a good idea, Josie. If Tony's not fit to go it might be better if you don't go either.'

'And miss out on one of the best dos of the summer! Oh, come on, Frankie, Tony won't mind. Gets him off the hook.'

'How would you explain me to Tony?'

'Did I mention that it's an open marriage?'

'A number of times.'

'We don't *mind* each other's bits of fun. So long as it doesn't get serious.'

'I'm working, Josie. PIs work seven days a week.'

'Oh, give yourself an evening off. Why not just have a nice night out with little Josie?'

Had he not wanted to go he'd not have kept on talking, but from the start he'd seen that this could be the break he was hoping for, a chance to find out the sort of people Mellors was in contact with, a chance, maybe, to throw a little light on the activities that brought him in a good deal more than his salary.

'You've gone quiet, Frankie. Does that mean you're thinking what a lovely time you could have with Josie at a party where the champers comes at eighty pounds a bottle?'

He smiled. 'OK, Josie, if you're sure it'll be all right for me to replace Tony.'

'You've made my day, sweetheart.'

'What time do I pick you up?'

'Sevenish. Come in a taxi and then we can both have a few.'

'See you later.'

'Maybe we'll go back to your place afterwards. With Tony poorly sick in bed with a shawl on he might be a bit grumpy if we come back here.'

Still smiling, Crane drove on. He had a lot to do. Saturday and Sunday were good days for catching people at home who tended to be elusive during the week. He'd not be picking up Josie in a taxi and not be taking her to his own place after the party. He'd be taking his own car and having no more than a couple of drinks. He'd need a clear head for what he might be able to pick up about Mellors at the house near the reservoirs. Enthusiastically available as Josie was he didn't want the anticipation of her body and busy legs in his bed to preoccupy his mind this evening.

FOUR

'Who is the woman with the tall, well-made chap over by the window? The way she's gazing at him she looks as if she wishes they were alone in a darkened bedroom.'

'If that's your woman's intuition it's working at full tilt. That's Josie Mellors, known to Dad as the nutty nympho. The last party we had she tried to get Dad into bed and when she drew a blank there she tried to get me.'

'That last sentence seems to be incomplete, namely, "but she drew a blank with me, too".'

Damien grinned. 'I haven't got Dad's skill at fending off women like Josie. I realized I was being made an offer I couldn't refuse. I just lay back and thought of England.'

'I see. Well that marks the end of our relationship. And you can whistle for your diamond ring.'

'I'm sure that's an attitude the late Elizabeth Taylor would have fully approved of.'

'The next time you see this ring it'll be on a chain round my neck. Why aren't you over there now, chatting her up for what I daresay she calls a roll in the hay?'

'I would but the big man appears to have proprietorial rights, for this evening anyway. No, I'll make do with you.'

'I'm afraid I'm not prepared to make do with you. Not now.'

'Ladies and gentlemen.' Damien's father spoke in a carrying voice and the sounds of talk and laughter began to die away. 'If I could just have your attention for a minute.'

He stood at the bottom of the big room with Tessa on one side and Damien's sister Mollie on the other. 'I think we're all here now,' Docherty went on, 'and I want you to enjoy the evening. There'll be a buffet in the dining room from half past eight, so just help yourselves and sit where you wish. I want to welcome you all here and say how pleased we are, Tessa and I, to repay the hospitality we've had from so many of you in the past.

'There's just one announcement I'd like to make and that's to tell you that Damien is engaged to be married to the young lady who's at his side. Tessa and I are delighted to welcome her into the family and we wish Damien and Melanie a very happy future together.'

'Well done, Damien!' Someone called from the back of the room.

'Lucky man, Damien!'

'When's the happy day?'

'Congratulations!'

People began to applaud as Damien and Melanie smiled around, Melanie pink-faced and self-conscious as she'd not been expecting Brendon to say those nice things, though she knew he was very fond of her, apart from fancying her in a way he couldn't quite conceal.

The applause ended and people pressed forward to shake Damien's hand and clasp Melanie's arm. And then the classical music began to filter softly from concealed speakers, which was one of the aspects of a Brendon Docherty party, in this case Mozart's Clarinet Concerto. Docherty now carried on his host duties of moving steadily but unhurriedly from couple to couple, while Tessa stood with a small group of her own friends and relations. Chatting and smiling, she still had the slightly preoccupied air of a woman concerned that everything was going to plan in the kitchen and dining room. A reliable and expensive catering firm had been engaged to prepare the food and circulate with the trays of drinks, but she had her misgivings.

*

'I've done such a silly thing, Frankie. When I was rushing to get showered and changed I completely forgot to put my knickers on! What if we were on the patio and there was a breeze that blew my skirt up I'd not know where to look. Can you believe that I could do something as silly as that?'

Crane could, quite easily. In fact he doubted if there would be any event she could go to, however grand, where she could be relied on to arrive knicker-intact.

She was wearing a summer dress in floral cotton with a scoop neck, short sleeves and a full, pleated skirt. The long fall of her glossy hair had received a lot of careful attention and Crane was reminded again of the woman in the old black and whites. He had a box set of *films noirs* DVDs and he'd checked out the sultry-looking actress in *A Gun for Sale* and found it to be Veronica Lake. It was as if Josie had used her as a model and it was a look that became her. It somehow went with the state she was in – knickerless and probably bra-less beneath the cotton dress. She could be in bed, anyone's bed, legs akimbo, in seconds.

'When we've had some supper, Frankie,' she began softly, then broke off to deftly deposit her empty champagne glass on a tray proffered by a young man in a white jacket and take yet another full one. When the waiter caught her scent and took in the neckline of her dress it was as if he sensed that economies had been made in the underwear department. He moved quickly away, eyes averted. 'When we've had some supper, Frankie,' Josie said again, 'and everyone's got rat-arsed why don't we slip upstairs for a little while? It's liberty hall at Tanglewood House, I'm sure no one would notice in this mob.'

It wasn't easy for Crane to keep the picture out of his mind of her slender naked body beneath his, her buttocks, he sensed, gyrating at the speed of a CD and Josie giving little squeaks of pleasure. It was why he'd been determined not to take her home later.

'We couldn't do that, Josie, take advantage of people who are giving us such lavish hospitality. It would be like treating the place as a cheap motel.'

She pouted a little. 'I had you down as a chancer, Frankie. But perhaps you're right. If anyone found out and it got back to Tony I'd never hear the end of it. We'll hang on till we're back at your place.' Then she added in the breathy tone that was so incredibly sexy in combination with her little-girl voice, 'But it won't be easy. I'll not be able to stop thinking about it.'

That was Crane's problem, too. Right now Josie Mellors was a distraction he could do without.

Mollie said, 'I'm so pleased about your engagement, Mel. I couldn't wish for a nicer sister-in-law.'

'Mollie, I'm absolutely delighted to be coming into your lovely family. And so good of your dad to say those things. It was completely unexpected.'

It was a day that had begun cloudy but the sky had cleared in the afternoon, as so often in an English summer, and the big room was flooded with setting sunlight. It enhanced the patterned grey-green wallpaper, the delicately painted plaster moulding of the high ceiling and the gilt-framed Canaletto prints. Almost all the men had taken off their jackets and stood about in shirt-sleeves; the women all wore summer dresses or tops and light skirts. They all looked to be well off, with many of the women wearing costly bracelets and necklaces, while the men sported gold or platinum cufflinks and Rolex watches. Some people were drifting out through the French window to sip their drinks on the patio. Damien and the two women watched Docherty's steady progress round the room, shaking hands, kissing cheeks, chatting for a few minutes.

'No one can work a room like the old man,' Damien said enviously as he watched his father's progress, a trim sturdy figure in crisp white shirt and chinos, thick dark hair neatly cut, listening in the enveloping way he had, as if the person he was talking to was of special interest and required his total attention.

'Watch and learn, little brother,' Mollie said. 'One day when you're standing for the North Division you'll need advanced glad-handing skills.'

Melanie smiled at Damien being called 'little brother'. Mollie, pretty-looking with dark curly hair, green eyes and a Celtic cast to her features, was several years older than Damien and one day really had been the big sister he'd looked up to from his playpen. 'Little brother' was an amusing term now when Damien stood head and shoulders above her.

'Daddy's *so* ambitious for you both,' Mollie said. 'He told me he wanted to live long enough to see Demmy as a secretary of state in the Commons and then appointed to the Lords. But he knew that to do that it would help if you had the right kind of wife. He said he couldn't think of anyone who'd fill the bill better than you, Mel.' She grinned. 'He's very dynasty minded. Wants to see the right kind of people running the country.'

Damien said, 'I never knew that. He's never put the slightest pressure on me but he was always so encouraging. Do politics and economics at university but don't try straight away for an internship to do research. Go into business for a few years to get a feel for what it's all about. It'll pay off, there are too many MPs these days who know sod all about the commercial world, that's why businessmen can run rings round them when they're buying these great computer systems.' He smiled. 'Well, that's Dad. And this evening he wants me to do the rounds myself, in the hope that one of these high-fliers can find me an opening. Hope you don't mind, Mel.'

'Of course not. I'm just pleased you're so ambitious. Life might get hard and hectic but I don't think it'll ever be dull. I'll stay here with Mollie and if you need me give me a high five. And if you go within two yards of the nutty nympho I'll throw this flower vase at your head!'

'I've got to, Mel. It wouldn't be polite not to. And I need to

thank her for her great kindness to me last time she was
here. . . .'

As Josie prattled on, becoming slightly incoherent with the
champagne she was putting away on an empty stomach, Crane
monitored Brendon Docherty's progress around the room, with
his warm smile that never seemed fixed or put on. He wasn't a
tall man but he carried himself erect and with his broad
shoulders, seemed to dominate the room. What was the
connection between Mellors and Docherty? Mellors worked in
the public sector and would seem to have little place at a do like
this, which seemed mainly composed of businessmen. Docherty
was clearly a very successful businessman himself. There was
this great house with its block of garages containing top of the
range motors, this limitless supply of expensive champagne,
outside caterers to prepare food that would almost certainly be
as perfect as the wine. Where did a man like Mellors fit into all
this?

Crane then noticed that Docherty's son was also beginning to
make the rounds of the room. He looked to have similar
mannerisms to his father; the engaging style, the ready smiles,
the ability to talk easily. He was a well-set-up young man, taller
than his father and leaner. His fiancée was a looker, too. There
was a lot of affection in the family, which Crane warmed to as
he'd always been close to his own parents. Yet he needed to bear
in mind that if Docherty knew Mellors well enough to invite him
into his house there could be an outside possibility that
Docherty's business activities weren't entirely kosher. But then
a lot of businessmen operated near the edge. And got away with
it.

'Hello, Josie! How nice to see you again.' Docherty stood in
front of them. 'I've not had the pleasure of meeting this
gentleman before.' He leant over and kissed her cheek, then took
Crane's hand, who introduced himself. 'Where's Tony?'

'How lovely to see you . . . again, Brendon. Tony's had an awful migraine. It's a sort of . . . headache where you get . . flashing lights in your eyes, feel as sick . . . as a parrot and think someone's using your head as a football and—'

'I know about migraines, Josie, Tessa gets them occasionally, I'm afraid. I'm sorry to hear it. Could he not have dosed himself with paracetamol and come along? I'd have made sure he was looked after.'

'Para . . . para . . . pain-killers don't seem to work, Brendon. Should have seen him. Poorly sick in bed . . . with a shawl on.' She began to giggle and then hiccuped.

For some time now she'd been leaving gaps in her sentences as if not quite sure where the next word was coming from. She was swaying slightly and it was obvious she'd guzzled a great deal of Docherty's excellent wine and not treated it as the pre-prandial it was meant to be, but Docherty was just as charming and attentive to her as to all the other women. Even so, with his lengthy experience of reactions and what faces were telling him behind the impression they were giving, Crane had been able to detect that Docherty's warm smile was concealing intense annoyance. There'd been an almost subliminal hardness in the man's eyes on hearing the news of Mellors.

'Frank's a . . . friend of the family, Brendon. Hope . . . you don't mind him standing in for . . . Tony.'

'Not at all, not at all. I hope we can give you a pleasant evening, Frank. I'm very sorry Tony's been ill, Josie, as I particularly wanted to talk over a couple of things with him. Give him my regards and I hope he'll feel a lot better in the morning.' He nodded and moved off.

Josie treated herself uncertainly to yet more champagne from the young waiter's tray. He seemed barely able to look at her in case he couldn't tear his eyes away from her cleavage. 'Let's . . . not stay too . . . late, Frankie. Let's . . . toddle off to . . . your place when we've . . . had a bite to eat,' she murmured, trying for her demure but inviting look and not quite making it.

'Hello, Josie, nice to see you again. Tony not about?'

It was Damien Docherty, working the room in the opposite direction to his father.

'Demmy, darling, how lovely. What a lucky . . . girl Maureen is to nobble a . . . handsome bloke like you.'

'Melanie,' he said, correcting her with as pleasant a smile as his father's. 'And I think I'm the lucky one to be engaged to a girl like her.'

'Whatever,' she said dismissively, in her lisping tipsy voice. 'Tony's got . . . a migraine. You get flashing . . . lights in your eyes and feel as sick as a . . . football and as if someone's using your head as a parrot—'

'I know about migraines, Josie, Mum has them now and then. Sorry about Tony.'

'Poorly sick in bed . , . shawl on.' She began to giggle again.

'I don't think we've met, sir. I'm Damien Docherty,' Damien said politely to Crane. As their eyes met Crane raised his eyebrows slightly and the other gave him a faint knowing smile, as if both in agreement that there wasn't much you could do about Josie.

'I'm Frank Crane, Damien, how do you do. I'm just a family friend standing in for Tony.'

'How do you do, sir. I'm sorry about Tony. Hope he's soon better.'

Crane said, 'We've just been talking to your father. You're both very welcoming to a stranger. I feel I know your father from somewhere. Would you mind me asking what line he's in?'

Damien smiled again. 'Not easy. He has an office on Well Street, which he spends long days in, but I've never been able to get a clear fix on what he does.'

'A one-man band?'

'He's involved in property and building deals, I know that. A lot of the people here are in the building business or as suppliers of materials. He's also connected to imports and exports but I couldn't really tell you in what way. He just hates talking about his work.'

'Will you perhaps be going into business with him?'

'Oh, no. Dad says it simply wouldn't work. He says he spends his life nosing out deals and operating on gut instinct. I'm just down from university and I'm hoping one of the people here might find me an opening if I make the right noises.'

'I'm sure you'll be snapped up, a young man of your background.'

'Well, fingers crossed. What's your line?'

'Frank?' Josie suddenly erupted. 'Frank's a—'

'Financial adviser,' he said before she could blurt out his real occupation. Like doctors, he was guarded about what he really did in general company. Doctors didn't want to hear about your grumbling hernia and PIs didn't want to talk about their prices or hear jokes on the lines of, 'Do you drink bourbon and wear a trilby hat and have a blonde called Mitzi with boobs this big as your PA, hur hur hur.'

'Not easy, I should have thought in today's tough climate.'

'I'm afraid you're right, but I plod on, hoping for better times.'

'Well, nice to talk to you. See you later. My regards to Tony, Josie.'

'See . . . you later, darling, if I can get past . . . Mildred.'

Crane watched him go. With his ready smile and his easy manner, there'd been quite a lot there to make him think.

'I . . . feel a bit . . . dizzy,' Josie said, giving a sudden lurch. Crane caught her, one hand on her back and one on her arm. What a bloody nuisance she was. But he supposed he had to remember that without her he wouldn't be here. 'Let me get you out in the fresh air,' he said. 'It's getting a bit oppressive in here.'

He bundled her out through the French windows and sat her down on the patio beneath a parasol. People were now moving back inside as it was time for the buffet. 'I'll get you something to eat, Josie,' he told her, knowing she was badly in need of food as ballast for the alcohol.

'Right you . . . are, lover. Where's my glass?'

'No more booze till you've eaten.'

'There's . . . masterful.'

He left her steadily hiccuping and went through to a busy dining room. There was a vast array of buffet foods and he filled two plates with a mixed assortment and went back to the patio, asking the young waiter, who was pouring coffee, to bring two cups outside. The patio was now deserted and Josie was laid back in her chair with her feet on another, shoes abandoned, singing quietly to herself.

'I want you to eat this, Josie, all of it. It'll stop the dizziness.'

'All . . . right, master. Do it . . . for you. Not really into . . . food.'

He could believe it. The two dominant aspects of her mojo seemed to be drink and dick.

He sat down beside her and was about to start on his own supper when he heard faint voices. One of them he recognized as Docherty's. He got up. Josie had suddenly found her appetite and was eating steadily, eyes down. The voices came from the block of garages to the left of the house. The up and over doors were at the front of the house, but there were access doors at the rear, one of which stood ajar. Crane moved quietly to this door and glanced warily in. Docherty and another man were sitting in a sports car, which had its top down. Fortunately, the car had been backed in and the men were facing to the front. Docherty now came over as abruptly different from the warmly outgoing host of the drawing room. He was speaking very forcefully and with a harsh edge to his tone.

'That bastard *owes* me. The house, the wheels, the place on the coast, money in off-shores, he'd never have got any of those things off his own bat. What's bugging the sod?'

'He says he's done enough and he's had enough, boss. Says he wants out.'

'*I* say when anyone goes and in his case it won't be for a long time yet. He should have been here tonight; I was going to have it out with him. Christ, the trouble is I need the beggar. I'll have him in the minute I can find a window. I'm up to here right now, that's why I put it off.'

67

'You're one busy man, boss.'

'I was counting on sorting it all out tonight and I could have done without that drunken twat of a wife of his rolling up with the latest screw. I suppose he's shafting her out of what wits she's got. Pouring my best champagne down her throat like tap water.'

'You might have a job talking him round. He's saying nothing will keep him on board. He wants his old life back.'

'Tough. He wanted the money so he came in. And once in, you stay in. You're not in a position to choose any more.'

'What if he *tries* to go?'

'There's no chance, Joe. We hold the cards, the full pack. I don't need to spell it out.'

'I know what you're saying.'

'I'll have him in next week, whatever has to go on the back burner. Right, let's move on. How's that other matter going?'

'The bogie's on leave. Back Monday and then we'll have a name and address.'

'Good. I'm not too worried. The way we're organized no one can crack the system. Go back in the house through the front door and mingle. I'll go in the back way. Best if you're just one of the crowd in there.'

'Got you, boss.'

Crane moved quietly and quickly back to the patio table. Josie had eaten all the food on her plate and now seemed almost back to her usual self as she sipped black coffee. She appeared to have remarkable powers of recuperation and he guessed it was the nervous energy she almost vibrated with.

'I do wish you'd told me you were going for a tinkle,' she said petulantly, back to speaking clearly now. 'I thought you'd started chatting up someone else. When that gorgeous young waiter came with the coffee I was very tempted to take him down under the trees for a quickie. I thought he should have some fun in life looking like that. I could tell he'd got the hots for me.'

Crane thought it must have been near impossible for him not

68

to have, if he wasn't gay. With her feet up on the facing chair the skirt of her floaty dress had ridden so far up her shapely thighs that had it gone half an inch further the waiter would have known for certain that she regarded underwear as an optional extra.

'Oh, hello again. I thought everyone had gone inside.'

Docherty gave them his warm smile and spoke in the same agreeable way as earlier, but in the last of the sunlight Crane caught the split second of wariness in the other's look of surprise.

'Oh, Frank brought me outside because I was a tiny bit overcome by the heat build-up in your lovely room,' Josie said brightly, as if the eight glasses of champagne she'd seen off had had nothing to do with it. She was the sort of person, and Crane had known many, who could give their own version of the truth and then genuinely believe it. 'Where did *you* pop from, Brendon?'

'The garage. I was just checking tyre pressures. I've got a long drive north in the morning.'

'Ooh, I wish I was going in that gorgeous Phantom of yours.'

'What a temptress you are, Josie,' he said, chuckling, 'but Tessa would take a dim view. We old married men, we have to toe the line.

He looked, in fact, very tempted as his glance flicked over her thighs to where her skirt only just concealed her Brazilian. But Crane could tell he was satisfied he'd not been overheard in the garage. Smiling and nodding he gave them a few more pleasant words and then went back to the drawing room.

It was now getting dark and Crane and Josie also returned inside. Josie took a glass of dry Martini from the young waiter's tray but sipped from it very sparingly, as if she'd moved on to her other preoccupation: how soon she could count on being given one on Crane's duvet. The waiter haunted their part of the room, clearly expecting Josie to want a drink every few minutes. It was as if he sensed he'd almost been handed ten minutes of gold-plated fun in Mr Docherty's back garden and perhaps if he hung about. . . .

As people had now eaten they tended to move around more and Crane found himself shaking hands and making general coversation with those who drifted into his orbit. But the big draw, to the men, anyway, was Josie. It was obvious her reputation had travelled, about the open marriage and her readiness to take off her knickers – assuming she actually had any on. The men strove to give an impression of casual friendliness but found it impossibly difficult to control their reactions to the incredibly sexy pull she exerted as they grasped her hand and kissed her cheek. Josie, basking in the attention, could have been lying topless on a sunny beach.

Crane smiled and nodded and made the right kinds of noises. Most of the men he chatted to came across as successful business types, but there was a small group of men in a corner of the room who tended to keep to themselves. They were well dressed and had the expensive watches but to Crane's acute eye they seemed not to be quite the same as the rest. The differences were very slight but he knew they were there. They had about them a certain guardedness. At one point he saw Docherty join them. As he talked, they listened almost deferentially, as if he was some kind of figure of authority.

Damien had confirmed that his father worked as a one-man band but Crane hadn't been able to buy that. Anyone who'd got together a business successful enough to provide this kind of lifestyle couldn't have done it without *some* staff, however tight the ship was kept. He wondered if the men in the corner of the room worked for Docherty and if the man he'd heard in the garage, but not clearly seen, was one of them. He had a lot of thinking to do about what he'd heard but couldn't do it right now with all the distractions. It would have to wait till he'd dropped Josie off home.

Not that he *wanted* to drop off a knickerless, bra-less Josie, who would now, in the frightful jargon, be gagging for it; but he had to remind himself that with the funny things going on around Mellors and Docherty it would be safest for the time being to keep her at arm's length.

*

'I didn't know you lived this way.'

'I don't. I'm taking you home.'

'No!' she shrieked. 'We said we'd go to *your* place!'

'You said that, not me. My wife is sitting at my place and she'd take a dim view of me rolling up with you when I'm supposed to have been working.'

He wasn't married and lived alone but Josie wasn't to know that.

'Oh, Frankie, you never said you were married. Let's go to the Ramada then. Look, ring your wife and tell her you've got to go to Newcastle or somewhere.' Her little-girl voice had lost its soft throatiness and now held a note of pleading urgency.

'Sorry, I promised I'd be in by midnight. She sees little enough of me as it is.'

'Frankie, you do *want* to make love to me, don't you? I know I've turned you on. I always know.'

'You turn *all* straight blokes on, whether your knickers are on or off.'

She began to giggle. 'Oh well, if we can't go to your place and you won't treat me to the Ramada we'll just have to make do at my place. Tony won't mind, really. It's an open marriage, you see.'

'I had a sneaky feeling it just might be.'

'There you are then. He'll be watching the telly while we're upstairs.'

At Bingley he right-angled up the hill, which took them to the Mellors's imposing house. The drive was lit up by the triggering of a security lamp as he drove the Renault into it. As they were getting out of the car, the front door was opened and Mellors stood there. He was dressed in a T-shirt and chinos. It was the first time Crane had seen him out of a business suit, but the casual clothes made little difference to the impression he gave of a nondescript and unassuming man.

'Hi, Tony,' Josie called. 'This is Frank. He stood in for you at

71

Brendon's. Brendon was very disappointed you couldn't make it.'

Mellors looked decidedly uneasy at this. He nodded to Crane without speaking. He gave no impression he'd been in agony all day with a severe migraine. Did that mean he'd not been able to face Docherty this evening and the migraine had been an excuse? In other words, he'd bottled it?

'Frank's just coming in for an hour, Tone. We'll not bother you. Go back to your telly.'

'I can't come in, Josie. I must get back home now.'

'Oh, *Frankie!*' Her shrill voice carried in the silent darkness. 'You *can't* rush off like this. Just come in for half an hour then.'

'Sorry, Josie. Another time.'

'Oh, Frankie, *quarter* of an hour!' she cried in a voice of near-desperation. Even Mellors looked taken aback as his gaze passed from Josie to Crane. Crane wondered if it was some kind of a first for him, too, Josie being brought back to the house by a man who then got in his car and went home. Josie's mouth had fallen open as if she simply couldn't believe that any man really could leave her without a duvet session; that *had* to be a first for her. It was with genuine regret that he re-started his engine; he really didn't want to go home on her. But instinct was telling him not to get involved at this stage and he trusted it. He would call on Colette tomorrow, his semi-detached girlfriend, to take his mind off Josie.

When he reached home he didn't go in the house right away. He turned on classic FM and began to do what he spent half his life doing: he sat in his car and thought.

'That was a really lovely do. I enjoyed it.'

'Dad always says to make a party go with a swing have plenty of good booze, plenty of good things to eat and turn a blind eye to where they wander off to, even if it's upstairs to have a kiss and a cuddle with someone they're not married to.'

The drawing room now stood empty of guests and the catering people were quietly removing glasses and plates and rearranging furniture. But the room still seemed to hold an imprint of the many people who'd filled it, the talk and the laughter, the endless movement, the unobtrusive background Mozart.

'The chap called Frank, who was with your close personal friend, Josie, he didn't seem to be slapper-bait – assuming Josie really is a slapper.'

'Josie could enter the Olympics as England's greatest bonker and be certain of a gold medal. Never been too picky, either, who she *bonked*. Well, you saw the blokes hanging round her after supper with their tongues on the carpet. But you're right, Frank doesn't really seem a Josie type.'

'He hasn't any looks worth talking about but there's something about him. Tall, strong-looking and a sort of capable air. And a smile that makes all the difference.'

'He looks like the sort of man who should really have been here with someone like you.'

'I couldn't have put it better myself.'

'He was only supposed to be standing in for Tony Mellors. A family friend, in gigantic inverted commas.'

'By the way, who were those men who stood together over in the corner and didn't seem to mingle very much?'

Damien smiled, shook his head. 'I keep forgetting how odd the old man's set-up must seem to anyone who's not lived with it all their lives. I've absolutely no idea who they are in Dad's scheme of things and am not remotely curious. They're just something to do with Dad and you know how tight-lipped he is. I read somewhere that novelists dislike talking about the book they're working on in case they somehow talk it away and can't put it back together. Maybe that's how Dad is about the business. He runs it all on instinct and if he tries to explain it in too much detail the instinct might dry up.'

She smiled. 'You could be right. Look, darling, I'm going to help your mum in the kitchen.'

'Mel, for heaven's *sake*. There are highly paid people to do all that.'

'She wants to do the glasses herself, says she can't trust caterers with the best glasses. See you soon.'

Damien watched her go, wondered if he should help with the many glasses, too. But just then the French windows opened and his father stepped in. 'Ah, Demmy, there you are. I've just been doing the rounds.'

It was part of his father's routine, checking that the garages and the outhouses were secure and the cars locked. Though he never gave that impression, his father was a very careful man. He now locked the French windows and came over to him. 'Good news. Charlie Murphy's got an opening that has your name on it, son. Go and see him next week and he's in a position to start you a week Monday.'

'Dad, that's *terrific!*'

'No one knows the brick business like Charlie. You'll learn a lot from him and his people. I didn't mention the politics but he did. He knows about your involvement with the Party. I told him if you managed to put up for a division it would probably be five to ten years down the road yet. He doesn't mind. Says the prestige of having a possible MP on the staff would be good for business.'

'Dad, you really are a marvel!'

They put their arms round each other. Just then, Mollie came in. 'Hey!' she said, 'If you're having a hug-fest can anyone join in?'

'I've got a spare arm, sweetheart.'

The three of them hugged and kissed. 'Sure,' Docherty said, his voice slipping into the Irish inflection he used with family and thickening with emotion. 'I couldn't have wished for a finer son and daughter.'

'Oh, Daddy, what about a finer *father?*' Mollie said. 'Marvellous holidays, this lovely home, private schools. We've been spoilt rotten.'

'Not spoilt, darling, never spoilt. I had two good plants and all I did was make sure they were put in good soil, were properly watered and got plenty of sun. All the rest you did yourselves.'

'Peter's really sorry he couldn't be here. He's so keen to expand his business. He's working on the books tonight. He's over the moon about your loan. It's going to make all the difference. He's going to start paying you back next month and at a proper interest rate, not a Mickey Mouse half of one per cent.'

'He mustn't, Moll. Tell him he just pays it back straight and only when he's in a position to. He's a good chap and he'll get on.'

'Oh, Daddy.' She kissed him fondly again on the cheek.

Damien said, 'We can never repay you, Dad, for the great life you've given us.'

'Your children don't need to repay, son. It's a one-way system. Your job is to give your own children a good life.'

Crane mulled over everything he'd heard outside Docherty's garage. He had a trained memory and could recall the details almost word for word. Mellors wanted to get out of whatever he was in and Docherty didn't want him to. Docherty had been able to provide him with a lavish life-style but what had Mellors done for Docherty that was causing Docherty to take a very tough line about him 'wanting to go back to his old life'? It sounded very much as if he had the power to force Mellors into continuing to do what he no longer wanted to do. Crane wondered if he could believe that there'd been an almost criminal undertone in Docherty's attitude. But how could that be? The man obviously lived in the middle of a very loving family. Crane could have him checked out but was certain he'd be found to be as clean as the expensive white shirt he'd worn this evening.

But what about the parcel Mellors had picked up from the old lady? It could have been quite above board but what if it wasn't? There was also the matter of a 'bogie' being on leave but when he was back they'd have a name and address. That sounded very much like a bent copper feeding a car registration number into the national computer and illegally supplying the details to someone who illegally wanted them. He wished they'd said who they wanted them for.

Finally there'd been the man called Joe who'd sat in the sports car with Docherty and the two or three men who'd stood in a corner of the drawing room looking, to Crane's eye, slightly different to the rest of the men. And who had been very respectful indeed when Docherty had joined them.

None of it looked good but he found it difficult to believe that Docherty could be any other than the man he seemed; a devoted family figure who'd got on. The trouble was, he *wanted* Docherty to be that person; he was finding it difficult to be objective. Yet Docherty had said that the way he had things organized no one could crack the system. What system and who did he suspect of trying to crack it? Was it the man that the one called Joe was keen to trace through a vehicle registration?

Crane got out of his car and let himself into his house. He was getting nowhere.

'Boss?'

'Go ahead, Joe, as long as you're on a landline.'

'Great party, Saturday.'

'Glad you enjoyed it. I had a lot of hospitality to repay.'

'This bloke who's been tailing Mellors, boss. I've got the info now. It's a guy called Frank Crane. He's a private dick.'

'Frank Crane. That's odd, there was a chap at my do called Frank Crane, but Damien said he's a financial adviser. Coincidence. So why should a PI be tailing Mellors?'

'He's got serious form. Used to be a bogie himself a few years back, CID.'

'Was he now. Is someone trying to stitch Mellors up?'

'Can't see it. Bogies yes; a private man no. Who'd be paying him to do that kind of work?'

'Well, he'd not find anything, not the way we have it. I need to think this through, Joe. Ring me back in half an hour.'

'Will do, boss.'

The phone rang exactly half an hour later. 'Me, boss.'

'I can't think what the guy's up to, Joe, but we can do without him giving Mellors the eyeball.'

'Might just see something he shouldn't.'

'Have your boys give him a kicking.'

'Leave it with me.'

'Nothing serious. No broken bones or head damage. They tell him to stop shadowing Mellors. Just that. They tell him if they catch him at it again they'll leave him in such a bad way he'll not be able to crawl as far as the gate.'

'I've got it, boss. And Mellors, what's the story there?'

'I'm getting him in on Thursday. They're fixing to send another parcel. France. Same routine. We've got another old lady in place. This will be the test for Mellors and he's got two choices: he either stays with us and does what he's told or he'll lose everything, I'll make sure of that. . . .'

FIVE

The three women sat in Cilla's flat. It was in Conway House, the same building where Linda had hers. Cilla had brown wavy hair with blonde highlights and a similar kind of prettiness to Linda's: clear blue eyes and well-shaped features. But the prettiness was flawed.

'The acid caught me on the right cheek,' Cilla said. 'Not full on, otherwise I'd have been in a right old mess.'

She spoke as if relieved to have hung on to the looks she still had.

'Oh, Cilla, I've never known anything like it. It must have been an appalling shock.'

Cilla gave a fatalistic shrug. Like Linda, all she really had was her looks and her figure and they'd even wanted to take those from her. The skin graft had been an excellent piece of work. The frightful scorching of the flesh on her right cheek had been completely concealed by a smooth, clear transplant, presumably from one of her buttocks. But it had left her face unbalanced and with a faint sheen that wasn't an exact match to the left side. Her right eye had been drawn slightly out of true. Despite the surgeon's skill, Cilla was never going to look the same as she'd once looked. But Melanie said, 'The surgery's marvellous, Cilla. You look as good as new.'

Cilla gave a wry smile. They were comforting words but they

both knew the minute changes to the right side of her face made it seem disproportionately uneven. 'It could have been a hundred times worse, Mel.'

Melanie said, 'Are you still having to do . . . the tricks?'

'Oh, yes. It's just that the choosey blokes with the fat wallets don't want to know now. I have to make do with what's left.'

They sat in silence for a short time in an atmosphere that, to Melanie, seemed tinged with the pain and suffering Cilla had had to go through. She said, 'Look, both of you, would you really like to get out of this frightful existence?'

Linda said, 'Like tomorrow, only that's never going to happen, is it? How can it, the way they're on our backs?'

'Linda, my boyfriend could make it happen. We've talked it over and given it a lot of thought. No, you weren't identified, I give you my word.'

For the next ten minutes she outlined the plan Damien had talked about when they'd sat in the pub. 'He'd pick you both up in the early hours and take you to Leicester. He's got an address where you could rent a flat that's not too dear. He'd cover your expenses for the first month. There's a good deal of unskilled work going, even today. It would give you a chance to make a completely new life for yourselves.'

Both women sat silent, mouths falling open. Then Linda said, 'Why would your boyfriend do all *that*? What's in it for him?'

Suspicion had become second nature in her now. In her short life she'd never known any man who'd ever done anything for nothing.

'There's nothing in it for Damien except the satisfaction he'd get from seeing you make a new start. That's the way he is. He hates to think of young women like you being in the hands of these frightful people.'

'Men don't *do* things like that,' Cilla broke out. Her suspicious streak was even stronger than Linda's. Understandably.

'The men *you* know don't. But Damien *does*,' Melanie said

firmly. 'I've known him a long time and I know how his mind works.'

'He wouldn't know us if he fell over us, Mel. Why would he want to help people he's never even met?'

'Because *I* know you and I know about the sad lives you're living and he takes my word for the things I've told him about you. Look, girls, you've got to believe me. By this time next week you could be in a different town, with no one knowing a single thing about your past lives.'

There was another silence, a longer one, as if the women needed time to get all this together. Then Cilla said tentatively, 'What do you think, Linda?'

Linda watched her for a good ten seconds, clearly thinking hard. 'I think we go for it,' she said slowly. 'We can trust Mel. She's not a bullshitter, doesn't say anything she doesn't mean.'

'Give yourselves a couple of days to think it over. Talk it through. If you decide to go ahead Linda can let me know. You'd only need to pack your bags on the night you thought it best to leave and until then you live exactly as normal.'

'It's going to take us a while to pay your boyfriend back for all this, Mel,' Cilla said uneasily.

'He'll not want paying back. Damien and me, we've been very lucky in having caring families and when we see how badly you've been treated we realize just how lucky we are. The man who threw acid at you, Cilla, should be in prison.'

'Both of them,' Cilla said bitterly, 'the one who threw it and the one who said it had to be done.'

'Do you know who these people are?'

'Oh, yes.' Cilla's face reddened unevenly, the colouring of the cheeks not quite matching. 'I know who they both are. But I daren't tell you, so don't ask.'

'She'll not even tell me,' Linda said.

'But everything that happens, everything, only happens because word comes from the top.'

Melanie said, 'The police should be told, Cilla. These awful things shouldn't be happening and no one being punished.'

There was fear in Cilla's eyes and she seemed to hunch into herself. 'The acid in the face, it was because I said I'd speak to the police. My . . . my bloke and me, we'd had a few. He said I wasn't making the tricks . . . exciting enough. There'd been complaints. One of them came down from the top.'

'You had sex . . . with *him*?'

'My bloke, he got very angry. Said it blew back on him if I didn't put enough into it. Because of the booze he'd had he let a name slip. He went as white as a sheet. "You didn't hear that," he said, "you never heard it. If that name got out and they traced it to us they'd beat us senseless". But I was spitting feathers, what with the gin and the sex I wasn't making sexy enough. I told him I'd go to the police and tell them everything I knew. And I knew a hell of a lot. Des, he couldn't keep 'is mouth buttoned. He bragged about what went on, 'specially when he'd been at the rum and a line up the nose, know what I'm saying? And I said I'd tell the police everything: the drugs, the illegals, the loan-sharking, the computer hacking, the prostitution, and I'd tell them who was the top banana 'cause now I *knew*. That's what got me the acid in the face.'

Shuddering, Melanie said, 'Would you really have gone to the police?'

Cilla shook her head. 'It was just the drink talking. What would the police have *done*? This stuff's been going on for years and the police have never been near. And everyone would deny everything, including the girls, and that would be that. But Des, full of drugs and booze, he *believed* what I was saying so I got the acid.'

'Look, Cilla, it all sounds like some kind of organized crime to me. If you did go to the police and told them who threw the acid and about the other things that go on you'd get witness protection. They'd put you in a safe house and—'

'I've heard it all, Mel. You might as well be dead. Cut off from your mates, on your own most of the time, new moniker, all that crap. I couldn't do it.'

'It wouldn't be much different if Damien got you to Leicester.'

'We'd have each other, me and Lin. We'd be able to live ordinary lives and make new friends.'

'We just want out, Mel, and no more hassle,' Linda said. 'Anything to do with the bogies would just bugger our lives up and they've been buggered up enough as it is.'

'Well, if you ever do feel you want to talk about it and can give me any names I'm sure Damien would be able to sort something out. He's clever, he'd know what to do. . . .'

It was another warm, sunny day. She opened the door as he was getting out of the car. All she seemed to be wearing was a man's shirt, striped in blue and white.

'Come in, Frankie. Great to see you.'

As usual, it was unlikely she'd be wearing any knickers or bra and his hands seemed to tingle with the urge to stroke her breasts and buttocks, satiny with a dusting of talcum powder.

'How about we cut to the chase, Frankie, and go for a nice lie down? Dumping me on Saturday like you did, it means we've got a lot of making up to do.'

'You must put on some jeans, Josie, we've got a lot of serious talking to do and we can't do it with you in just one of Tony's shirts.'

'Oh, come on, a nice lie down first and you can do all the talking you like then, promise.'

Her long fair hair was glossy with brushing and as usual she'd taken great care with the false eyelashes and the dark-red lipstick. It was with a considerable effort that he forced himself to turn away and walk into the sitting room. 'No, Josie, you're paying me to work for you and the whole point of working for you seems to be getting lost. There are things I've *got* to talk to you about.'

'You can be such a *bore*,' she said, pouting. But she trailed off and rejoined him a few minutes later, the shirt tucked into a pair of white linen trousers. She said, 'I thought you'd told me he wasn't messing about. Just taking the tea-girl to lunch.'

Crane sat down in an armchair, knowing that if he sat on the sofa she'd sit close to him with a hot, overlapping thigh. Josie half-laid herself on the sofa, displaying most of her cleavage through the only partly buttoned front of the shirt. He said, 'I'm pretty sure there's no other woman, but Tony *might* be involved in other things you should know about.'

'Christ, not other *blokes!*' she hooted. 'Don't tell me he's turned a fiver each way.'

'No, he's not bi-sexual either, as far as I can tell, but he might just be dabbling in things that are definitely illegal.'

She raised her eyebrows slightly but that was all. 'Well, that's *obvious*, Frankie. You don't think all this stuff comes from the peanuts the council pays him: this house, the motors, the seaside place, the cruises—'

'You . . . *know* he's into funny money in a big way? Has he told you how he makes it?'

'Never says a word. Just gives me the money I need for clothes and a new motor when I want a change. I don't even work. Tony says there's no point.'

Crane had already guessed that any kind of work would severely restrict the freedom that was essential to her dedicated pursuit of a demanding sex life.

'Look, Josie, you must have your own ideas about how Tony is able to make so much money.'

She shrugged indifferently. 'He works in planning so he'll know a lot about property that will be useful to guys like Brendon Docherty. Brendon wanted Tony there at the Saturday do. Best not to back out of an invitation to a Docherty piss-up when Brendon can throw the goodies your way, but Tony just didn't want to go. I told him it was a bad move.'

It handed him a surprise that she could have got so much together intuitively to reach more or less the same conclusion that he had himself, though in his case with a great deal of plodding observation and hard thinking. 'You reckon Docherty is using Tony's expertise about properties and re-development?'

'Not half. I mean you don't get to be as rich as Brendon selling firewood, right? That great house near the reservoirs, the lifestyle. What a *fantastic* bloke he is.'

There was an intensely wistful note in her little-girl voice. Docherty was clearly the one she yearned for above all others, despite being ready and willing to make do with men like Mellors or himself or even, when it came to the crunch, any man at all, really.

'Josie, if Tony and Docherty are involved in illegal activities something should be done about it.'

'How do you mean?'

'The police should be informed, that's what I mean.'

Her mouth fell open. 'The *police*? Because they're making a few bob on the side?'

'If they're running some kind of scam with taxpayers' money then it has to be stopped.'

'Frankie, all I'm paying you for is to check the bugger out for another woman. How he makes his living is sod all to do with anything.'

'If he's making a crooked living it's got a lot to do with me. I'm an old CID man and a big part of the job was trying to ensure the public wasn't ripped off.'

'Frankie, they *all* make a bit on the side. Even the MPs fiddle their expenses. It's just the way life is.'

'Not with me, it isn't.'

'What could you do about it, anyway? With a clever bloke like Brendon pulling the strings and Tony looking like a guy you'd trust with the Crown Jewels, no one's ever going to be able to tell if they're fixing the odd deal.'

She'd hit the bull's eye. How would he ever be able to prove anything with men as cautious as those two? But her lack of concern for the way she came by the gilded life she was able to lead depressed him.

'Oh, Frankie. . . .' She wafted a hand over her face and undid another button of the shirt as if the room was getting unbearably hot. 'Just relax, sweetheart. It really isn't worth worrying about.' She got to her feet with a pantherish grace and held out her hand. 'Come with me and I'll take your mind off things. You really are badly in need of cutting yourself some slack.'

'Sorry, I've got to move on.'

'*Frankie*! I thought we'd agreed you'd stay for an hour.'

'I didn't agree to anything and I can't spare the time. But I want you to think carefully about what Tony might be getting himself into. It could turn ugly, believe me. I feel sure he didn't begin his career wanting to involve himself in dodgy activities.'

'Tell me about it. If I'd not pushed him and nagged him we'd still be living in a semi and driving second-hand cars and having holidays in Margate. We'd be nowhere.'

He watched her in silence. It was a syndrome he'd known before; the feisty, manipulative woman and the partner who was clever but lacked drive. She really didn't care how he made his money as long as he made plenty of it.

'I'll see you later, Josie.' He got up and made for the door, not sure there was really any point in seeing her again. Mellors wasn't involved with another woman but was definitely into crooked activities. Josie lived happily with that and would be of no use in getting her husband's collar felt. Not in the totally amoral world she inhabited.

'Frankie!' she cried, 'please don't go, not yet.' She bounded after him as he walked quickly to his car, plucking at his jacket. 'I'll pay you double if you'll stay another half-hour.'

He smiled wryly. It was a first for him, being offered money to provide sex. He opened his car door, slid in. 'I really can't find the time, Josie. You'll have to make do with the gardener.'

'For Christ's *sake*, Frankie, he's in his seventies! I don't think he's had the bloody thing out since the millennium.'

They sat once more in the Dochertys' dining room with its view of trees in full leaf and its sounds of muted birdsong through open windows. Tessa, with her usual preoccupied air, had cooked the usual excellent dinner of lamb and a starter of Dover sole. Melanie, again, sat next to Brendon.

'Let me top you up, darling,' he said, pouring from a bottle of Sancerre. 'Sure, it does my two eyes a power of good to see yours beginning to sparkle so nicely.'

He gave her his warm, enveloping smile that contained that faint wistful hint of desire she was getting used to. She supposed that it was only to be expected that a vigorous man like Brendon should have a high sex drive. She thought of the party when the women had found him so attractive as he'd moved from one group to another, their eyes lingering on him as he'd made his steady progress; the perfect host, with not a single woman, it seemed, whose first name wasn't carefully stowed in his capacious memory.

Yes, he was a highly charged man, but that was the way he was made. Yet she also sensed in him that fondness that was similar to the fondness he had for his son and daughter. It was very, very pleasant after a long day in the crisp factory to luxuriate in his affection, knowing that the only woman who really figured in his life was the one he'd been married to for all these years – plump Tessa, who Melanie knew from old photos to have once been very pretty with a lovely figure.

'Tell me, Mel, the young woman you mentioned last time you were here. She had a boyfriend who knocked her about. Is that still going on?'

'Oh, it all seems to have quietened down now and she's managing to stay bruise-free.'

'I should think so, too. Some of the things that happen these days. Wasn't I only reading in the paper not long ago about a poor kid getting acid thrown in her face. This isn't Manchester or London, it's a respectable town. What's going on, Mel?'

Melanie caught Damien's eye across the table and he gave her a faint conspiratorial wink.

'It's a different world to the one we were brought up in,' Tessa said sadly. 'Drugs, domestic violence, all these young kids having babies by different men and then expecting society to house and feed them.'

'You're right, Tess,' Docherty said. 'Who could have thought things would go this way? And to have acid thrown in your face. Probably some boyfriend she'd told to get lost. I was going to offer to pay for the reconstructive surgery to be done by a top man, it upset me so much. But then the public started chipping in and they set up a fund. I sent them five hundred pounds and there was soon enough in the kitty to put her face to rights. But the swine who threw the acid should have had acid thrown in his own face. And if it blinded him, all to the good.'

He'd grasped his wine glass so tightly that Melanie thought it was in danger of shattering. He was so goodhearted and she was quite sure that if there hadn't been a public fund for Cilla's surgery he really would have picked up the tab. Her eyes met Damien's across the table again. 'Oh, well,' she said, 'let's hope she got over that frightful injury and her life is going to improve. . . .'

'I didn't want to tell your parents about *our* involvement. The girls were almost paranoid about their names not being used.'

'You're right, best to keep schtum. Well, you know what Dad's like about keeping his mouth shut, but Mum can be a bit chatty with her sisters. Best if no one knows except us.'

They sat again at the side of the upper reservoir in the evening silence. Ducks were making for the boundaries to settle for the night and the sheet of water was becoming as still as glass. Damien said, 'What's the situation with the girls, have they made a decision?'

'They're still brooding about it, psyching themselves up. It's a big step to take, starting a completely new life away from a town they've lived in all their lives.'

'My Leicester pal, he can recommend a decent place for them to stay. The woman who owns the house has a flat that's available. Naturally, she's said it's first come, first served, but she's agreed to let Clive know if anyone else wants to take the lease. In which case I'll pay to keep it reserved for when the girls are ready.'

'It's very good of you, Demmy.'

'Clive also says he believes he could line up some work for them. His uncle owns several short-order restaurants and staff vacancies come up fairly regularly.'

'I'll tell Linda tomorrow, it'll help to focus their minds. If they have somewhere to live and work to do I'm sure they'll be ready to take the plunge. It would give them breathing space and a chance to sort out their lives. They might even find some kind of happiness. I hope so – they deserve it.'

'You don't think they might be tempted to go back on the game?'

'Difficult to tell. I'm just hoping they'll be so sick of tricks and punters and the money going to pimps that it'll have put them off the game for good.'

Crane had worked late and it was dark when he got home. He gave a weary sigh. It had been yet another cheating husband of a middle-class woman who was in a position to pay him to confirm what she suspected. He couldn't wait for the day when he never had to shadow another well-heeled middle-aged man and his dazzling PA. It was usually a matter of making sure that at the end of a lengthy wine-floated dinner the pair definitely occupied the same hotel room. Firm evidence had to be supplied to an anxious wife. If mobile phone photos could be produced of the pair in circumstances that could only have one possible interpretation then that was all to the good. Or to the bad, depending on where you were sitting.

He put his car in the garage, locked up and made for the back door of his house. Suddenly, two men appeared, almost soundlessly, in front of him. They were heavily built. His heart lurched. He knew this could only be bad news.

'You Crane?' one of the men grunted.

'What's . . . that to you?'

'We ask the questions, pal.'

'All right, my name's Crane. What—'

'You've been tailing a bloke called Mellors. Tony Mellors.'

Crane watched their shadowy faces in silence, thinking fast. He knew now that Mellors was definitely bent; maybe these two thought he was checking him out because of his illegal activities. He decided to go for injured innocence, to insist that the reason he'd been tailing Mellors was for what he'd been originally hired to do. 'Look,' he said, speaking as calmly as possible, 'I don't know what it's got to do with you but I've been keeping an eye on Mellors because his wife thought he might be having it off elsewhere. What's the problem with me trying to find out if he is?'

The men watched him for a few seconds. Then the one who did the talking said, 'We don't want you tailing him at all, pal. It stops right now and you'll do yourself a favour if you forget you ever heard Mellors's name.'

'What do I tell his wife?'

'Nothing, seeing as now you can't even remember who he is.'

'The woman's paying me, she'll want answers—'

The first man pushed him hard in the chest, sending him staggering backwards. As he tried to regain his balance he stumbled over the second man's raised leg and fell heavily to the ground.

The talking one said, 'Just in case you *don't* forget Mellors, Crane, we're going to give you an idea of what's going to happen if you can't get the guy off your mind.'

The kicking started then. Crane hunched himself up and clenched his teeth. He could have tackled one man, even though they were obviously skilled heavies, but with two of them it was best to let them get on with it. The kicking was very, very painful but it was inflicted by experts. The kicks landed on his thighs and buttocks and upper arms but none touched his head, spine or genitals. And the kicking didn't last *too* long, even though time seemed to be distorting seconds into minutes.

'OK, pal, that's the warning. You ever go inside a mile of Mellors again and you'll not walk for a month.'

'And then you'll probably need a zimmer.' The second man spoke for the first time.

'And you'd not want no brain damage. Brains are funny things to get right again.'

'If they ever do.'

'Can I give you a hand up, pal?' the first man asked in a ludicrously caring tone. 'You'll be as right as rain in a day or two.'

'I'll . . I'll see to myself,' Crane gasped painfully.

'OK, Switch, we're out of here.' The men padded off as silently as they'd come.

Crane had pitched from the driveway on to the back lawn. He lay there for some time, breathing deeply as the waves of pain passed through his body. He was going to feel bad for a few days but he could move all his limbs, so he knew nothing was fractured. He also knew there was nothing he could do about it. He could provide a rough description of the men but it would mean little or nothing to the police. And it wouldn't be a good idea involving the police anyway, not if he didn't want to find himself on crutches. He'd simply have to accept that he did a job that could occasionally be dangerous. He stretched his throbbing limbs again, almost ready to begin the agonizing process of levering himself to his feet. He gave a twisted grin. He now knew for certain that Mellors's bruises, as shown to him on Josie's photo, hadn't come from an S&M session. Like Crane's they'd come from a thorough kicking by those two state-of-the-art specialists.

SIX

'Boss?'

'Go ahead, Joe.'

'Crane. He's been seen to. No harm done, they never get carried away.'

'Good. If he used to be a cop he'll know the cops won't break sweat about a harmless kicking. How did he react?'

'He reckoned he was only tailing Mellors because his wife thought he might be playing away.'

'Playing away! It's supposed to be an open *marriage*. Christ, she's even tried to get me into bed half a dozen times. I'm not saying I'd not like to give her one, who wouldn't, but I just don't sleep with the women of men who work for me.'

'Well, that was Crane's story.'

'I daresay he was levelling. If Mellors really is playing away seriously it could leave that fuckwit of a wife of his on her uppers, cash wise. He'd take an entire way of life with him. She's got no other means of support, no livelihood. She's got so much on lining up the next shag-fest, it doesn't give her a lot of time to go to an office.'

Joe chuckled. 'The boys are pretty sure he wasn't bullshitting. Private dicks do do the sort of stuff he says he was doing.'

'OK, Joe, I think the boys have probably got it right, and if he's had the gypsy's warning I think we can forget about him. I doubt he'll be back.'

'They spelt out what would happen if he did.'

'We can't have the sod seeing something he shouldn't. Not an ex-CID man.'

'Too right.'

'Now Mellors himself, Joe. I've had him in, spent a long time with him. As you said, he wants to go back to his old way of life. I asked him what he'd use for money. He said he gets a decent salary and they'd just have to live inside it. I pointed out that Josie was very high maintenance but he said she'd just have to accept a lower standard of living.

'I told him very calmly and firmly that I wasn't running a corner shop, that he came voluntarily into a set-up that paid him top whack for the things he did for us.'

'How did he take it, boss?'

'He was scared. I didn't take an aggressive line but he knew I meant what I said. Once in, I told him, you don't get out.'

'Do you think you scared him enough to handle the French drop?'

'No. I want you to do it, Joe. You and me, we both know we're making do. No one can do these things as well as Tony – that respectable honest-John look of his – but I've sent him off and told him to think about what I've said very carefully.'

Docherty sighed. 'The trouble is, he scares easily but he has a stubborn streak. I could tell I wasn't getting the message across. When Mrs Thatcher was in office, Joe, and thinking of giving a back-bencher a promotion, do you know what she asked her closest aides: "Is he one of us?" In other words was he a dyed-in-the-wool Tory who thought the way she did, no wishy-washy left wing ideas.

'Well, that's what we have to ask ourselves about Tony Mellors: Is he one of us? And he just isn't.'

'He wanted the money, boss, no one *made* him come in.'

'He wanted the money because that trollop he married was never satisfied, and not just because she could never get enough dick.' He was silent for a few seconds. 'So if Tony's saying she'll just have to manage on his council salary maybe he's had enough of never being able to keep her satisfied. Maybe he really is having it off elsewhere and Josie was worried enough to hire a gum-shoe.'

'If Tony's not one of us what's the form?'

'It depends. I've given him a day or two to think it over, but if he still won't do what he's told we can't have any loose cannons. I'm beginning to think with Tony what you see is what you get, a bloke who can't live with what he's made himself do. He might, just might, begin to feel so guilty he needs to put his hand up.'

'Christ, you don't think—'

'I work on gut instinct, Joe, always have, and my instincts are telling me that if Tony really is going to throw a wobbly on us he'll need to be taken care of before he can do any serious damage.'

Crane had a bad couple of days. Hot baths and Arnica helped. He'd not taken any time off but carried on as usual, if slowly. It wasn't possible for him to sit at home doing nothing. He took on work that allowed him time to sit in his car, waiting and watching. He didn't attempt to shadow Mellors again; he was quite certain that the men who'd delivered his kicking had meant what they said.

He spent a lot of time thinking through the Mellors's situation. Going by Josie's photo, Mellors had been given a kicking that was identical to his own. Why was that? It seemed the heavies were employed to ensure you did as you were told. Was that the case with Mellors? He thought over the talk he'd overheard in the garage at Tanglewood House. About Mellors wanting out. Wanting out, it was now pretty clear, of crooked activity. And had he been wanting out even though he'd had a kicking?

Mellors looked so *ordinary*. Thinning hair, unremarkable features, a rather slight build. He had the sort of face that you simply couldn't associate with any kind of wrongdoing. Which had to be why he was so valuable to Docherty and why Docherty couldn't let him go.

But what if, at the start of his career, Mellors had been exactly what he'd seemed, a hard, conscientious worker, who was totally honest and reliable and liked the security of a public sector job? Before, say, Josie and her demands had tempted him, perhaps very much against his true nature, to go for the funny money.

Josie, after all, was an incredibly attractive woman. Could it be that Mellors had found it very difficult to believe that a woman like her could be attracted to a man like him? But what if Josie had had a secret agenda? Perhaps not too bright but very cunning, she'd known exactly what she wanted from life. Mellors may not have been a natural choice for a woman like her but perhaps she could sense he was going places in the planning department and she knew he was so in love with her, he could be manipulated. In those early days of the relationship Crane could quite see a man like Mellors being in the grip of an obsessive attraction. And perhaps Josie had wanted so much in the way of a costly lifestyle, and could be so persuasive, that Mellors had realized he'd need a lot more than his salary to satisfy her endless demands. When Docherty had come into the picture, perhaps he'd picked up on the same vibes as Josie, that here was a man, strategically placed in the council, who might be open to a little delicate leverage.

This was all conjecture. But Crane had always worked on hunches and often, he was right. Perhaps Mellors really had stopped wanting to live his crooked life. What if the decent, ordinary man he'd always seemed to be was still there, maybe struggling to get out from inside the man who wore eight hundred pound suits and drove expensive cars? And what, if he was striving to return to being the man he'd once been, might he do about the guilty conscience the past few years could have hung on him?

Crane suddenly sat up in his car, wincing with the pain that still lurked in his buttocks and thighs. He'd spent half an hour thinking through a situation that might just possibly be true. But if *his* mind was moving in this direction, what about Docherty's? He was a clever man and one of his most valued employees wanted to adopt his old way of life. How would he handle that? Surely it must have occured to him, as it had to Crane, that Mellors now had a great deal of information stored up in his head of the crooked set-up Docherty was running. Information that could be very dangerous if it got into the wrong hands.

Stalin had had a way with people he mistrusted: no man, no problem. Surely Docherty's mind couldn't be running on those kind of lines. But if it was, what could Crane do about it?

Docherty said, 'Sure, wasn't I only saying to Tessa the other day that if we'd had another daughter I'd have wanted her to be like you, Mel.'

'You and Demmy seemed so right for each other,' Tessa said. 'I could see you as a daughter-in-law from the first day I met you.'

Damien, across the table, grinned and rolled his eyes, but Melanie said, 'I'm very touched. I couldn't be coming into a nicer family.'

They were eating another of Tessa's delicious dinners, escallops of veal cooked in what Tessa said was the Viennese way and drinking Docherty's expensive wine. Dinner with the Dochertys was getting to be almost a daily event as Melanie's parents took a lengthy holiday at this time of the year, so when she got home from the factory she had to make her own meal. Tessa had simply said, 'You must eat with us, Mel, we always love having you here. It's as easy to cook for four as for three.'

She'd been welcomed so warmly by the Dochertys and she had to admit how much she enjoyed the lifestyle: the food, the wine, the big elegant house.

'You'll be finishing at Manchester next year then, Mel,' Docherty said, with his warm, embracing smile that she now accepted would probably always hold that hint of sexual desire.

'Are you still aiming to teach?'

She nodded. 'I'll need to tack on a teaching course but it shouldn't be more than a year.'

'It's a wise choice. You'll make a very good teacher. Any school in mind?'

'My ambition's the Girls' Grammar, but I daresay I'll have to make a start in the foothills and the way things are going, even that might not be all that easy; an awful lot of graduates after a very few openings.'

Docherty sipped his wine and was silent for a short time. 'St Dunstan's, Mel, I'm on the board of governors. I know when the vacancies come up. When you're going through your training I could do a bit of discreet lobbying for you. It's a good school and would give you worthwhile experience for having a crack at the Girls' Grammar in due course.'

'Oh, Brendon, that really is very thoughtful.'

'Looking after your loved ones is what it's all about, honey.'

Tessa had cleared away the dinner plates and now brought in strawberries and cream, a cheese board and freshly percolated coffee. Magician-like, Docherty had produced a half-bottle of Sauterne to complement the fruit and poured a little for Melanie into a separate glass. 'Now then, Demmy and Mel,' he said, 'we need to think about a place of your own for when you're married. I know it won't be for at least another year but there's no harm in getting your eye in.'

'If you're aiming to help us to buy one, Dad, I shall insist on paying you back once I'm in a position to.'

'Look, son, we've been through all this before. I bought Mollie a house and we've always treated you both the same. I've been lucky and I've been able to get a few bob to one side. It makes sense to spend some of it now and reduce the inheritance tax. So instead of paying me back, give some money to charity. One of the local ones that help the poor.'

Melanie sipped the sweet wine. What a great life she was having since she'd been drawn into this marvellous family. She couldn't repress a twinge of the old guilt, though, that every part of her life should be near-perfect when almost every part of Cilla and Linda's was frightful. So frightful that it meant starting life from scratch in a different town. She and Damien would do the very best they could for them. She felt she owed such a debt to the poor sad creatures they'd become because of all the good things that had been showered on her. It was like having two fathers; Brendon and the one at home. She felt she was beginning to love them both equally.

'Will you be having a little of the Bric now, Mel, and another drop of Bordeaux?'

'How will I ever be able to face beans on toast when I'm back in digs?'

Docherty began to laugh and patted her hand. 'Don't even think about it. Just live one day at a time, that's what I do. And before I forget, Tessa and I think it would be a good idea if we all had a long weekend on the coast before very long. How does that sound?'

'Oh, that would be lovely! I've been longing to see the sea.'

'I must have read your mind. Well, it won't be this weekend but perhaps next.'

'I'll tell Mollie in the morning,' Tessa said. 'I'm sure she and Peter will be up for it.'

'Terry Jones.'

'It's me, Terry, Frank.'

'How're you doing, Frank?'

'Not bad. Terry, could you spare me half an hour in the morning?'

'I could find a window about eleven. Would that be all right?'

'There are a couple of things I'd like to run past you.'

The next day Crane faced Terry Jones across his desk in the central police station. DI Jones had been Crane's boss when he'd worked for the force in the CID. They had a lot of time for each other. Jones had given him a great deal of help in setting up as a PI when he'd had to leave the force and Crane owed him.

'It's about a bloke called Mellors, Terry, Tony Mellors. He works in the council planning department.'

Crane went on to outline his involvement.

'Drugs in parcels sent to little old ladies,' Jones said in a musing tone. 'They've dug that one up, have they. I thought we'd knocked that one on the head fifteen years ago.'

'I reckon it's got to be drugs. And they use Mellors because he looks so incredibly trustworthy and honest.'

'I'm sure you're right. Born criminals do have a tendency to *look* like criminals.'

Crane then told Jones how he'd been warned off about shadowing Mellors and given a kicking in case it slipped his mind.

'Go on! No damage, I hope.'

'I was in a lot of pain but these guys were experts in damage-free methods. The thing is, I'm certain Mellors has had a kicking, too, and I wondered why a criminal gang would do that to one of their own.'

'Because he wasn't toeing the line?'

'My feelings.'

Jones was a CID man and Crane had once been a CID man; their minds worked on similar lines. He explained his theory about why Mellors might possibly be in danger. 'From what I'm getting together on him he looks to be very much the type who might have attacks of conscience, maybe even feel he has to blow the whistle. And if the man who is pulling the strings is thinking along similar lines. . . .'

Jones said, 'And let me make an inspired guess who you think *is* pulling the strings. A bloke called Brendon Docherty who lives in some style in the biggest house on Tanglewood Drive.'

Crane stared at him for several seconds in stunned silence. 'You *know*?'

Jones grinned. 'Sorry to pre-empt you, Frank, you've worked very hard in your single-minded way to get your info together while we've had it handed to us on a plate.'

'A . . . snout?'

Jones, a big, heavy man in a dark suit, levered himself out of his chair, crossed to the window, turned round. 'There are some things even snouts won't touch, as you know. No, this was one of Docherty's own people. He felt he was as good as Docherty and should have been getting a bigger share of the dibs. Docherty told him to sod off. It made the guy keen to see Docherty brought down. He said he'd speak to us, but only if we didn't try to swing any charges on him. It would be on a snout basis only. We agreed. He'd only meet us up on Baildon Moor, where he could be absolutely certain he'd not been followed. He told us everything: Docherty's property deals, the dodgy tenders, the drug-running, the illegals, the young kids they groom for prostitution, the loan-sharking, the internet raids on people's bank accounts. He told us Docherty gets a cut from every single activity and the reason they all give him a cut is because of his incredible talent for spotting a winner and setting these things up. They're in at the sharp end but he's the brains. He operates through a team of two or three men who he pays well. They're the only ones who know he runs the show. There may be one or two lower down who have an idea but if they do they keep very schtum. Nothing ever ties Docherty to anything and we in the CID certainly didn't know. The ship couldn't be kept any tighter. Step out of line and you get a kicking, step too far out and you're in a wheelchair. Did you read about the young kid who had acid thrown in her face? Well the order for it came down from Docherty. Just in case any of the other girls were tempted to talk to us. And one of Docherty's perks, by the way, is to be the first to give the girls one when they've just been turned on to the game.'

Crane was silent for some time, finding it difficult to cope with all this new information. 'I just can't get it together, Terry. I had him down as a businessman who'd gone a bit bent. Dodgy property deals, maybe even a spot of drug-running, but this . . .' he shook his head. 'He comes over as such a charming *bloke*. He throws parties for people who all look to be ordinary business folk.'

'You've *met* the guy?' It was Jones's turn to look taken aback.

'By a pure fluke.' He explained the circumstances of his taking Josie to Docherty's party in place of Mellors. 'Mellors was pretending to be unwell but it's becoming obvious he was wanting to distance himself from Docherty's set-up. And Docherty was very angry that he hadn't shown.'

'Well, the guy up on the moor told us his charm's a big part of the act and he does run a thriving legitimate business apart from the crooked stuff. He has a flair for knowing what he can ship in from abroad that will sell and what he can ship out that will sell in other countries. He's good with the stock market too, and can suss out promising start-up companies that are seeking venture capital. He never stops working and he's very, very secretive. Worth a good few million, he reckons, the bulk of it in off-shores.'

'I've had some shocks in my life,' Crane said, 'but not many that compare to this. Successful businessman, settled marriage, two fine kids, son and daughter, both in their twenties. That's what you *see*. I'm sure none of them have the remotest idea what a bastard they've got as husband and father.'

'There are only about six people who know what the bugger's about and two of them are you and me. He knows how to play the society game; gets involved in local affairs, puts his hand in his pocket for the local charities and so forth. According to our informant they all think he's Mr Very, Very Nice Guy.'

'What will you do about him?'

'Not a lot. Me and the super, we've given it a heap pf brainstorming.' Jones came back to his desk and slumped into his chair with a heavy sigh. 'You read *The Sunday Times*, yes? Well, remember a few weeks back there was a story about a villain who was so big and ran such a complex operation the Met felt they just didn't have the resources to tackle him. Well, on a smaller scale that's our problem. They don't come more astute than Brendon Docherty. We could nail half a dozen of his pavement guys tomorrow but nothing is ever going to lead us to him.'

'But surely this can't go on. Not with all the info you've got from the horse's mouth.'

'It's cash, Frank. You must know Cameron's government's taking a knife to the police. Calling for cuts in recruitment, retiring senior men who'd sooner stay on, all that. You can guess what it would cost us in officers and money if we made a play for Docherty, with no guarantee of a successful outcome. It would leave the other departments on reduced budgets. It's not something we let on about to the general public but that's the *real-politik*. We just can't tackle Docherty till the economy's back to where it was in 2005 and when will that be?'

Crane thought for a few seconds. 'This guy who coughed about all this,' he said slowly, 'he wouldn't accept a plea bargain to go to court?'

'We tried that and he didn't want to know, just not prepared to go inside even for a nominal. Apart from which, the guy's disappeared. I just hope he's done a runner and didn't end up in the footings of one of the new office blocks Docherty's had a hand in.'

'So it would have to be someone in his organization who's prepared to cough and is ready to face the music.'

'If you're thinking in terms of one Tony Mellors, who may or may not be ready to put his hand up and go in the slammer, with someone like Docherty do you think he'd ever live long enough to stand in a witness box?'

The Dochertys possessed several cars, one of them being a 4x4 which Damien had borrowed. He drove the big vehicle to the narrow road that bisected Heaton Woods. He pulled off the road and on to a strip of parking, doused the lights and turned off the engine. 'We could try to sleep,' he said, 'but I daresay we'll find it pretty difficult.'

'Near impossible, I should think,' Melanie said, 'but we'll be able to make up for it tomorrow.'

'And get our Circadian rhythms back in order.'

'Whatever they are.'

'They're as old as mankind. Basically, they ordain that people should be awake during daylight and asleep during dark. That's why people who work nightshifts never fully adjust to going against their rhythms and are prey to all sorts of odd illnesses.'

'The things you know, Demmy.'

They went on talking quietly in the darkness for another half hour and then Melanie began to doze and eventually so did Damien. He had set his mobile to wake him at 2 a.m. and he was quickly alert. When he keyed the ignition Melanie also awoke and he drove along deserted roads to the Willows Park estate and Conway House. Both women were waiting just inside the main door of the building and Damien carried their bags and stowed them in the back of the 4x4. 'OK, girls, in you get.'

They settled themselves into rear seats of the big motor in silence. Melanie said, 'Your minders, where are they?'

'It was their night for Seventh Heaven,' Linda said sourly. 'To sweet-talk two more poor bitches into putting out for ten per cent of the asking price.'

Damien drove rapidly to the ring road, which would put them on to the M62 going east and the M1 going south. Linda and Cilla talked quietly to each other, subdued, it seemed, by the impact of the dramatic changes tonight would bring to their lives.

There was a good deal more traffic on the motorway; delivery vehicles grinding along in the nearside lane and a surprising number of saloon cars, often with loaded roof-racks. 'Holiday season,' Damien said. 'People heading for the south coast or the Continent without tailbacks.'

'Bad news for *their* Circadian rhythms.'

He drove steadily on as names disappeared from illuminated signs: Barnsley, Rotherham, Sheffield, Nottingham. About a hundred miles down the M1 he took the turn-off for Leicester.

Neither of them knew much about the town but Damien had keyed the postcode into his satnav and a soft female voice directed them to the road where the house was situated where Cilla and Linda were to live. It was a road of well-maintained. three-storey terraces and a light was showing in the front ground-floor window of the one that matched the postcode.

As he drew to a halt, the front door opened and a middle-aged woman stood in the glow from the hall light. She came down the garden path as Damien got out of the 4x4. 'Mrs Fisk? There was really no need to get up so early. We were quite ready to wait until a more suitable time.'

'Oh, don't worry about me, sir. I'm a poor sleeper at the best of times. I thought it might help to get your young ladies in their flat so that they can catch up on *their* sleep.'

She gave a reassuring impression of homeliness. Round-faced, stockily built, she wore a flowered pinafore over a dark dress. 'If you'll follow me.' She led them into a wide hall and up thickly carpeted stairs to the first floor, where she opened the door to the flat. The first room was a living area, very clean and containing a small dining table and chairs, a three-piece suite, a flat-screen television and a sideboard on which stood fresh flowers in a glass vase.

She then showed them the other rooms: a galley kitchen, a bedroom with twin beds and an en suite. She talked all the time she was showing them round, explaining how all the equipment worked. 'I got a few things in for the girls' first day. There's bread, eggs and milk and a couple of ready meals for dinner. There's a takeaway round the corner and a little Asian shop that sells just about everything.'

'It's lovely, Mrs Fisk,' Linda said, 'It's just what we wanted.'

She sounded very relieved that they were here at last with no one to know where they were and in such attractive accommodation with a woman who seemed so motherly.

'Why don't you girls do your unpacking and settle yourselves in while I have a word about the details.'

She took Melanie and Damien back downstairs and into her own quarters, another pleasant living room, comfortably furnished with several well-cared-for pieces that looked to be antique and a well-stocked bookcase.

'Do sit down,' she said. 'You must be ready for a hot drink; I've had coffee percolating.'

'Coffee would be so welcome, Mrs Fisk,' Melanie said.

'Help to keep us alert on the journey back,' Damien added.

Mrs Fisk bustled off and was back in seconds with the coffee things on a tray and a plate of mixed biscuits. When they were all sipping the excellent coffee, Damien took out his cheque book and detached a completed cheque. 'This is the deposit plus the first month's rent, Mrs Fisk. I have a friend in Leicester who believes he may be able to fix them up with jobs. It will probably be checkout work or waiting tables but it should pay them enough to cover the rent and their other expenses. If there should be any difficulties with the rent let me know and I'll sort it. This is my card.' He handed it over with the cheque.

'Thank you. And the girls, they've had problems?'

'They got in with the wrong men through no fault of their own. They both want a clean break and a fresh start. I can't say too much and the girls may tell you more in due course.'

Melanie said. 'You look like the sort of person people *do* tell things to.'

Mrs Fisk smiled. 'I'm the repository of many, many secrets. And I'm very good at keeping them. I'll keep an eye on them. I shan't obtrude but I'll be there if they need any help or advice.'

'That really does put our minds at rest.'

They finished their coffee and then Damien said, 'Well, we'd better be heading back, Mrs Fisk. We'll just pop upstairs and say our goodbyes.'

The flat door was opened by Linda. Both she and Cilla were in dressing gowns. She said, 'We're aiming to crash out for a few hours, Mel. We can't begin to thank you for bringing us to this nice place. And Mrs Fisk, she seems great.'

'She'll be a lot of help when you're finding your feet.'

Linda threw her arms round Melanie, Cilla did the same to Damien. They were both a little weepy. 'Oh, you *two*,' Cilla said with a half-sob. 'I can't believe it, I just can't *believe* it. You've been so kind, so *generous*. No one's ever done anything like this for us before, not ever. We'll pay you back. One day, when we're on our feet, we'll pay it all back.'

'Don't worry about that,' Damien said. 'Just sort your lives out, work hard and have a little fun. That's all the repayment we'll ever need. My Leicester friend will be in touch, I'll call on him on our way back. I've told him nothing about your background. Just said things have been difficult and you want to make a new start. He's pretty sure he can find some kind of work for you. I could probably arrange for him to call round this afternoon if that's OK.'

'That's fine, Demmy. Tell him we'll do anything that'll give us an earner.'

'Good. Well, all the very best, girls. Any problems just contact Mel or me.'

'We'll never, ever forget your kindness, Demmy.'

'Goodbye, girls and good luck. You deserve some.'

As they turned to the door, Cilla said, 'Mel, could I have a quick word? Just you. Sorry, Demmy, it's a woman's thing.'

'That's OK. I'll wait in the car.'

When he'd gone, Cilla turned to Melanie, hands clasped so tightly together the knuckles showed white. 'The man, Mel, the one who runs it all up there. We're safe now, Linda and me, so I can tell you. Demmy, he's so clever he might be able to do something about it one day.'

Linda said, 'This man controls everything, Mel, nothing can be done without his say so. And what he says has to be done must be done.'

Cilla then let a name fall into the silence.

It gave Melanie the worst shock she'd ever known. She could

feel her heart pounding and had an impression her stomach was filling with iced water. 'No, Cilla, you're *wrong*! It can't be, it can't *possibly* be!'

SEVEN

Crane spent an uneasy couple of days. He mulled over the things he'd learnt about Docherty. All he knew for certain was that Mellors wanted to get away from Docherty's set-up but an impression was emerging of a man who seemed to be having attacks of conscience and the big question was what he might be aiming to do about the things that were *on* his conscience. More worryingly, what was Docherty going to do about a man who wanted back his old way of life? A man who knew too much. Much too much.

As usual, much of this was conjecture, but if he'd got it right he felt Mellors was badly in need of some impartial advice. Crane knew he couldn't stand by and do nothing about a man who could be in serious danger. He picked up the phone and keyed the number of Mellors's house. A female voice answered that wasn't Josie's.

'I . . may have a wrong number. I'm wanting to speak to a Mr Mellors.'

'No, this is Mr Mellors's house. I'm the cleaner. Mr and Mrs Mellors are at their house on the coast.'

'I see. Would you have a phone number for it or an address?'

'I'm afraid I haven't.'

She'd have both the number and the address and normally he'd have approved her caution; this time it left him cursing. He seemed to remember Josie saying something about a weekend place at Sandsend. He could make a guess that one of the small houses in the village wouldn't have satisfied Josie; she'd have set her heart on something much grander. She'd have wanted something big and detached, maybe standing a little away from the village itself.

It was early evening of a day of hazy sunlight through thin cloud. He decided to take a chance and drive across to the coast. There was none of his work that wouldn't wait till tomorrow. He rang Maggie and told her of his movements. When both of them were out of the office anyone calling on his landline would automatically transfer to Maggie's home. He then set off, driving on the Harrogate Road as far as Poole, where he took the A659, which led him through fine open country to Tadcaster. From there he drove to Malton and then on via Pickering to the North York Moors, a sea of violet heather. As usual, he was plunged into an intense nostalgia for his youth, when he would be taken in the family car to those marvellous holidays in Whitby or Scarborough. Crane had had a very happy youth and childhood, even if manhood hadn't been up to much. He left the moors behind him, bypassed Whitby and drove on to Sandsend, which was to the north, midway between Whitby and Runswick Bay. He detected no large houses on his way into the tiny village and drove through it and up the slope beyond. Where the land levelled out again he caught a glimpse to his right through iron gates of a big detached, screened by a high wall.

He drove on a short way, then did a three-point turn and came back to the tall gates. They were locked but there was a speaker system and a button to press. He pressed it. The unmistakeable little-girl tones of Josie's voice came irritably out. 'If it's the groceries I particularly asked for them to be delivered this morning.'

'It's not the groceries, Josie, it's Frank.'

'*Frank!*' she shrieked. 'You've made my day! Come in, come right in.'

The gates began to slide apart. He got back in his car and

drove along a driveway to the house. It was long and two-storeyed with white-painted stucco and a roof of green-tinted pantiles. It was reached through well-cut lawns and flower-filled borders. From the rear it would have excellent sea views. A door already stood open and Josie came bounding out to meet him.

'Frankie, what a wonderful *surprise*! How did you find us?'

'You said you had a weekend place in the area. I looked for a holiday house. It's a very nice one.'

'It's not bad,' she said indifferently, 'but it's so *boring* here. Sea and sand and walking on cliff tops. God! I didn't want to come. I mean the nightlife in Whitby and Scarborough is worse than Grange over frigging Sands. I want Tony to sell this and use the money for a place in Provence. But now you're here it makes *all* the difference. I've been thinking about you ever since we got here. Can't get you out of my head, Frankie, and I'm sure it's the same for you. Well, that's why you're here, isn't it? You'll stay for the weekend, won't you, in fact stay the week. We've got plenty of rooms. Rooms are one thing we're not short of.'

She gazed at him, her long glossy hair stirring in the breeze. She wore a white beaded top over jade trousers and looked as ravishing as ever. 'I can't stay, Josie. I'm here because I need to have a word with Tony.'

Her face fell. He was beginning to get used to the way her emotions flickered so rapidly and clearly to the surface. You always knew the way her mind was working. 'But you *must* stay, Frankie, at least for the weekend. What do you want to speak to him about? If it's about us being under the duvet together he'll not mind. I did tell you it was an open marriage, didn't I?'

'I believe you did once mention it. Look, Josie, I'm not here to sleep with you. I'm very worried about Tony. He could be in serious trouble.'

'He *knows*! He knows he's in trouble. That's why we're in this Godforsaken dump. I can't think why I let him build the place here when we could have had a nice house in France. The trouble, well it'll blow over in a few days if we keep our heads down.'

'I'm not sure it will. Tony's wanting his old life back, yes? I'm pretty sure the man who runs the crooked set-up doesn't like people wanting to opt out.'

'Brendon? Oh, he's just a big pussycat, really. He'll not be cross for long and then he'll talk Tony round. He's very persuasive. And Tony knows we couldn't begin to manage on just his council salary.'

'I may have it wrong but I don't think Tony's in the mood for being talked round. Does Docherty know where this place is?'

'Tony may have told him. He was so pleased when he saw it finished and the garden laid out. And then he seemed to lose interest. I'm not surprised. There's either a wind strong enough to knock you over or it's pissing it down. If we'd just gone to France in the first place.'

'I think he lost interest because of where the money came from to buy it. And I reckon he lost interest fairly recently.'

Her transparent features showed bemusement, as if Crane was outlining a concept her brain was unable to cope with. She shrugged. 'Oh, come inside and have a drink. Then we'll have some dinner. You must be hungry.'

She led him into a spacious hall, hung with land and seascapes of the local area. They then crossed to a long room at the rear of the house with floor to ceiling windows and fine views over a sea calmly blue in the evening light. The room was as expensively furnished as the Bingley house, with woollen carpets and patterned rugs, comfortable chairs, bookshelves on the back wall and a drinks table with cut-glass decanters. Mellors sat on a sofa, a look of alarm crossing his features when he saw Crane.

'You remember, Frank, Tony, don't you, from when he brought me home from Brendon's party? He's come all the way over here to speak to you. I'm going to get the dinner going. It won't be anything like what those lovely blokes off the telly do, Frank; it'll be whatever comes to hand in the readymeal line.'

'I more or less live on them,' Crane told her. He guessed that Mellors did, too, as he was unable to vizualize Josie in a pinafore wielding a basting spoon with a bead of perspiration in the little groove above her top lip.

Mellors hadn't spoken but continued to watch Crane uneasily. He was dressed in T-shirt and chinos but, as on the night after Docherty's party, didn't really look right not wearing one of his tailored suits. Crane wasn't invited to sit but did so in an armchair facing Mellors.

'I'm a private investigator, Tony, who was once in the CID with the Bradford force.'

A startled look now replaced the unease. 'Josie— I thought she told me you were an FA.'

'Protective colouring. It's best if people don't know you are one unless they're hiring you.'

'And you . . . you were with the police?'

'A good few years back. But I keep in touch with old colleagues.'

The unease and shock had now been replaced in Mellors face by what could almost have been a look of relief. 'What . . . what do you want with me?'

'Josie engaged me to keep an eye on you. You once came home with bruises on your backside. She thought you were getting your S&M sessions with another woman.'

The startled look was back. 'How did she know about the bruises?'

'She took a photo of them when you were asleep.'

Mellors digested the information in silence, eyes flicking to Crane's and away several times.

'But it wasn't a caning, Tony, was it?' he said gently. 'It was a kicking – by two of Docherty's heavies.' Mellors's face was having a workout this evening, running through more expressions, it seemed, than it probably got through in a week.

'How . . . how much do you know?' he said, almost in a whisper.

'Quite a lot. The valuable information you were feeding Docherty about properties destined for the schedule that he could buy cheap and sell dear, the dodgy tenders you nodded through, the parcels of drugs you collected from innocent old ladies. I'm sure there's a lot more I don't know about but I don't think I need to go on.'

It was wide-eyed alarm again and Mellors's hands were trembling. He got up shakily and crossed to the drinks table where he poured himself a large brandy. 'Do you . . . want a drink?'

'A G&T.'

Mellors poured again, the tonic bottle tapping a tattoo against the rim of the tumbler. He put down Crane's glass on a side table, slumped back on to the sofa and took a gulp of almost half the glass's contents. 'What . . . what are you going to do?'

'There's not much I can do. Look, the police know about Docherty, they know all about him; the whistle was blown on him by one of his own people, who then legged it. Either that or Docherty saw him off. And Docherty is such a clever man they know there's nothing they can do about him right now without firm admissable evidence, and where's that going to come from?'

If it gave Mellors any kind of relief it was hard to tell. He sat with bowed shoulders, taking regular sips at what was left of the brandy. 'Why . . . why are you here then?' he said after a silence, in the same low voice as before.

The door suddenly swung open and Josie burst in. 'Naughty!' she cried. '*Naughty!* Drinks in the drawing room for the gentlemen while the skivvy slaves over a hot oven. A nice big G&T for Josie, if you per-lease.'

Mellors didn't look up. It didn't seem he was ignoring her, more that he was too preoccupied to register her words or even her presence. Crane got up and mixed her a large one.

'Thanks, sweetheart. Can't sit down, have to keep an eye on the spuds and the broccoli. At least I think it's broccoli; I soon get lost with veggies if they're not peas or carrots. Anyway, it's green. And we're going to have a strawberry flan to finish with. I think I'll open a bottle of champers. In fact, two bottles. One goes nowhere, not for three, just barely moistens your mouth. What's wrong with Tony? He looks as if he's won the rollover but lost the ticket.'

'I think he's upset that I know so much about his activities.'

'Oh, *that* carry-on. Just put it out of your heads, both of you. Don't want to spoil the evening. Brendon's sure to come round. He can't do without Tony. Just do as he asks, Tone. I mean, doing these odd jobs for him has given us a great way of life, hasn't it?'

Again, Mellors didn't react. Crane wondered if there was more to it than his preoccupation with his own problems. He seemed almost to give an impression he'd stopped bothering to listen to Josie, anyway, much of the time. If this was the case it left Josie indifferent. She'd almost seen off her gin and handed her glass to Crane. 'Just sweeten it up, darling. A good helping of the Gordon's and just a dash of tonic is how I like them. I'll take it through to the kitchen. Dinner in about twenty, assuming I've set the timer right. I'm not too great around cookers, Frank, to be honest.'

Crane had no difficulty believing that and watched her charge off with a faint smile. Then he turned to Mellors. 'You asked me why I'm here before Josie came in. I'm here because I'm pretty certain you're no longer wanting to dance to Docherty's tune and Docherty isn't happy about that.'

Mellors's haunted eyes met Crane's and he rubbed his jaw compulsively. 'I just want my life back,' he said in that near-whisper voice. 'I never put a foot wrong till I got mixed up with Docherty.'

'And it needed a lot of money to keep Josie happy.'

Mellors seemed aware it was a statement not a question. He was silent for a good ten seconds, then finally nodded. 'No more, Frank. It was the worst mistake I ever made. I'll never involve myself with him again.'

'I doubt you'll have a free hand to make that decision. You must know that getting in with a man like Docherty means you don't get out. The way I see it, and I may not have it right, is that Docherty doesn't want to lose a key man but could be more worried that you'll go to the police and get it all off your chest.'

Mellors's head shot up in a sharp glance. Then he fell into one of his lengthy silences. 'I can't live with it any longer, Frank,' he said at last. 'You can't believe. . . . I was well brought up. My parents, they scratted and scraped to give me a private education. I did well. Passed my exams. Got made a prefect. Good career in the council. I wanted to serve society. That's how I'd been brought up. My father used to say, if you've had a good home life and education try to put more into the rest of your life than you take out. That was the way he was, God rest him.'

His voice had become uneven and he looked to be not far from tears. 'I . . . I *am* going to the police, Frank. I can't live with myself.'

Crane nodded. He could see Mellors as he'd once been, quiet and unassuming and wearing a well-pressed school blazer. A boy who listened carefully to teachers and always turned in homework on time. He'd have been regarded as a model pupil by staff, who'd have difficulty recalling his face or even remembering him at all once he'd left school. He'd have been the exact opposite of those chirpy characters whose deadpan wit could make the class hoot with laughter, always took a leading role in the school play and who were ordered to the head's study on a regular basis. *They* were the ones you could see working on the wrong side of the fence, not obedient, industrious types like Mellors.

'Going to the police, Tony, it's not going to be as easy as that.'

' I don't understand.'

'If Docherty got wind of you going within a mile of a police station your life wouldn't be worth twopence.'

'No, Mel, *no*! It can't be, it can't possibly *be*. For Christ's *sake*!'

'She gave me his *name*, Demmy. She *described* him.'

'She's got him mixed up with someone *else*. He's not the only man of Irish stock in this bloody city.'

'What can I say, Demmy, what can I *say*? I'm just telling you what she told me. Her pimp let his name slip. She was told to have sex with him and the description exactly matches.'

Damien couldn't stay still. He paced up and down the breakfast room of Melanie's parents' house, his face drained of colour with shock. Melanie had kept it to herself on the way back from Leicester, not wanting to distract him from his driving. And it would have distracted him. Dreadfully.

'I don't know how you can begin to *think* it!' he cried, turning at the end of the room and striding back again, to bring his face close to hers. 'I don't know how you can even think it, some gossipy rubbish from a tom.'

Melanie forced herself to stay calm, though she'd spent all morning feeling as baffled as he now was. 'Demmy, it's not a *question* of me thinking it. I'm simply telling you what Cilla told me. There's no *point* in shooting the messenger. I can't get it together, either.'

'She must have got the name wrong. *Must* have.'

'Perhaps she did. Both the name and the description.'

'The description could fit a dozen men.'

'All right,' she said in a low voice, 'let's just say she got it all wrong.'

She sipped the strong coffee. She'd not eaten all morning and still couldn't face food. She'd been looking forward to the weekend so much, but she suspected it was going to be one of the worst she'd ever known. They'd been going to spend the morning catching up on their sleep and were then going to drive to the Dales for a pub lunch and a hike before putting up at a B&B for the night. They'd not be doing that now. Damien was back to his endless pacing up and down the room, shaking his head every few seconds as if to clear his mind of the frightful things he'd been told.

'Sit down, Demmy. I'll make some fresh coffee.'

'It can't be right, Mel, it just *can't* be right. I mean, you know the man, you *know* him. He's my dad! I've looked up to him all my life.' He picked up his coffee with a hand that shook so badly some of the liquid slopped over the side.

'Please stop marching about. Sit down and let's try to talk about it, rationally.'

'*Rationally?*'

But eventually he sank down on to one of the chairs at the little circular table that stood in front of the window. He looked to be all in and it was nothing to do with missed sleep. A couple of hours' sleep now, as planned, and they'd have been fine, they were young and healthy. She wanted to put her arms round him, comfort him. She wished she'd not told him, had instead told herself it was all a matter of mistaken identity, just as Damien was striving to do now, and simply carry on as normal until Cilla's words were only a fading memory. Surely it would have been easy to forget them in the warm, caring atmosphere of Tanglewood House.

But she knew it wouldn't, not with the kind of shock she'd been given today. She knew quite certainly that Cilla had got nothing wrong. The name Docherty wasn't one you could be mistaken about. And the description, it fitted Brendon to the smallest detail. She grimaced. If she had been prepared to carry on as normal it would have meant Brendon always at her side at the dinner table, giving her those glances that meant she was desirable to him that he couldn't entirely conceal. But it wouldn't be because she reminded him of an old girlfriend; it would be because he just wanted the same sort of sex from her that was provided by the many call girls he had access to. She felt nauseous.

'Look, Mel, it's my *dad*. How would you feel if someone said those things about your dad?'

'I'd be blown away, you know I would. But I really do feel we have to try and discuss it as calmly as possible and decide what we can *do* about it. . . .'

'I came here to think it over,' Mellors told him, 'and get away from things back at home.'

'Does Docherty know where this house is?'

'He knows I've got a place on the coast. I didn't say exactly where. I might have mentioned Sandsend.'

'Tony, if I could trace your weekend house from knowing it was near Sandsend it'll present no problems to Docherty's people.'

Fear yet again crossed Mellors's face. 'You don't think they'll come *here*?'

'I don't know. I've spent a lot of time trying to work out the way your mind was working and Docherty's. Well, I seem to have got it right with you and my thinking about Docherty is that he'll want to make sure of your silence. It's difficult to know quite what he'll do but my instinct is to get you to a safer place than this. A place he can't possibly know about.'

'Such as . . . London?'

'No, you need to be near the Bradford police. That's if you've definitely decided to talk to them. Do you *want* to talk to them?'

'You said my life wouldn't be worth twopence if I went near them,' he said uneasily.

'It wouldn't if you tried to go it alone. But I could find a place for you and Josie that only I would know about. I could get you into the central police station and the police would be able to arrange witness protection for you both.'

'Would that mean a new identity?'

'For information on this scale everything would be changed. Identity, National Insurance number, driving licence, the lot.'

Crane began to see what was definitely a look of hope on Mellors's face. He could imagine the relief he must be feeling. He guessed that with a new name, Mellors would be able to make himself a new man, a man who, once again, really did give the impression that what you saw was exactly what you got; a decent, able, hard-working type who could be trusted with the Crown Jewels.

Crane said, 'I have a friend. She lives in Gargrave in her own place. We go directly from here to Gargrave and she'll put you up. We go from there the following day directly to the police station and my old boss, Detective Inspector Terry Jones will handle it all from there. They'll keep you and Josie well guarded and when it's all over you'll simply disappear to a different town with a new identity.'

Mellors sat back on the sofa as if relieved of near-unbearable tension. 'You can't believe what it means to me to hear that.'

'You'll have to go inside yourself, Tony, prison that is, but if you're going to inform on Docherty's set-up it'll be a nominal sentence. Your counsel will play the card that you were under considerable duress to do the things you did and it will all go down well with the jury.'

Mellors nodded. 'I've been a criminal so I deserve to be punished. I'll give the police my total co-operation.'

'Good. Just keep it in mind that in two or three years you'll be able to start a new life.'

'I'll never stop thinking about it.'

'Your biggest problem now is what's to be done about Josie.'

Damien crouched over the breakfast table. Melanie could sense the pain he was in. This was the man she loved and his pain was her pain. She got up and put her arms round him. 'He's been almost like another father to me, Demmy. I just can't get it together.'

'What can we do, Mel? What on earth can we *do*?'

She moved her chair so they were sitting side by side, took one of his hands in hers. 'We've got to talk about it, try . . . try to get it straight in our own minds.'

'But you can't believe it, can you? Any of it.'

'Linda and Cilla, they've been very silly getting involved with those people. But they aren't stupid. You met them, saw how keen they were to start again. I wish I *could* believe she'd got it all wrong, but I can't. If you've had acid thrown in your face you tend not to get things wrong.'

'I feel sick,' he said in a low voice. 'How anyone could do that to a young woman. They're barely human. But to make out the orders came from *Dad!*'

'I made her repeat the name again and again. I made her describe him half a dozen times. How did he have his hair? How did he speak? The colour of his eyes, the shape of his features, his build, the clothes he wore. I was positive she must have it wrong. But she couldn't be faulted on the smallest detail. The so-called boyfriends might knock them about occasionally, but injuries like acid-throwing would only ever be done if it came from the top.'

'Did Cilla know he was my father?'

'No. I only ever used your Christian name with them.'

'What do we do, Mel?' he said again.

'We really can't just go on what Cilla says, I realize that. We need to check it out.'

'How do we do that?'

He spoke in a vague tone she'd never heard before, as if his mind was so full of the ghastly shock he'd been given that there wasn't much left to cope with anything else. She squeezed his hand. 'We need to try and find out exactly how he spends his time away from the house, what he really does in his office and who he mixes with. It would be a start if you could get hold of his mobile and see what's on his inbox.'

It seemed almost to be an effort of will for him to take in what she was saying. 'I . . . I never see his mobile and . . . and as for what goes on in that office of his. . . '

It gave Mel a return of that icy sensation in her stomach. There was such an ominous feel now about the wall of secrecy Brendon had mounted around himself. What *did* he do to be so wealthy? How *did* he spend those long hours in an office where he seemed to have no staff, not even a PA? Would it hold up to scrutiny? She just didn't want to go there, even though she knew they must.

After a lengthy silence, Damien spoke again. 'Let's forget it, there's no way either of us could find out how he spends his working life.'

'You're right. It needs someone who specializes in that kind of work.' Melanie poured more coffee. They were existing solely on coffee. She got up. 'I'll be back in a tick.'

When she returned she was holding a copy of the Yellow Pages. 'It will have to be a private investigator,' she told him. 'Someone who'll find out what we need to know and not ask too many questions.'

She leafed through the directory, then studied the entry of an investigator who'd taken out an impressive advertisement in its own box. 'This chap looks as if he'll do. Says he covers all aspects of investigation: bad debts, lifestyle checks, suspected fraud, domestic problems and so forth and promises a fast and efficient service. He's called Frank Crane.'

'The name rings a bell.'

'Wasn't the man who was at your dad's last party called Crane? The one who was with the Josie woman.'

'That Crane was an FA.'

'Coincidence. He's got an office in the Old Quarter.'

'I'll contact him. I can't believe I'm doing this.' His forehead was creased as if he was suffering intense physical pain.

'It would help to prove he lives an ordinary, blameless life.'

But would it be ordinary or blameless? She couldn't get it out of her mind; Cilla paling and only being able to speak the name Docherty through trembling lips.

'Dinner won't be long, boys,' Josie said, bursting into the drawing room again. 'At least not according to that bloody timer. Just sweeten my drink up, Frankie, there's a good chap. The shampoo's chilling nicely.'

Crane fixed her yet another hefty G&T. When she'd cantered off he wondered just what could be done about a loose cannon like her. Mellors gave a sigh. 'I wish I'd never met her,' he said quietly. 'I'm not putting any of the blame on to her. It was all my own doing, but if it hadn't been for Josie I'd still be the man I used to be.'

'She does seem to be rather one on her own.'

'I was crazy about her. I'm not now but I was then. I couldn't believe anyone so very glamorous could want to marry me. And so . . . seductive. She made the running; we were in bed the first weekend I took her out. I couldn't think of anything but her and her body. I was obsessed. I wanted to give her things for all the happiness she was giving me in those early years. But nothing was ever enough. First a new motor for her, then a bigger house, then expensive holidays on the Riviera. Then it was cruises in the best accommodation and why couldn't we have our own weekend place? My salary was going nowhere.'

'How did Docherty latch on to you?'

'I'd occasionally be taken for a meal by one of the builders. They'd just be a sort of thank you because their tender had been accepted. It was all above board and I always recorded them. One day Docherty was at one of the dinners. He's a very clever operator. He can somehow get things out of you you'd not realized you'd let go. He'd casually mention an area where redevelopment was a remote possibility. I'd think I wasn't giving the slightest hint it was destined for the schedule, but he was able to gauge my reactions even so. Anyway, in one of these cases he bought up a great many properties at a knock-down price and eventually sold them to the council for a hefty profit. He invited me to lunch, handed me an envelope. It was stuffed with fifties. One of his sidekicks took a photo of me opening it on a mobile, though I didn't know at the time. Docherty had me. Even so, with all that money, I could buy things for Josie. He'd guessed I'd reached the exact point where I was corruptible.

'After that, all the valuable inside information went directly to him. And then he wanted me to pick up the packets of cocaine. Organize the loan-sharking. Get the illegals into respectable digs and arrange fixed marriages so they'd be able to stay in the country and draw social security benefits. Cyber crime. He talked me into everything, Frank, because I knew my way round computers and looked so, well, respectable. My face, as far as

Docherty was concerned, was my fortune.'

It was as Crane had thought. How could a man with a face and demeanour like Mellors be a bad hat? He said, 'Docherty would have his work cut out replacing you.'

The other nodded, finished his brandy. 'I know. That's why I got the kicking. I saw him recently in his office. He was coming over as nice and nasty. No one can do nice and nasty better. He said if I stayed with him he could make me a really wealthy man. He then showed me the photo of me taking out the fifties from the envelope. He told me that if I didn't stay with him the photo would lose me my job. I didn't care in the end. I knew I'd lose my job anyway once I'd talked to the police. I didn't care. I knew if I was going to be able to live with myself I'd have to own up.'

Several table lamps ignited themselves, sensors, it seemed, reacting to fading daylight. The two men sat in silence for some time and then Crane said, 'Does Josie know any of this?'

Mellors gave him a look of resignation. 'Josie closes her mind to anything she doesn't want to think about but she knows all the goodies couldn't come from my council salary. She fools herself into pretending I do little jobs for Docherty that are just a bit iffy. She's convinced my break with him is something that's going to blow over and the money will start rolling in again.'

'She's going to take it very badly when she sees you're serious.'

'I don't care about that, either. She's had a very good run with me and now it's over. I just don't care what she does. She'll be all right. She's totally self-centred and always lands on her feet. She killed the love I had for her a long time ago with her incessant demands. Not just the money and the toys but, well, in the bedroom. It was marvellous at first with a woman as attractive as she is, but when it never ended, when I just wasn't in the mood after a day working for both the department and Docherty, it just became an exhausting chore.'

He gazed towards the painted screen that stood in front of the fireplace with unfocused eyes. 'So then, when I wasn't satisfying her sexual demands on a nightly basis, she said we needed an open marriage. I was very hurt and upset at first but on the other hand it took the pressure off me when I could go to bed and just sleep. As you probably know she soon gained a reputation as the village bike.'

Crane said, 'As I told you, the reason she hired me was because she thought you were getting your caning sessions elsewhere.'

Mellors gave a short backward toss of his head. 'The caning was her idea. She thought it would spice up the marriage. Well, I'm only human and odd as it is I found I did have rather a taste for it. But as usual she wanted too much and refused to accept how weary I got from my long hard days.'

'Did she really have a thing about the canings? That neither of you could do it with anyone else, for all the open marriage.'

He nodded. 'Anything went except the S&M. It had to be special to us. It was sort of symbolic, if you know what I mean. What she was really worried about was that I might leave her for someone else, with the money and the lifestyle going with me. She comes over as scatterbrained, which she is most of the time, but she has a cunning streak and knows I've got money that's untraceable in off-shores.'

Crane studied this quietly spoken, diffident man in the lamplight. What a sad, twisted, scary existence his life had become since he'd first laid eyes on the dazzling creature Josie must have been and become overhelmed by her magnetism. A life of crime to satisfy her material demands and no respite from the physical ones when he crawled wearily under the duvet.

Josie crashed into the room for the third time. 'It's all ready, boys, can you believe it! I'll just have another quick G&T, Frank, and then we can put the nosebags on.'

As Crane stood at the table mixing her latest drink, a bell sounded in the hall. Mellors started. 'There's someone at the gate,' he told Crane uneasily.

'Probably the bloody groceries,' Josie said, 'that the halfwits should have delivered this morning.'

123

'It won't be the groceries,' Mellors said, 'not now.'

Crane felt sure he was right and shared his uneasiness. Who could possibly be out there that they weren't expecting so late in the day?

EIGHT

They went into the hall and Mellors keyed the speaker. 'Who is it?'

'It's . . . it's Heather, Tony.'

'Heather! What on earth—'

'It's . . . it's about the Monday meeting. There's a report they're wanting that I can't finish without your help.'

'The Windy Edge development? I left notes in the file.'

'I'm so sorry. There are several I don't fully understand. If you could spare me an hour to go through it. . . .'

'I'll open the gate, Heather. Drive in and pip your horn so I can close them.'

Looking completely mystified, Mellors pressed another key.

'Your little seccy,' Josie said dismissively. 'What on God's green earth can bring her all this way about a bit of paper? The way the council works I'm sure it doesn't matter if it's done this month or next.'

'She can be overzealous,' Mellors admitted. But like Josie, Crane thought it decidedly odd that his PA would drive seventy miles to talk to her boss when she could have rung or emailed him. The car horn sounded and they heard the car crunch to a halt. Mellors opened the front door.

Heather walked up to them, a troubled look on her plain, homely features. She wasn't wearing her office clothes but even her casual ones had a sensible look: a plain white shirt, a beige cardigan and brown, straight-leg trousers. 'I'm so sorry, Tony, I decided we'd need a little time together to get the details right. And with the meeting scheduled for ten on Monday. . . .'

Crane had a strong impression she was concealing the real reason she was here by the feeble-sounding excuses she was making. He felt that Mellors was also of the same mind.

'We're just about to eat,' Josie said brightly, 'but you must share our simple repast. There's plenty.'

'You're very kind, Mrs Mellors. If you're sure I'm not—'

'Drink? Your tongue must be hanging out after that drive over the moors.'

'Oh, er, a small sherry, please.'

Josie picked up a decanter that contained some dense brown liquid that looked as if it had rested undisturbed since they'd first moved in. Heather didn't see her contemptuous smile as she poured the sherry but Crane did. Josie didn't seem particularly surprised about Heather's dash from Bradford and hadn't appeared to pick up on a reason for her presence that didn't really hold water. But she seemed not to have the slightest interest in Mellors's working life.

'We mustn't let her drink alone,' Josie said cheerily, 'we'll have one more. The dinner's on a low light.'

Crane guessed that mastery of the low light had been the first to be developed of Josie's limited culinary skills. She began enthusiastically pouring gin for herself and Crane, brandy for Mellors. Crane felt he could let himself go a little. He'd not meant or wanted to stay overnight but it seemed it could be for the best with the arrangements he'd need to make about Mellors.

'By the way, Heather,' Mellors said, 'this is Frank Crane, a friend of ours.'

'How do you do,' she said, taking Crane's hand. 'I believe I've seen you in the pub Tony and I sometimes go to for lunch.'

126

'The one at the bottom of Hustlergate? Yes, I do go there now and then.'

She had a good memory even though when he was working he tried to make himself as anonymous as possible.

'You must stay the night,' Josie told her. 'You can do the report in the morning.'

'I'd not want to impose, Mrs Mellors. I could find a B&B.'

'Nonsense, we've got plenty of rooms. More bedrooms than soft Mick.'

'Yes, you must stay, Heather,' Mellors said. 'You can't go searching around at this time of night.'

Crane, too, was in favour. The Mellors might have an open marriage but surely in front of his very seemly PA Josie would want to give an impression of a normal relationship and restrain herself from hammering on Crane's door. But would she? He drank some of his G&T and glanced at her in her beaded top and jade trousers. She was so desirable and it certainly wasn't that he didn't want to share a bed with her; it was just that he had a lot on his mind and knew she'd be a distraction that right now he could do without.

'Well, let's go and eat,' Josie said. 'Bring your drinks.'

Heather had taken barely a sip of her sherry. They crossed the hall to a dining room, perhaps half the size of the drawing room. It had a chandelier with crystal teardrops and walls expensively decorated in a soft green matt paper and hung with more landscapes. The table was oblong and extendable and laid with mats, glasses and silverware and the chairs were reproduction Regency. Tonight, the room was lit only by wall lamps and table candles in ornate holders. Josie set out a fourth place for Heather.

For all the impression she gave of haphazardness in the kitchen she'd managed to get together a decent crab and lobster starter with warm crusty rolls. 'Would you open the champers, Frankie, seeing as you're near the stand?'

He fished one of the bottles from an ice-bucket, dried it and carefully eased out the cork. He made to pour into Heather's glass but she put a hand over it. 'Not for me, Mr Crane. I'm not much of a drinker.'

'How do you *cope!*' Josie exclaimed. 'Who was it said, those people who don't drink, when they get up in the morning that's as good as they're going to feel all day?' She gave a peel of laughter and drank deeply of the champagne Crane had just poured.

'Would you like an orange juice, Heather?' Mellors asked solicitously. 'Sparkling water?'

'Water would be nice, Tony, but please don't go to any trouble.'

Mellors got up, went to the sideboard, opened a bottle of water and poured it into a cut-glass tumbler. On returning to the table he had his back to Josie but Crane saw him give Heather a glance of such fondness and warmth that he suddenly realized that this was the woman Josie had hired him to trace. Heather had never really been in the equation with either Josie or him, but it was clear she and Mellors were in love.

'Give me a top-up, Frankie, would you?' Josie said, waving her empty glass. 'Me and champagne, a love affair that will never end.' She gave another peal of laughter.

'This is a lovely house, Tony,' Heather said quietly, glancing round the spacious room.

'Boring, Helena, boring,' Josie broke in. 'There's nothing to *do*. Whitby's a graveyard with roads and Scarborough's not much better. It was a big mistake building the place. We shall sell it and maybe just use hotels in future. We'll be quite happy in hotels as long as they have five stars and Grand or Royal or Ritz in the title, won't we, darling?'

Mellors barely reacted and Josie said to Heather, 'Tony's a bit low in his mind, Helena, he's had a falling out with one of his friends who brought him a lot of business. But it'll all blow over and things will soon be back to normal. I know the chap and he'll not want to lose Tony's expertise. My glass seems to have got itself empty again, Frankie. Back in a tick.'

She took off the first course plates on a tray and returned with the servings of the ready meals, which were a Chinese chicken dish with additional vegetables of jacket potatoes and French beans, which cleared up the uncertainty of the green vegetable being broccoli. It was all a little odd but Crane, living alone, often made himself rather odd meals and though Josie had begun to lurch a little the food looked to be well cooked and tasty.

'Well, this is nice,' Josie said as she lowered herself uncertainly on to her chair, 'company instead of just Tony and me sitting here like bookends. I was sure I asked you for a refill, Frankie.'

'And I gave you one,' he said, smiling. 'You drank it while you were going backwards and forwards to the kitchen.'

'Better top me up, then, and if we're getting low open the other bottle.'

She then began to eat with good appetite. Crane was also very hungry now but Mellors only picked at his plate and Heather also ate sparingly.

'What did you think of that last *Britain's Got Talent* then?' Josie asked eagerly, of no one in particular. 'Isn't Simon Cowell *gorgeous*? My mama always said you can't trust a man who parts his hair down the middle but I could trust Simon whichever way he did his hair.' She drank more of her wine. 'Even if he had it in a *ponytail*,' she added firmly as if to clinch the matter. 'What did you think of the dog woman, Helena?

'I'm . . . afraid it's not something I've watched, Mrs Mellors, and the name's Heather,' she said in a tone of gentle correction.

'Oh, well, whatever turns you on,' she said dismissively, holding out her glass for Crane to top up. 'And call me Josie. Can't do with that Mrs Mellors crap.'

Crane could quite see Heather not being a *Britain's Got Talent* fan. As Josie prattled on in a world of her own Heather and Mellors no longer bothered to conceal the loving glances they gave each other and seemed to regard Crane as being part of their conspiracy.

With an effort, Josie stood up and began noisily to gather the dinner plates and to reel off with them to the kitchen. Heather also got to her feet. 'I'll give her a hand, Tony. It's a lot to do on her own.'

'Jolly good of you, Heather,' Mellors said, his eyes lingering on her fondly as she left the table. 'It's about now she starts breaking things.'

Heather took away the vegetable containers and came back shortly afterwards with dessert dishes on which were neatly cut slices of the strawberry flan and a cheese board. She did everything with an air of calm competance. Josie then crashed back in, coffee pot and cups on a tray, everything jingling. The tray was beginning to droop at a slight angle and just as it seemed the pot and crockery would land on the carpet Heather moved quickly forward. 'Oh, do let me give you a hand, Josie, you've done such a lot this evening,' she said helpfully, firmly seizing the tray and putting it safely on the sideboard.

'Thanks, Emma, I came over a tad dizzy just then. Can't think why.'

'It will pass off if you sit down,' Heather said, pulling out Josie's chair and giving her a supporting hand. 'Perhaps I could give you some coffee.'

'No, I'll just have a last glass of champagne. And what do we do after dinner? I've got a couple of naughty DVDs I could fish out. That'll be a laugh.'

Only, it seemed, to Josie. Crane, Mellors and Heather ate in silence as Josie chattered unstoppably on. Heather had now unobtrusively taken over at the table and cleared it calmly and quickly when the meal was over. She then took the coffee tray into the drawing room and poured cups there. Mellors patted her shoulder gratefully, looking as if he longed to take her in his arms. The naughty DVDs weren't to be inflicted on them after all, as Josie wandered away and didn't come back.

'Probably sleeping it off,' Mellors muttered, on a note of relief.

The three of them sat companionably in the lamplight and then Mellors said, 'You might as well know, Frank, that Heather is the other woman that Josie hired you to find out about.'

'I had rather gathered that. I only ever saw Heather as your PA and nothing more. And Josie never suspected, not for a minute.'

'That's because I could never be regarded as a glamour girl, Mr Crane,' Heather said with a faint smile.

'Thank God,' Mellors said feelingly.

'And the name's Frank, Heather.'

Crane felt Mellors should have married someone like Heather in the first place. They seemed so right together with their unremarkable looks and he guessed they had a great deal in common: books, music, back-packing holidays, and caring natures. They were Joe Average and partner like most of the couples you saw in the street.

'I shall divorce Josie, Frank,' Mellors told him. 'I'll do the best I can for her but I want an end to the relationship.' He turned to Heather where they sat together on the sofa. 'I've a lot of explaining to do, Heather, about Frank and what he's going to do to help me.'

The two men began to outline the situation: from how Crane had been hired by Josie to check on Mellors, and with his police training how he had uncovered Mellors's crooked activities, to how he was now to arrange for him to make a full admission to the police and expose Docherty's set-up.

She listened intently and showed little or no surprise. Crane guessed Mellors had already confessed to her the details of his past.

'Heather had already found out what I was doing, Frank,' Mellors said. 'We worked closely together and she'd cottoned on to what I was up to. She tackled me about it and that was when I began to want to get back to being the man I'd once been. We both knew if we were going to have a future together I had to make a new start.'

131

Heather took one of his hands in hers. Crane had rarely seen such a look of devotion as passed between them.

'I'm afraid it's not going to be easy, Heather,' he said. 'Tony's been involved in criminal activity and he'll have to face a prison sentence. But as he'll plead guilty, express remorse and make a full exposure of Docherty's network I doubt he'll be inside for long and whatever the sentence it'll be reduced for good behaviour.'

'I'll be waiting for him,' Heather said softly, 'however long he needs to be in prison. And the real reason I'm here now is that I just had to see him; he looked so very worried this last week.'

'I don't deserve you, Heather,' Mellors said, his voice wavering, 'and you don't deserve this mess of mine you've been drawn into. If I'd only met you ten years ago.'

Emotion was bringing out naïvety. Ten years ago he'd not been able to get Josie out of his mind. There'd have been no contest then between the dazzling, sexy woman he'd married and sensible, self-effacing Heather, even though she'd have been exactly right for the kind of man he really was.

She now said, 'We'll sort it all out together, Tony, and once it's over we'll have the rest of our lives.'

'I'll not have a job, you know. No income from the council, no bent money from Docherty and Co.'

'*I'll* have a job and I own a house. And when you come out of prison you'll find *some* kind of work, a clever man like you.'

Crane said, 'I should point out, Heather, that Tony will need witness protection. Docherty's a very dangerous man and the main thing on his mind will be how to silence him. The police will need to give Tony a new identity and find him somewhere to live in a different area.'

'Wherever he goes I'll go, Frank.'

'In the meantime he and Josie will have to go into hiding while I sort it out with my old colleagues in the CID. Once he's with the police they'll take good care of him until the case can go ahead.'

'Into hiding?'

'I have a friend who lives in Gargrave. She'll take them in till we can ship Tony down to the station.'

'Why don't they stay with me? No one knows of our relationsip, mine and Tony's. Everyone thinks I'm simply his PA.'

Crane thought about it. It seemed a good idea. Better than troubling Colette, who would take them in because of their friendship but who, understandably, wouldn't be too keen. 'If you're willing to do that it would simplify matters.'

Mellors yawned, looking suddenly very weary. Crane wasn't surprised; he'd had a lot on his mind and it would have taken it out of him. He said, 'It might be best if we all turned in, Tony. We can sort out an action plan in the morning.'

He looked relieved. 'All right with you, Heather? I can lend you some of Josie's pyjamas and there are toiletries in your room's en suite.'

'I've got an overnight bag in my car,' Crane said. 'I'll just go and get it.'

He went out through the front door and opened his boot. The earlier hazy cloud had cleared and it was a calm, moonlit night. As he took out his bag and brought down the tailgate he had a strong sense that he wasn't alone. He locked the boot and glanced warily about him. He could detect no other presence. He wondered if it was simply the way his nerves were reacting. Mellors was here to get away from Bradford and think things through. And Docherty being the careful man he was, and maybe thinking the way Crane suspected he was thinking, might have decided to send some of his people over here. It was impossible to guess. With a final glance round, he went uneasily back to the house.

Mellors showed them to their rooms, hoped they'd sleep well and went off to his own. The room Crane had been given was also an en suite and so he took a leisurely shower. He hoped he *would* sleep as insomnia dogged his life, especially when he had things on his mind. He put on pyjamas, got into the comfortable three-

quarter bed and switched off the bedside lamp. The second the room was in darkness he had the feeling that he'd had outside, that he wasn't alone. But this time he really wasn't alone. The bedside lamp was re-lit; standing at the bedside was Josie, wearing just the top of a pair of pale-green pyjamas. 'Gotcha at last,' she murmured in her little-girl voice. 'Move over, big boy. . . .'

She undid the buttons of the top, took it off and dropped it on the floor. She stood before him, smiling and naked, her long sleek hair freshly brushed. She was in excellent shape for her age, which he put in the early thirties, with firm rounded breasts, a slender waist and smoothy silky thighs. It still amazed him, as it had at Docherty's party, how rapidly she was able to oxydize alcohol, it was as if that vibrant body needed only a couple of hours to burn it off. She spoke clearly now and the slackness had left her features. She got quickly into bed with him and the lamp was doused a second time. She, too, came fresh from the shower and smelt of a very delicate scent that seemed to increase her desirability, if that was possible.

'Off with the jimjams, Frankie.'

She began deftly unfastening buttons. He knew he couldn't get out of it this time, and this time he didn't want to. She was one sexy woman and he'd been in a state of ill-defined tension all evening. It would relax him. So he let Josie treat him to some of the best sex he'd ever had. There was no aspect of the act that she'd not brought to a peak of polished perfection. The fondling of her delicate fingers and the way she seemed able to use her toes also like fingers so that he never knew where the next caress was coming from; the revolving of her soft buttocks and the knack she had for control of the action that ensured orgasm was lengthily delayed. Crane could only admire and enjoy such incredible expertise and the dedicated attention she'd spent so much of her life doggedly devoting to it. She was a one-trick pony but what a brilliant trick it was. It left smoke and mirrors nowhere.

He eventually eased himself off her quivering body. He was now in a very pleasant state of relaxation and could feel himself more than ready to drift into sleep. 'Well,' Josie murmured with a throaty little giggle, 'that makes for a nice start.'

Nice start! Her fingers were already feathering his genitals again encouragingly. He should have known that Josie didn't do sleep, not when she was in a bed that came with a man. Why sleep when you could bonk? He knew he wasn't going to be allowed to fritter valuable bonking time away on mere sleep. But he needed sleep now. They were in an isolated house, Mellors was a man on the run and Docherty might have decided something needed to be done about it.

He stilled her busy hand. 'Look, Josie—'

There was a sudden noise from outside. It had a metallic ring to it as if one of the cars had been struck with an implement. He got out of bed and padded to the window. Carefully parting the curtains slightly he looked out. He could see nothing that moved.

'What's going on, Frankie? Please come back to bed.'

'Did you hear that noise?'

'Noise? We get all sorts of noises in this place. We're on the main road; it could be anything. Come back to bed, sweetheart.'

He began rapidly getting dressed. 'We could be in danger and I need to know if there's anyone out there. Go and tell Tony to get dressed and come downstairs. Don't put the lights on.'

Even as he spoke he knew Mellors was not a man who could respond quickly in a crisis, he was simply not in the tough-guy league. But he knew he might need some kind of help and Mellors was all there was.

'Oh, *Frankie!*' she wailed softly. 'Just when we were having such a lovely time.'

Crane went downstairs. She could be right, it might have been a noise coming from a vehicle on the road. But it had sounded too close to the house and when he'd gone out to the car earlier he'd felt he sensed a definite presence. But if it was one of Docherty's people why make such a noise? It could have been accidental but what if it had been made deliberately? So that someone would go and investigate? Which would have to be Mellors as no one would know Crane was here. Unless he'd been clocked as he'd gone out for his overnight bag. Crane knew he had to find out for certain. If they were in trouble they needed a plan.

In the hall he hesitated. Going out through the front door wasn't a good idea. The same applied to the back door. He moved into the drawing room, lit by moonlight through windows at which the curtains were undrawn. His trained mind automatically memorized every aspect of a room he went into and he'd earlier noted that this room had French windows. It opened on to the right side of the house. It was both locked and bolted but the key was in the lock. He drew the bolt and turned the key. He began to inch open a half-panel. He wished Mellors would come down, he might need whatever help he could get. When the half-panel was fully open he stepped out on to the flagged pathway. The only sound was a whisper of a tide either ebbing or flowing. He edged towards the front of the house. The moment he reached the corner a torch was flashed in his face and then instantly extinguished. A voice he'd heard before said, 'We told you to keep away from Mellors, pal, and what would happen if you didn't.'

He grasped Crane's upper body in a bear hug, pinning his arms to his side. The man was big and strong but Crane was also big and strong and he knew exactly what to do to free himself from this manoeuvre. But in the part of a second he braced himself he heard soft footsteps behind him and from the corner of his eye glimpsed a weapon being raised. With every ounce of his strength he swung the man who pinioned him through a hundred and eighty degrees so that their positions were reversed. It was too late for the other man to arrest the downward swing of a baseball bat and the man who held him received full on the side of his head the blow that had been meant for Crane. As he fell to the ground his accomplice, thinking fast, raised the bat again and took very careful aim at Crane's head. The bat was just about to begin its second swing when that man, too, took a blow to his own head with what appeared to be a thick hiking stick. The man staggered but didn't fall and so the stick came down again and again. The man went down this time but the blows kept coming.

'All right, Mellors!' Crane shouted. 'For Christ's sake don't *kill* him.'

'Why not, they'd have killed you,' a woman's voice said breathlessly.

It was Josie. She gave the man one more blow then burst out laughing. 'I *enjoyed* that, Frankie! This is turning out to be a fun night, isn't it. I've not had as much fun since I jumped in a pool with half a rugby team, all stark bollock naked.'

He had to smile. She might be a nympho and not entirely right in the head but without her quick thinking he could have been seriously injured. 'Josie, I can't begin to thank you enough for the risks you took but it should have been Tony and me.'

'He doesn't do duffing up,' she said, still giggling. 'Not in his genes. He comes from a long line of civil servants.'

There was no contempt in her tone. She seemed to accept Mellors exactly as he was. As they stood over the prone bodies, Mellors himself emerged from the French windows. He looked at the two men and gave a perceptible shudder. 'I'm sorry, Frank,' he said, 'I was in a really heavy sleep and it took a little while to come round. Not that I'd have been much help,' he added sadly. 'I'd not have known what to do.'

'Not to worry, love,' Josie said, 'me and Frankie got it sorted.'

Crane detected a note of affection in her voice for the man who found certain things beyond him, such as mixing it with thugs, and to whom no blame should be attached. The protective fondness was rather touching. It must always have been an odd relationship, even if close in the early years. But then, as he knew from experience, there were oddnesses about most relationships once you got behind the façade.

'Tony, the garage. It's lockable?'

'Yes, not that we seem to use it for cars.'

All the cars were parked at the front of the house: Mellors's Jaguar, Crane's Renault, Heather's Fiat. Crane said, 'Can you give me a hand to drag these two in there? They'll come round eventually and maybe find a way out but by then we'll be long gone.'

'It's brick-built, has no windows and a very strong door.'

'Good.'

'If . . . if they *can't* get out it could be awkward. We can't leave them to die in there,' Mellors said through lips that trembled slightly.

'I agree. Dead bodies could cause problems we can do without.'

'I suppose they'll use mobiles, though the signals aren't very good round here.'

'No, we'll be taking the phones with us. We need to get well away without them contacting anyone.'

'But if they can't get out—'

'Tony, these seem to be two of the outfit's best bouncers. Docherty and his people will know they've been here and if they don't turn up tomorrow or get in touch they'll check the place out. They'll not want to lose them.'

Mellors nodded. He was still very uneasy; these past weeks had not been a good time for him. They began dragging the men to the garage. Crane fished out their mobiles from their pockets and then Mellors locked up. 'They could have been brain damaged,' he said. 'That baseball bat, my stick—'

'So could I if it hadn't been for Josie. I don't want them dead but the kind of career path they're on, possible brain damage goes with the job description.'

Heather had now joined them and stood pale and frightened

in the moonlight. Mellors put an arm round her and led her back into the house where he began to explain quietly what had been going on. When he'd finished, Crane said, 'We go now as fast as we possibly can and it would be best if we went in one car, mine, as three will be too conspicuous at this time of night. We can arrange to pick yours up later. I'll drive directly to your house, Heather, and Josie and Tony will stay with you till I've sorted out the situation with my CID friends.'

'I want to go home,' Josie said firmly. 'I don't feel comfortable in other people's houses. And what's all this about the CID?'

'I'm turning myself in, Jo,' Mellors told her. 'I've been a crook these past years and I can't live with it any more.'

'Oh, for Christ's *sake*, Tony. A few iffy jobs for Brendon. Who's to know or care?'

'I do.'

'Josie,' Crane said, 'you've seen how these people carried on tonight. Do you think they'd have left Tony in one piece? Or any of us? This nice holiday house, the motors, the cruises, they all come out of funny money and at bottom Tony simply isn't that type. You know it's the truth, and now he wants to go back to being the kind of man who can live with himself.'

'In the slammer? If he puts his hand up that's where he'll go.'

'I know that,' Mellors said, 'and I'm ready for it. I'll talk it all through with you when we get to Heather's.'

'Oh, Tony, why *spoil* things? We have such a nice life. Let's go to Brendon and apologize for upsetting him. I'm sure he'll not want to lose you.'

Mellors said, 'My mind's made up, Jo. I'm sorry this life has to end. Frank has it right, I'm just not criminal material. You've had no involvement of any kind in the things I've done, but if you hadn't been quite so demanding I'd not be a crook. We'll talk it all through at Heather's.'

'We'll not be talking anything through at Heather's because I'm going home,' she said bluntly.

Crane said, 'That'll be the first place they'll look for Tony. If you're there they'll force you to tell them where he is. It won't be nice.'

'I am *not* staying at Heather's.'

Crane glanced at his watch. 'We'll sort it out later. We need to get right away – now.'

Mellors quickly brought down two suitcases and stored them in the boot of Crane's Renault, then locked up the house. They all got in the car, Josie taking the front passenger seat next to Crane, as if by right. He was glad to have her at his side; sooner her in a tight corner than Mellors. He drove past the tall gates, which had been keyed into the open position, and out on to the deserted road. He'd gone only about fifty yards when they came to a car drawn up on to the opposite verge – a Honda estate. 'Their car,' Crane said. 'I've got the keys, two sets. We need to disable it, Tony, just in case they do get out of the garage.'

'But if you've got the keys—'

'There just might be a third set hidden somewhere in the vicinity. Never underestimate these people. What do you think, we remove a couple of wheels?'

They got out of the Renault. 'I know a quicker way,' Mellors said. 'Give me some keys.'

They crossed to the Honda and Mellors opened the driver's door and released the bonnet. Propping it up he felt inside the engine compartment and diconnected something. 'The car's disabled now,' he said. 'It'll not move without this.' He held up a part in the light of Crane's torch. He seemed to assume Crane would know what it was but Crane had a blind spot about the insides of cars beyond checking oil and water and was only grateful that Mellors had proved to be a car anorak.

They got back in the Renault and Crane drove steadily along the coast and then from Whitby headed inland. He'd stowed both the phones of the men in the garage in his side pockets and the right one suddenly began to vibrate; its owner must have muted the bell tone. When the vibrating ceased there was a pause of about ten seconds and then the mobile in his left hand pocket began to vibrate. Eventually that, too, ceased. The calls would be from someone wanting a progress report. But the men they wanted a report from lay unconscious in the garage of the holiday home of someone who could now be assumed to be a marked man. What would they do next? Crane wondered. They weren't the types to just sit there.

They came to Blue Bank and began the steep low-gear climb to the moors. They were now in the early hours and could make rapid progress. They were halfway across the moors when a car came towards them, the driver not dipping its full beams courteously though Crane had dipped his.

'A bit early,' Josie said, 'even for people wanting clear roads.'

A bit too early for Crane's peace of mind, too. The other car was going very fast. He wished he could have angled his car away but on this road there was nowhere to go; the densely heather-covered moorland flowed to both sides of the road like a strong tide. Then the other car began to slow and the headlamps were suddenly dimmed to half-lights. As the cars passed each other, Crane saw that the driver of the car had his window down. The driver looked very closely at Crane's car before passing on. Inside that second, Crane clamped his foot to the throttle and checked his rear-view mirror. The other car was doing a rapid three-point turn.

'What's going on?' Josie asked eagerly.

'More of Doherty's people. I've got the mobiles of those two in the garage in my pockets and they've been vibrating. If they're not answered the gang will know there's been trouble.'

'How could they possibly get people out here so quickly?'

'Because Docherty leaves nothing to chance. They'll have had back-up people in Pickering.'

Crane was driving as fast as he dare. The following car was a long way behind. If he could get to Pickering he would feel safer, though at this time of night would anywhere be safe? His rear-view mirror gave him a partial view of Mellors in the back, hunched and frightened. He was beginning to realize just what it was capable of, the company he'd been keeping. He caught a glimpse of Heather, also very scared-looking and drawn into herself like a small animal instinctively trying to make itself insignificant to a predator.

'This is great fun!' Josie burst out, as the car finally zoomed off the moor. 'Just like *French Connection.*'

NINE

Melanie awoke with the inevitable troubled mind. Damien lay at her side asleep but she knew it wouldn't be a deep sleep, they didn't do deep sleep any more. They had the run of the house as her parents were still on holiday. She knew only too well that Damien would rather be here than at home.

Last night came back into her mind. They'd gone to St Dunstan's. It had been the evening before Tessa's birthday and Brendon had arranged for Father Casey to say a special Mass to which they could invite family and close friends. It was a tradition now as Tessa took so much pleasure in being given her own service.

Melanie had been in the middle of the little gathering with Damien. She was a non-believer but she'd found it comforting to be next to him in the half-light and listening to the responses. She badly needed comfort in this dreadful time, though she knew it only served as a sticking plaster to a wound that needed stitches. Damien prayed endlessly. She could barely restrain herself from putting an arm round him and stroking his face. He was in such a depth of misery.

Father Casey had gone to the front of the altar at one stage to thank Brendon for the unstinting support he'd given to the church in so many ways and to wish Tessa a happy and holy birthday in the bosom of her close and loving family.

Then Brendon had gone up to the altar, thanked the priest for agreeing to say the Mass and said a few touching words about his long and happy marriage to Tessa and the two fine children who'd come out of it. 'To sum up,' he'd said, 'Tess, apart from being such a good wife and mother, has been, quite simply, my best friend.'

Glancing across the aisle, Melanie had seen Tessa dabbing her eyes with a tissue. She felt bemused and as their eyes met she knew Damien shared the same confusion. She'd seen Brendon blessing himself with holy water, she'd seen him knelt in prayer, she'd listened to the affecting accolade he'd made to Tessa and in five minutes she'd see him take Communion.

Yet she couldn't get out of her mind poor Cilla having acid flung in her face and the way she'd named and described Brendon as a man who'd had sex with her, outlining with total precision the man Melanie had just seen on the altar: stocky, powerful and with a face you didn't forget.

Damien awoke. Eyes open, he lay expressionless for several seconds until the usual pain crumpled his face and he sat up, pale and lost. 'Oh God, Mel,' he muttered, 'dear God.'

She, too, raised herself up, her back to the headboard. 'I know, Demmy, I know.'

'The way you saw him last night, that's the way he's always *been*. The way he appreciated Mum and looked after her, they were . . . they were lessons in how a marriage should work. This was how decent families went on. Mel, he can't be, he can't possibly be that other man, not someone who goes to Mass and talks about Mum like that. Surely, surely, *surely* he can't.'

Melanie had never known such unhappiness. The pain never ended. If they weren't talking about it they never stopped thinking about it. They were both having to take tablets to get any sleep at all and they had so little appetite they were beginning to look drawn, haggard, even. Damien refused to go near Tanglewood House and spent all his time at her parents'.

She stroked his cheek, kissed him, got out of bed. They slept together but made love only rarely and in a preoccupied way. It pushed everything aside, the endless brooding they did about Brendon. She padded into the kitchen, filled the percolator and set it going. They still drank endless cups of coffee. She put slices of bread in the toaster; they had to try and eat *something*. She wondered if she should boil a couple of eggs but put them dispiritedly back in the fridge – just be a waste of eggs. They might be able to cope with cornflakes. She shook some into two bowls.

Damien came silently into the kitchen. He looked so different from his normal self, so ghost-like. It was absurd but she almost felt that if she put a hand out to him there'd be no bone and tissue to touch. She'd read that unhappiness was aging and she had the proof before her eyes in his pale, worn features. She knew it applied to her, too, not that she could bear to look at herself in the mirror.

'What do you want to do today, Demmy?'

'I'd like to go on to the moors. Might take our minds off things.' He forced a twisted grin. 'Maybe give us an appetite for tonight.'

She nodded wanly. It was Tessa's big birthday party tonight, with most of the people who'd been at church.

'Try not to think about it, your dad, until you've seen the investigator.'

He watched her across the table. 'If none of us, me, Mollie, Mum, ever knew about any of these things he's supposed to have done, what chance will a PI have?'

'If he can't find things out he's in the wrong job.'

'And what if he does find things out? What do we do then?'

'What *can* we do? We'll have to think . . . to consider going to the police.'

'But what about *Mum*? It would break her up. She'd never be able to live with it. She's spent all these years thinking how lucky she's been to marry a man like Dad.'

Melanie gazed over the back garden with unfocused eyes. And so it went on, the endless circular discussions, as if this frightful time would never end. She wondered dismally if there was the remotest possibility it ever would.

Crane drove rapidly through a silent Pickering and on to the Malton road. He knew the area well and was keeping a good distance between the two cars. But sooner or later their pursuer would pull some move that would put them in danger. If they got close enough they might even try a bullet through a tyre. They'd certainly be armed.

He squealed round a bend that put the following car's headlamps out of sight. They were driving past farmland and all at once he got lucky; the wide gate to one of the farms stood open. Braking sharply he shot through the opening and on to an unmetalled track.

'Cool move!' Josie cried, as excited as a child on a fairground switchback.

'It looks to be an arable farm,' Crane said, glancing round in the moonlight. 'If there are no prize bulls to nick I suppose an open gate doesn't matter too much.'

He had doused the car's lights and as he moved steadily along the earth road he kept checking his rear-view mirror to see what the other car did. As he'd hoped, a few seconds later he saw it hurtle past the opening and continue along the main road. Relieved, he was able to take stock of his surroundings. Ahead, there was a dark mass that could have been a farmhouse. The fields they were passing contained crops and a little further along they came to some outbuildings. There were three of them, set back, and at the third one he drove the Renault round the side of it and halted.

'This puts the car out of sight from the road,' he said. 'This is the position as I see it. Docherty's people have gone straight past and as I was a good way ahead of them I'm hoping they'll think I'm still ahead of them on the main road. That should keep them going for a good few miles. But in the end they'll twig I must have pulled off and they're going to turn round and check out the turn-offs. That could also take time. Tony, I want you and Heather to stay here in the car. Me and Josie, we'll take a look round.'

'Wouldn't . . . wouldn't it be better if we all stayed in the car?' Mellors said agitatedly. He was very frightened. He was caught up in a way of life that had always made him feel guilty but had now turned into a nightmare.

'These people are out to get us, Tony. They're now running very scared you'll get near the police. Sooner or later there's a strong chance they'll decide we must have come along here and we need to decide what to do about it. Just stay put with Heather and I'll try and sort something out with Josie.'

'See you soon,' Josie said chirpily as she and Crane got out of the car. She seemed not to know what fear was. Dressed in trousers, T-shirt and zip-up jacket she'd taken her hair back in a ponytail and gave her usual impression of vibrating with energy. 'We should be tooled up,' she told him. He wondered which American film she'd picked that up from.

The men locked in the garage had had guns, which Crane had removed the shells from and put in the car's boot. He daren't think what might happen if Josie got near one, considering the blows she'd given out to the gangster's head with the hiking stick.

They walked quickly back to the gateway, looking in on the outhouses as they passed. The one behind which Crane's car was parked was a large barn. It was used presumably for storing harvested crops and hay but at present it just held an elderly rusting Volvo. In the next outhouse there was a tractor.

'Trusting bloke,' Josie said. 'Open gate, unlocked barns.'

'The Volvo's not worth stealing and the tractor will have modern ignition so that the only things that'll move it will be the keys that came with it.'

The last outhouse, the one nearest the road, contained what seemed to be some kind of a pit with a cover held in place by counter-sunk bolts.

'What do you suppose this is?' Josie asked.

He shone his torch over it. 'Could be an inspection pit. The farmer will probably have basic mechanical skills and be able to make car and tractor repairs so as not to hold up the work.'

They walked on to the entrance, where he closed the five-bar gate, which squealed from want of oil. 'That might put them off. They should figure we'd not have had the time for someone to get out of the car and open the gate in case we were spotted.'

'Maybe they're not that bright.'

She had a point. They walked back to the outhouses. 'That pit,' she said, 'let's have a look at it.'

'With what in mind?'

'I'll tell you when I've seen it with the lid off.'

They went into the building and while Josie held the torch Crane drew back the bolts on the cover and lifted it away. The pit was about six feet long and two and a half feet wide and between five and six feet deep. Josie examined it for some time in silence. 'What if,' she said, 'instead of that lid it was covered in some of the plastic sheeting that's in the corner?'

'Go on.'

'If those men do come here they'll think we're hiding in one of these barns. This one's the first they'll come to. What if they walk across the floor and fall into the pit because it's only covered in plastic?'

It was a good idea. The men crashing into the pit in the darkness and the cover quickly replaced and bolted down. 'Nice one, Josie. The problem is they might not walk over the pit.'

'So we arrange things along the sides so that they'll have to move along the place where the pit is.'

He glanced round the room. A lot of equipment was stored here: wheelbarrows, picks and shovels, forks, rakes, hedging tools. 'We'll give it a try.'

The room had a generally untidy look and the way they proceeded to scatter equipment added to the picture. First they covered the open pit with the sheeting, keeping it in place by weighting it with some of the hardware. Then they disguised the sheeting with some sacking that had come to hand. Then they ensured that the only clear space among the tools was the pit area. When they'd finished there was no trace of the pit in the moonlight that glowed through the only window.

The building was equipped with power and light and he tested the overhead globe rapidly to ensure it was in working order. He then saw that there was a door in the back wall. He went through it and found it led to a lean-to section. It contained a table and several folding canvas chairs. There was also a socket and an electric kettle. It was perhaps a place where farmhands could eat a sandwich lunch. There was an overhead bulb in this room, also in working order. He turned the light on then went back to the main room, closing the door to the lean-to. As he'd hoped, a sliver of light showed beneath the door, which stood out in the gloom. 'If they come in here,' he said, 'they'll see that little strip of light and want to investigate. The pit will be directly in their path.'

'What a night!' she said gleefully. 'You can't believe how much I'm enjoying this. What a life you lead, Frankie. I'd love to work with you when we're back home. What do you say?'

He grinned in the darkness. He'd always been a one-man band but if he ever did work in partnership she'd certainly have been in with a chance. She was nerveless, tireless and able to think on her feet. 'Josie, this is not what the job is about. It's all wall to wall bad debts and missing persons and tracing legatees and checking out lifestyles and keeping an eye on men who might be playing away.'

'I'm so glad Tony wasn't playing away. This has been lots more fun.'

'Not so damn funny if men start pointing guns at us.'

'Oh, we'll be all right. You're such a big strong man. You always know what to do in a crisis.'

He wished he felt as confident in himself as she did. He'd been in dangerous situations before but he'd had his CID training.

The hardest lesson he'd had to learn had been to keep his cool when in the sort of position he was in now. Grace under pressure, as Hemingway had it.

At the back of the room stood a set of ladders that could be combined in different ways He fixed them together so that they stood at a height just above his own. He then draped more of the sacking over them. 'We hide ourselves behind these,' he told her, 'wait, and speak only in whispers.'

'Wasn't it funny,' she whispered, giggling, 'me thinking Tony was having his bottom caned by a special girlfriend when all the time he'd just had it kicked because he'd not do as he was told. I should have known; he'll never leave me, Frankie. Who could give him what I give him and look like I do? Now, I reckon that plain-Jane Heather fancies him rotten. I ask you, driving seventy miles about a stupid report. Have you seen the way she looks at him? Poor bitch, I suppose she might very well pass for forty-three in the dusk with the light behind her.'

She was full of surprises. He'd not have thought she'd ever heard *Trial by Jury*, let alone be able to quote from it. She was being cruel. Heather had the sort of homely features that made her look a little older than her age, but she could only have been in her thirties and had a good figure. And a kind heart. Josie had an unerring instinct about Heather's feelings for Tony but a blind spot about Tony's equally strong feelings for Heather. When this business with Docherty was all over Josie had a big shock coming. He wondered how she'd handle it.

'How long do you think we'll have to wait?' she whispered. 'Have we got time for a quickie? All this excitement's putting me in a right old fruity state. I could even make do with a wall job.'

She squeezed his thigh invitingly. He said, 'Sex doesn't go with men who are almost certainly tooled up, as you put it, and could be creeping around outside right now.'

'It's so boring, just waiting.'

'I spend half my life just waiting.'

'It could be ages before they get here. And ages before we can get our kit off again.'

He gave a wry grin. He wondered if there could be any situation, any at all, that wasn't somehow guaranteed to put her in a sexy state. He knew he had only to give her an encouraging word for her to be lying, legs akimbo, on a mound of sacking, even though she was prepared, at a pinch, to make do with a 'wall job'.

'Frankie.' The whisper had become wheedling. 'You will think about letting me work with you, won't you? I could be a decoy girl, one of those women who can provide proof to a wife that her old man is having affairs.'

Some decoy girl, he thought. Genuine decoy girls didn't actually have sex with straying husbands, they just went through all the moves that led up to it. They made secret recordings and took compromising photos on their mobiles. But the whole point to Josie would be actually encouraging the bloke to give her one. Or three. Or half a dozen. There'd still be the recordings and the photos for the wife to use in the divorce case but the poor sod would at least have had the best jump of his life.

He let her burble on. He'd thought her prattle might distract him but found it eased the tension a little. He glanced at his watch. It had been only a short time since they'd driven off the road but as usual the minutes seemed to be acting like hours. 'Quiet, Josie,' he whispered a short time later. He'd heard something and wondered if it could have been the squeal of the farm gate. If it was would they drive on to the track as he'd done? He thought not; they'd probably want to move as quietly as possible.

'Do you think they're here?' she whispered gleefully.

'I don't know. We listen and wait.'

They listened and waited for what seemed a very long time. She quivered at his side in silent delight, ready for anything the night might throw at them. She'd had a lot of luck with the hiking stick and didn't realize that things might not continue to go well. He was very uneasy about the absence of activity since the gate had squealed, if it had been the gate, and only wished he could have shared Josie's insouciance.

Then the door began to creak slowly open and in the moonlight he could just make out the shapes of two men. They began whispering; he could just make out the words in the deep silence. 'See the light under that door?' one of them said. 'We'll take a shufti. Watch your step with all this gear.'

They began to move quietly over the only clear path across the littered room. Suddenly there was the heavy slumping collapse of what could only be men falling into a man-trap. Crane was positioned near the switch that turned on the overhead light. He flicked it on. To his total dismay he saw that only one of the men had fallen. The other teetered on the edge for a moment but then regained his balance. He was holding a gun that Crane knew to be a machine pistol. It would hold enough bullets to kill off half of Pickering.

'Christ, Benny, I've fallen down a bloody hole. Give me a hand.'

'Hold on, Pete. That guy Crane's here with Mellors's woman. I've got them covered.'

'I think I've broke me sodding leg.'

'Just give me a couple of shakes to sort this out. They've tried to set us up.'

The standing man knew how to handle a crisis. He never let his eyes move from Crane and Josie and was clearly thinking fast. He said, 'Where's Mellors?'

Crane said, 'He could be anywhere by now.'

'Do me a favour, Crane. You were all in one car. You wouldn't let Mellors go off in it.'

'I sent him back to Pickering to contact the police.'

'That's bullshit. He's around here somewhere.' He fell silent for a short time, then said, 'Look, Crane, you and the woman don't figure in this but we need Mellors. He'll not be hurt but we need to sort a few things out with him and they're urgent. Just tell us where he is and you two can scarper, right?'

Crane stayed silent. He knew that he and Josie were in exactly the same danger as Mellors; they all knew too much now and they all had to be silenced one way or the other.

'I'm waiting, Crane, and I'm not going to wait long. I've got an injured mate down here. If you don't tell me what I want to know this gun will do the talking. You'll find walking very, very difficult with a shattered knee-cap.'

Neither of them spoke. Had Josie blurted out Mellors's location he'd not have been surprised and not have held it against her. For all her incredible self-confidence she had to be very scared. Crane was, and though his own mind was in overdrive he felt there was nowhere to go.

'OK,' the man said, 'I'll count to ten and if neither of you coughs one of you gets a sore kneecap. Or it could be both of you with sore kneecaps. I'll think about it while I'm counting.'

'Let them go, they're nothing to do with any of this. It's me you want and now you've got me. Let them go.' It was Mellors, standing in the doorway.

The gunman had been startled but rapidly adjusted to the situation. 'Good thinking, Mellors. If I'd had to come searching for you it would have got me very angry and when I'm angry my fists seem to lead a life of their own. Go and stand with Crane and your missus.'

'You are going to let them go?'

'There's no big rush. I've got things to do first.' He took hold of Mellors's arm and pushed him towards Josie and Crane. 'How are things down there, Pete?'

'The fucking thing's broke, I'm sure of it.'

'I'll get help, don't worry.'

'Quick as you can. Feels like the sod's on fire.'

The gunman was dividing his attention between the man in the pit and those who stood against the opposite wall. There wasn't much left over for him to be aware of someone else who'd just appeared behind him in the door-way. It was Heather, small, frightened and as white as A4, but looking very determined. She was grasping a small thick log that looked as if it might have come from the farm's fuel store. She raised it but instead of trying to strike the gunman from her height she rammed him in the small of the back with all her strength. He still stood at the edge of the pit. He teetered, cursed, instinctively stretched out an arm to grab something to regain his balance, but there was nothing to grab and he pitched headlong into the pit to join his partner, who screamed in even more pain as the other's body slumped on top of his.

'Well *done*, Heather!' Crane cried, 'That was one hell of a risk you took.'

'I couldn't just stand by,' she gasped, 'not when these frightful men were . . . were. . . . Are you all right, Tony?'

Mellors had sagged against the wall, sucking in air. A few seconds ago he must have felt certain he was going to be shot and now he was out of danger. 'Heather,' he said in a strangled tone, 'I'll be forever in your debt.'

Crane, on an emotional roller coaster himself, also breathed deeply. He didn't like to think what might have happened to them but for Heather. What courage she and Mellors had been able to find in themselves. He glanced at Josie. She was grinning, her chirpy spirits fully restored, not that it looked as if they'd ever really left her. She seemed to see her present life as a sort of Hitchcock film in which people encountered all sorts of danger and were constantly on the run but where everything turned out fine in the end with Cary Grant yanking you up on the monument.

She said, 'I wonder if he's broken his leg, too, the man who's just gone in the pit. If one's broken his left leg and the other his right, they should be able to get about with an arm round each other. What has two heads and two legs and eats fish and chips?'

There was a great deal of noise coming from the pit. Cursing, groaning, cries of pain. 'Tony,' Crane said, 'The cover to the pit's over there. We need to get it in place fast and bolt it down. We need to be careful to keep out of sight as they're both armed. Or were. Follow me.'

He took a step forward and then yet another figure stepped

from the darkness into the barn. It was a stocky man dressed in dungarees and a jerkin. He held a shotgun, which was pointed steadily in their direction. 'Stay right still, mister, in case this gun goes off.'

Crane's spirits hit zero yet again. He'd always assumed that Docherty's heavies worked in pairs and that tonight's pair were now in the pit. But he'd been wrong.

This time there'd been a third man.

TEN

They'd driven to the pub called Dick Hudson's and parked Damien's car there. They crossed to the track that led to Ilkley Moor and walked along it hand in hand. It was a day of drifting cloud with a forecast of scattered showers but they'd packed waterproofs. There was also a strong breeze as so often up here and they were glad of its scouring freshness. It seemed to give an illusion of clearing their minds for a time of the trauma that dogged their present lives. There was also something of the old exultation about being quite alone in this high open land that seemed to stretch endlessly in every direction.

When they'd covered about a mile, Damien said, voice rising against the gusting air, 'If the PI does . . . find things out about Dad, I shan't expect you to stay with me, Mel. It would be too much to ask, expecting you to marry a criminal's son.'

'Demmy, for heaven's *sake!*'

'But don't you see, it would taint you for ever. If he went to court it would be in the papers and then all the rumours would start: how could he do those things without his family knowing; how could they live in that big house with that lifestyle and not know where the money came from? And it would be just as bad for you. People will say you married me because of all the crooked money.'

'Stop, Demmy, *stop!*' she cried, pulling him round to face her on the track. 'Nothing is *ever* going to alter the way I feel about you.'

'But you'll not be getting the man you thought I was. If Dad is a criminal and the police get on to him I'll not have anything like the prospects I have now. I'll not be able to take anything from him ever again. We'd have to buy a house out of what we could scrape together ourselves, and as for the Party, would they ever nominate me to a seat, a man from a criminal family? They'd think I must have known what he was, just like everyone else.'

They began to walk again. 'Demmy, do you remember when we first met? At university, the bottle party. You asked me out and I knew then you were the one. And don't forget, I'd no idea then about how you were placed: Tanglewood House and the motors and the lavish parties – I only found out about all that later. But I loved you for yourself, a man I thought needed to scratch around for a fiver like all of us.

'And I have to admit, when I found out about your background, it came as a relief to know we'd have so much help buying a house and all the other freebies. But . . . but it was always *you* that mattered, never the money. And now we might have to go it alone and so what, we'll just be in the same boat as all the rest. We'll be applying for jobs where we'll be one in a hundred but we'll get jobs in the end without your father's help, you'll see.'

He grasped her hand and they walked on in silence until it was time to return to Dick Hudson's. She sensed him to be calmer as if the clear air and the exercise really had helped to ease his mind a little. They sat in the pub, had a single drink and ate sandwiches for which, for the first time in days, they had a good appetite.

'We'll share the pain, Demmy,' she said, laying a hand on one of his, 'always. It's what it's all about, isn't it, being a couple? If it *is* true about your dad we'll rent a flat and buy a house when we can afford one.'

'And go to the police if. . . .' The sentence dangled.

'I don't know. I really don't know. We'll have to think about it. I'm tempted to say let's just walk away.'

'Not easy. Me and Dad, we've always been so close. He'd want to know why I was giving him the cold shoulder.'

'Don't say anything at all, just give an impression you're not happy being around him. He's astute. I'm sure he'll put two and two together.'

'I think I'd *have* to go to the police, Mel, if he really is doing these vile things.'

She nodded slowly. It was clear he was coming round to accepting what she herself was convinced was the truth, however bitterly unhappy it made him. 'I think you're right, I think they'd have to be involved.'

'It's Mum I'm really upset about. If there was a way things could be done without her knowing anything. . . .'

'She'd have to know if it came out, both her and Mollie. And all your relations. I'm afraid that all that would be left for your mum would be the happy years she's had up to now.'

'Poor Mum, I'd do anything to spare her the truth.'

Later, Melanie was to remember those words very clearly and to wonder if they had any bearing on what actually happened.

They sat at a plain square table in a large farmhouse kitchen. The farmer's wife had made them bacon sandwiches and mugs of coffee. It was still some time until dawn and Crane felt the night seemed to be taking twice as long as normal because of all the things that had happened.

'I sometimes take a walk round in the early hours,' the farmer told them, 'or my son does. There've been a couple of tractor thefts along the road. Ours won't move without the key but they tell me the beggars still have ways of taking them off. So we keep an eye out. That's how I came on the Renault.'

'We're very sorry to have put you to this trouble, Mr Ketch. You'll be needing your sleep after a day on the land.'

'Farmers live with broken nights. We catch half an hour's sleep when we can during the day.'

'The same goes for farmers' wives,' Mrs Ketch added, smiling.

'It's been difficult watering the crops with the long dry spell,' the farmer's son put in. 'No point in doing it with all that sun. We've had to wait for darkness and let the land cool down a bit.'

Mr Ketch was a man on the short side but strongly built with bluntish features deeply tanned from his outdoor activities. His son was taller and leaner with a similar tan and fair hair bleached almost blond by the sun. He was a good-looking young man and was mesmerized by Josie. Josie, too couldn't take her eyes off him and gazed with that knack she had with a man she fancied of giving an impression he was the one she'd been waiting for all her life and had just been laid aside by a *coup de foudre*.

'We'll keep an eye on those two,' Mr Ketch said. 'Don't worry.'

'This really is very good of you.'

They'd given the farmer a version of the truth. Mellors was a local government official who a criminal had tried to involve in corrupt practices to do with property and compulsory purchase orders. Mellors had told the man that he was going to report these approaches to the police. The men in the pit, over which the cover had now been fitted, had been sent to threaten him with violence unless he agreed to keep the police out of it. Crane had explained all this to the farmer, referring to his time with the CID and Mellors had quietly backed it all up, his face and demeanour, as usual, his finest card. The farm people had accepted everything they'd been told, asking for only the odd word of clarification now and then.

After this, Crane had rung Terry Jones, who, like the Ketches, was used to broken nights, and explained the situation. Jones was delighted that Mellors was going to give him everything he needed to know for Docherty to be brought in and charged. He was now arranging with the local police to pick up the men in Mellors's garage and the men in the pit. The situation would be sorted out when the day got going.

The men in the pit had been made, at the end of a shotgun barrel, to place their handguns on the floor at the side of the pit. The pistols had been drawn away with a rake.

Crane glanced at his watch. 'I think we should be moving on, Mr Ketch. You can leave it all to the police now. This is my card, which gives all my numbers. One of those will always find me. I can't begin to thank you for all the help you and your son have given us. And thank you, too, Mrs Ketch, for your hospitality.'

'You've got a lovely farm,' Josie said softly, giving Leo, the farmer's son, the big-eyed, misty gaze she'd probably perfected at twelve, when her favourite cousin had first tentatively fondled a gratifyingly welcoming thigh. 'Do you do bed and breakfast?'

Mrs Ketch shook her head. 'We manage to make a decent living and I help when we're getting the crops in so I'd not really have time for—'

'But I'm sure we could take *one* guest, Mum, if it was Miss Josie here,' Leo cut in.

'And I'd be no trouble,' Josie assured her. 'I'd not want the great British breakfast; tea and toast would be fine.'

'Well, in that case I suppose we could think about it,' Mrs Ketch said without enthusiasm. It was clear she, too, was picking up on the vibes Josie was giving out, which weren't easy to miss, and wasn't keen on what she was making of them.

'I'll give you our number,' Leo said eagerly, wrenching at the drawer of a cupboard and scribbling on a scrap pad. 'Farm number and my mobile number.' He handed the paper to Josie. 'And come back soon.'

Crane knew the poor devil would be a long stop and that she'd only ever be back in the unlikely event of facing a weekend with no one around to take her knickers off for. Even now he could only marvel at her rigid sense of priorities. Her husband faced a prison sentence and they'd been threatened at the holiday home by one pair of thugs and chased across the North York Moor by another, their lives at risk throughout, but the crucial matter on Josie's mind was to ensure an unbroken supply of duvet fodder.

They all moved out to the Renault, the Ketches walking with them, Leo clearly struggling to cope with a genuine *coup de foudre* of his very own. He took Josie's arm solicitously to help

160

her into the car. She gave him a final misty-eyed, adoring smile and when settled, puckered her lips and blew him a kiss. This left him in a state close to a catatonic trance and, glancing at Mrs Ketch, Crane knew that Josie would never ever eat breakfast in his mother's kitchen, even if it would have been only tea and toast.

There was handshaking all round and a few minutes later they were back on the road in the dawning light. The drive to Bradford went smoothly and rapidly with no further shocks or hold-ups. Crane drove first to Harden, a small village on the outskirts of Bradford where Heather owned a modern bungalow. She and Mellors got out of the car but Josie stayed behind. Crane sighed. 'It would be the best thing all round, Josie, if you both stayed with Heather. In fact, it's essential for your own safety.'

'No, I need to be in my own home. And you and me, we've got unfinished business.'

'You don't seem to understand the danger you're in. Tony's going to give the police a full statement of all the crooked activities he's been involved in and who was pulling the strings. A man like Docherty will do anything in his power to silence him. If you go to your own house that's the first place Docherty's people will look and they'll threaten you with violence if you don't stop Tony talking to the police. That's how these people operate. Believe me, I know.'

He knew his words were having no effect. Anything she didn't want to know she simply pushed out of her mind. 'All right,' she said, 'I'll stay with you at your place.' She grinned. 'Best deal, anyway. I can't wait to carry on where we left off and I'm sure you feel the same.'

'I'm not going back to my house. That's the second place Docherty's men will be checking out. They've probably figured that as ex-police myself I'll be involved in delivering Tony to the central station. I'll be staying with a friend of mine in a place as anonymous as Heather's.'

'Then I must be in my own house. It would be too inhibiting to stay at Heather's. I'd not be able to do the things I want to do.'

Crane knew he had no need to ask what they'd be.

'You *must* stay here, Josie. I can't let you put yourself in certain danger by going home.'

'I'll come with you, then, to your hidey-hole. I'm sure your friend wouldn't mind. Probably be glad of the company.'

'My friend is female. You'd not be welcome.'

'Ah-ha, like that, is it? We could have a lovely threesome. Girl on girl can be fun, too, while you're getting your breath back, especially if there are some really exciting fingers on the go. I've done it before; she had one of those state-of-the-art dildos. The things she could make it *do*: vibrate, go fast, go slow, revolve. Wowee!'

He wondered if there was the smallest aspect of sexual activity she'd not thoroughly explored, including dogging. She'd told him earlier she was a member of the Mile High Club. He couldn't help smiling at the thought. Her current boyfriend had had a friend who owned a small plane. He'd taken them up to the requisite height and then rocked the plane gently from side to side while they got on with it in the back.

'It was tremendous fun, Frankie, and when we were back on terra firma we couldn't wait to go up again. But my friend's wife cottoned on and couldn't wait to put the kybosh on it.'

'Some wives can be quite narrow-minded about their husbands wanting to enrol other women in the Mile High Club.'

'Miserable cow.'

Josie now said, 'You're smiling. Does that mean we *can* go and have a bit of fun with your girlfriend?'

'No, it doesn't. It's not in my line or hers. Now go in the house with Tony and Heather where you'll be *safe*. I can't let you stay in your own house.'

'Well, you'll have to come in with me, for an hour or two at least. Heather will give us a room where we can—'

'Out you get – *now*. I'm a busy man and there's a lot I need to catch up on.'

'Tell me about it. When do I catch up on what we didn't do at the weekend place?'

Crane got out, walked round the car and opened the passenger door. Beyond Josie to dissemble, her sour face said it all as she reluctantly joined him on the pavement. Heather and Mellors still stood at the gate of Heather's house, unable to have heard the discussion in the car but looking as if they knew Josie was being troublesome. They had an air of resignation about them, as if longing to be alone together and not having to fit their relationship around Josie's trying and difficult personality.

'Tony,' Crane said, 'Try and chill out as best you can. I'll be back for you day after tomorrow, OK?'

'That's fine, Frank, and thanks for everything. I've put you to a great deal of trouble and I'll not forget it.'

'Don't worry about any of that. I'm an ex-cop and I can cope with it. We'll keep in touch on mobiles. See you later. Goodbye, Heather . . . Josie. . . .'

They'd taken a lot of care with their appearance. They'd showered and washed their hair and Damien wore a new pale-blue shirt and chinos and Melanie a simple green abstract-print dress. She'd also spent time brushing and styling her hair from a central parting. Among the birthday guests at Tanglewood House they must have looked exactly the same as usual. But Melanie knew a closer look would have detected the faint shadows beneath their eyes brought on by the lack of sleep. They also both had a slightly strained cast to their features that they tried hard to conceal behind warm smiles and cheerful words.

Brendon Docherty was in his usual genial form, kissing women's cheeks, clasping men by the arm, finding a welcoming word for each of their many relations. He was standing with Tessa and kissed her fondly when Mollie took a birthday snap.

Melanie decided he had to have the kind of mind in which the life he lived to make all that money must be able to be partitioned off when he came home and not allowed to affect the

163

man he was there: loving, warmhearted, kind, thoughtful. Two different men seemed to live in Brendon.

She watched him as he began to move among the people in the big drawing room, with its soft wall lights and the music playing Mozart's 20th Piano. This afternoon she'd wondered again and again how she'd react to Brendon now that she knew so much of the other side of his life. One week he'd been one of the finest men she'd ever known; the next the most dreadful. Sooner or later he'd put an arm round her and have one of those jokey, flirty chats they usually had and give her one of those glances that told her how fanciable he found her to be. She couldn't control a shudder of repulsion, barely able to cope with the thought of being touched by a man who'd once ordered acid to be thrown in a girl's face. But she steeled herself to being the same Melanie he'd always known, cheerful and chatty and going along with a harmless flirtation with her fiancé's attractive father.

And then he was at her side. The usual arm round her waist, the usual kiss on the cheek. 'Ah, 'tis a picture you look tonight, Mel, in that pretty dress. Lovely to have you here again. Will I be topping up your glass?'

'No thanks, Brendon. I need to go steady with this delicious champagne.'

'Krug,' he said, smiling. 'As the evening goes on we'll be down to the Moët. A bit like the marriage feast at Cana in reverse.'

She forced herself to laugh gaily. 'Tess seems to be enjoying her birthday party,' she said, nodding to where Tessa stood, shaking with laughter with two of her sisters.

'Ah, she's a wonderful woman, to be sure,' he said softly, seeming almost moist-eyed as he looked at the woman he'd been married to for so long. 'When I'm with you, Mel, it's like being with Tess as she was thirty years ago.'

She had to force out of her mind the image of this man in bed with vulnerable young women, who'd been groomed for prostitution.

'You spoke about her so movingly at the special Mass,' she said, the words helping her to give him some semblance of the man she'd once thought she knew.

'I owe a long, happy married life to Tess,' he said simply. 'I've been blessed.'

'I'm sure she owes as much to you, Brendon.'

This was dreadful. Try as she might she couldn't quite get a warm inflection into her words or conceal a slight impression of reserve. Docherty turned back from the room. 'Are you all right, my love? You seem a little on the pale and peaky side. And Demmy looks a bit under par, too, now I think about it.'

'I've . . . I've had rather a shock. A close friend from uni, she was . . . she was killed in a car accident. We were like sisters. It left me a bit low.'

'I'm so very sorry.' He patted her arm. 'And Demmy knew her, too?'

'It was a bad blow for both of us. But I was so cut up I suppose it rubbed off on him.' She knew it didn't sound very convincing that the death of a friend could give her and Damien the abstracted air neither of them could entirely disguise. But a car death was the story they'd agreed on.

Docherty gave her a sharp glance, as if he'd picked up on the slight false note. He had a look she'd not seen before: wary, searching, sceptical. But then he said in his usual tone, 'Ah well, my love, I'm afraid these awful things happen now and then and they always give us such a turn.'

Melanie could feel herself beginning to colour but at that moment a small red lamp began to wink over the door and the piano music was interrupted by a soft chiming. Docherty grimaced. 'Never send to know for whom the bell tolls,' he muttered, 'it *always* tolls for me. Be back soon.'

He darted off and Mollie, who'd been standing nearby, came over to her. 'His study phone,' she said. 'The light and the chimes go off all over the house.'

'Oh, I see. Do . . . does your mum answer it when he's out?'

Melanie asked, as casually as possible.

'Glory be, no way! The answer service takes the message. Anyway, he locks his study. He says if the cleaner goes in she disturbs his papers. I should think you're beginning to learn how pathologically secretive he is about that business of his.'

Melanie looked away to mask the sadness Mollie's words had given her, knowing that she could have told her that her father had an awful lot to be pathologically secretive *about*, apart from the business deals.

'Hello.'

'It's me, boss.'

'Go ahead, Joe.'

'Two of the boys nailed by the bogies at Mellors's weekend place, two more nailed at some farm out Malton way. They'll not cough, we can be sure of that, but they might go inside for threatening behaviour and packing shooters. They've not got a lot of form but they've all got some.' Joe enlarged on the sketchy details he'd been able to put together.

'And the PI was involved?'

'From what I can make out.'

'Where is he now?'

'Can't trace him. Can't trace Mellors or his wife. Can't trace no bugger.'

Docherty was furious but he didn't let loose the expletives that trembled on his lips. He had to stick with his resolve not to let his anger show, had always to give the impression he had an answer to everything. He usually had.

'Right,' he said calmly, 'this is what we do. We let things ride for the time being. Sooner or later they'll all have to surface. When they do we'll have them. I'm positive now Mellors is aiming to blow the whistle. If he does start grassing we'll have to be absolutely certain he never makes it to a witness box. Whatever it takes.'

'I'm with you, boss.'

'I used him more than was wise, Joe, because of him looking like a Sunday school teacher. He's got a fix on every side of the business.'

'Like you said before, he's never been one of us.'

'I knew at the time I was taking a chance on him. The only thing that kept him in place was having to keep that nympho bitch of his happy.'

'I'll keep in touch, boss.'

'Every day, Joe. Make sure someone keeps a lookout for when Mellors or fire-pants gets home. . . .'

Mollie said, 'You know Dad's taking us to the coast next weekend?'

'Your mum did mention it.'

It was the last thing in the world she wanted, a long weekend in the company of Brendon, but she knew they'd have to go, that she and Damien would have to carry on, for the time being, with the charade.

Mollie laid a hand on her arm. 'Peter and I were wondering what we could give Dad that would be a nice surprise and show him how much we all love him. But it's the old problem: what do you give a man who's got everything?'

'I believe members of the Royal Family have the same dilemma. I read that they tend to give one another very simple things.'

'Exactly. Anyway it's his birthday next month and Peter suggests that maybe we could get Patrick Coogan from the Irish Club to sing at the party. Mum and Dad have the cassette and play it such a lot. Of course, Patrick's a big showbiz name now but he might do a private gig if the price was right. Dad would love that.'

With difficulty, Melanie forced a smile. 'What a lovely idea!'

She didn't think she could take much more of this. She just wanted to go home and put it all behind her. Mollie was bubbling with enthusiasm and clearly expected the same of the friend who was going to be her sister-in-law and who she was certain loved her father as much as she did herself. She gave Melanie an uncertain glance as if sensing the pit of depression she was on the verge of sinking into again. 'Are you a bit under the weather, Mel?'

She nodded. 'I was just telling your dad, a friend I was close to died in a car accident. I'm sorry if I seem a bit withdrawn. If . . . if Demmy seems a bit other directed, he knew her, too. It's been an awful shock for us.'

They both glanced to where Damien stood, giving an impression of being alone despite the knot of people he stood amongst. Alone and he, too, in his private hell. Mollie looked puzzled. A friend dying tragically young was very sad but not in the same category as the death of a parent or a partner. 'I'm so sorry. I can see it's given you both a bad shock.'

Docherty was back and he now put an arm round each of their waists. 'Well, a daughter and a daughter to be. So glad we all get on a treat. Now you and Demmy have written next weekend into your diaries, Mel, yes? I've booked a three-bedroom suite, Friday to Monday. We'll have a great time.'

Melanie felt physically sick.

Crane's mobile rang. 'Frank Crane.'

'It's Tony, Frank. Josie's gone. We thought she was in her room but she must have called a cab on her mobile and crept out. She's been very restless ever since you went.'

'Where do you think she'll have gone, Tony? Home?'

'I'm certain it'll be home. I've tried ringing her but all I get is her voicemail on both landline and mobile.'

'Leave it to me, I'll sort something out. Terry Jones will be ringing me back on a call I made earlier. I'll tell him Josie's probably gone home, ask him if he could have your house watched.'

'I'd not want anything to happen to her, Frank.'

'I'll make sure it doesn't. See you tomorrow.'

Crane closed his mobile. 'Josie's done a runner. She'll be in a serious state of denial. She'll be needing a bloke in her bed like a crack-head needs a rock.'

'She sounds a real character.'

'She's a one-off. Self-centred, cunning, manipulative. The only terms she'll live on are her own. I have to admit to a soft spot for her. She can be funny and resourceful and if it hadn't been for her quick thinking I'd have had my head bashed in.'

He was sitting over a glass of wine with Colette, whose Gargrave cottage was providing him with a temporary refuge until he could deliver Mellors to Terry Jones. He and Colette went back. They tended to meet on a weekly basis if they could fit each other into their packed schedules. There were no ties in the relationship and neither wanted to live on a closer basis due to their life-styles and the emotional baggage they carried from the past.

'How do you always seem to find yourself involved in these criminal cases, Frank?'

'They never start that way, that's the trouble. This case was just supposed to be Josie thinking Mellors was having his bottom caned elsewhere. It was an open marriage but bottom-caning wasn't part of the deal, it had to be exclusive to them. Anyway the case got into a bigger league when I cottoned on to what Mellors was really up to. Other PIs would simply do the job and walk away from any complications, but me,' he said shrugging, 'it's the old story, once a cop. . . .'

She poured more wine. Earlier, they'd eaten dinner together in the kitchen diner of the small cottage. Crane could have a few drinks as he'd not be driving any more tonight. He could tell her everything about his cases knowing nothing would go any further. She said, 'You deliver this Mellors chap to Terry Jones and he gives him a complete rundown on Docherty's activities?'

'That's the plan. The CID know all about Docherty but with budget cuts under the new government they don't have the bodies to mount a full-scale operation on him, which is what it would need.'

'And Docherty's too big?'

'The biggest. And keeps his head so low behind the parapet that not even his family have a clue about the life he lives.'

'How big is the family?'

'Wife and a son and daughter, both in their twenties. Great house near the Tanglewood reservoirs.'

'It's going to be a terrible shock for the family when it all comes out.'

'If it comes out. He could live the life he lives now until he's a grand, white-haired old man taking his grandchildren to feed the ducks, and no one will ever know what an evil bastard he used to be.'

Colette shuddered. Several years ago, living in the south she'd found herself involved with men like Docherty and she knew just how evil they could be. She put a hand over one of Crane's. But for him she'd now be dead.

ELEVEN

Maggie said, 'There's a Damien Docherty to see you, Frank. No appointment.'

Puzzled, he looked up from the report he was putting together, glanced at his watch. 'I could find ten minutes, Maggie, show him in.'

'Would he by any chance be any relation to Brendon Docherty?'

'He would indeed. The son. I can't imagine what he wants with me.'

The tall, good looking young man he'd met at Tanglewood House stood before his desk. He, too, looked puzzled. 'It is you. The man I met at Dad's party. But you said you were an FA.'

'Cover when I'm at social outings. Like doctors keeping quiet about it. They don't want to know about your stomach ulcer and I don't want them asking if I can help in tracing a stolen dog.'

Damien tried to smile. He looked very pale and tense.

'Sit down, Damien. How can I help?'

Damien sat. He wore a look that Crane knew well, it meant he was thinking hard about a choice of words. 'This . . . this is going to seem a very odd request.'

'Then it'll be like about fifty per cent of the other requests I get.'

The young man was silent for several seconds, still, it seemed, searching for the right words. 'You . . . you met my father at the party. He's, well, he's a very secretive person about the work he does. None of us really knows exactly what it is. We . . . we've tried to pin him down but he's got the gift of the gab and can talk a lot without saying much. It *seems* to be something to do with property deals and imports and exports. We . . . we just wondered if you could throw some . . . some kind of light on it.'

' "We" being?'

'All of us: Mum, sister, fiancée. It . . . it just seemed that if anything were to happen to him, an accident or a heart attack, say, we'd not . . . we'd not know how to go about keeping his business afloat.'

Damien's hesitant words seemed to indicate that he knew what he was saying didn't make much sense. It handed Crane a problem. He wondered if Damien had somehow got to know about the dark side of his father's activities and wanted Crane to be able to tell him his suspicions were groundless. There was a look of desperation in his eyes that he'd seen before in the eyes of those middle-class women who engaged him, hoping against hope that he'd somehow be able to bring back confirmation that the gorgeous PA was nothing to do with her husband's sudden bouts of overtime.

He watched Damien for some time in silence. He had a decision to make and it wasn't easy, but he trusted his instincts and they were telling him that it might be best if Damien knew for certain the truth about his father and maybe stopped trying to force an illusion that Docherty was what he seemed: an authentic successful businessman and a loving father. If he was given the plain truth it would be a terrible blow but it would release him from the ambivalent existence he now looked to be living. Knowing the exact truth would mean he'd be in a position to somehow decide how he was going to deal with it.

'I'm sorry, Damien,' he said at last, 'very, very sorry to tell you that your father is the biggest criminal on the local police's books.'

Damien went even paler and began to gasp as if struggling for breath. 'How . . .' he croaked, 'how can you *possibly*—'

'I was once in the police, CID. I've still got colleagues there who trust me with this kind of information. It's a matter of limited resources that they haven't mounted a full-scale operation to get your father behind bars. But the sad truth is they know every crooked line of business he's involved in. Everything.'

Damien suddenly crouched forward in his chair as if he'd been punched in the guts. Crane came round his desk and put a hand on his shoulder, then said quietly, 'I think I'm only confirming what you've already got wind of.'

Damien straightened up, took out a handkerchief and began to dab his forehead, now moist with perspiration. 'I've . . . I've only known for a very short time. I couldn't get myself to accept it. Just . . . just what has he done?'

'Everything in the crooked line you've ever read about. Drugs, illegal immigrants, prostitutes, fraud. He had a very profitable line going with a man called Tony Mellors on property scams. Mellors is in the planning department. Your father's cover for all this is a legitimate business importing and exporting a range of goods which is also very profitable.'

'My *God*,' he groaned. 'What's going to happen to him, Frank?'

'One day the police are going to find the money to tackle his set-up.'

He could have told him that the dismantling of his father's organization could, in fact, come very soon once Mellors had told the police all he knew. But that information had to remain confidential as too much could go wrong before any court cases could be mounted and it was also essential that no details of Mellors's pending interrogation leaked out. To anyone.

'What do I do, Frank,' Damien burst out, 'knowing all this ghastly stuff about him? What can I do?'

'I think I'd try and behave around him as if everything was normal. If he found out what you know now it's impossible to guess how he'd react.'

'It's what Melanie and me are trying to do. It's not easy.'

'Your fiancée? She knows too?'

In an almost toneless voice he began to give Crane the details of Melanie working at the crisp factory, of getting to know Cilla, who'd had acid thrown in her face and who'd told Melanie about Docherty when they'd taken the young women to Leicester. 'It was pure coincidence,' he said in a voice almost a whisper. 'If Mel hadn't gone to the factory for vacation work I'd still know nothing about his hellish life.'

Crane detected the note of regret in his voice that Melanie *had* gone to work at the factory. If she hadn't his father would still be the man he'd always known. 'Frank, I used to think I was one of the luckiest blokes alive. A dad who helped me every foot of the way. A private education and then guiding me towards economics and politics, knowing well before I did that I'd be suited to a political career. And no money worries so I could concentrate on my future.

'Then overnight, from having all that fantastic luck I wake up to find I've got the worst luck of anyone.'

He got up distractedly and paced to the window, which gave a diagonal view from the Old Quarter to Leeds Road. 'Those people walking about down there, whatever their backgrounds, no one has a father who's the worst bad lot in town.' He gave a half-sob, eyes glittering with tears. He'd clearly had a very bad time this past week. Crane joined him at the window, put a hand on his shoulder again. 'I know, Damien, I know how you feel.'

'You don't, Frank,' he muttered, 'no one does.'

'Look, I have a father I'm very close to. He gave me a lot of his time. I know I'd feel exactly as you do if he'd turned out to be a wrong'un.'

'If he'd only concentrated on his *honest* work. With his brains he'd have done just as well.'

Crane nodded but had reservations. The black economy paid no taxes. The money that Docherty pulled in from the many strands of his criminal network would put in the shade those captains of industry who took home a million or so a year, taxed at the top rate.

'I really am very sorry about all this, Damien, and that I couldn't give you anything for your comfort.'

He nodded bleakly. 'I was praying you'd be able to, though I knew you wouldn't. Deep down, so deep I'd almost buried it, I knew it was true, what Cilla had told Mel. Somehow I've just got to learn to live with it, having a father who ordered acid to be thrown in a kid's face.'

Crane stood at the window when he'd gone and watched him walk into Leeds Road. Shoulders bowed, he was almost shuffling. Poor chap. The current advice to people having crises in their lives was to deal with it as best you could and then move on. But how was Damien ever going to be able to move on from his father being a top villain? How would he ever be able to go into politics? Would any firm he worked for ever be able fully to trust him? Surely he must have had *some* idea, people would say, of where all that money was coming from. He sighed, went back to his report, which had to be in the post today. He suspected he was only thinking the same things that Damien would never stop thinking.

'OK, Maggie,' he called, 'ready for typing.'

She came in, picked up the papers, handed him the desk diary. 'I'll make sure it goes today. If necessary I'll finish it at home.'

'How would I cope without you?'

'That young Docherty chap looked very upset on his way out.'

'I had to give him the hard facts about his dad. I only confirmed what he already knew. He came to me as a last resort.'

'Poor boy, he'll never live it down if he stays here. I came across similar cases when I was in the force. He'll need to change his name by deed poll, give himself a new background and move to another town.'

'You're right. If it ever comes to it I could get Jason to put together a CV that'll clear up his background and produce the sort of documents that would need to go with it.'

'Good thinking, Frank. One day he might be very glad he came to see you.'

When she'd gone he sat for a few moments in thought. Mellors had been waiting for him when he'd arrived at Heather's house, shaved, hair neatly combed, dressed in one of his good suits. Heather had been at his side, her hand in his, a sad look of devotion on her homely face. 'Best of luck, darling,' she said gently. 'I'll be praying for you.'

He kissed her tenderly. 'It'll be over one day,' he said, in an equally gentle tone, 'and then we'll have the rest of our lives to spend together.'

He got into Crane's car, angling the passenger wing mirror so that he could see Heather standing at the gate of her bungalow till she was out of sight.

'It'll keep me going,' he said in a low voice, 'the thought that she'll be waiting for me. And if the witness protection people give me a new name and a new address in a different town it'll seem like I'm starting as a new man.'

Crane nodded with a wry smile. All the lives that would change dramatically if what Mellors was going to tell the police this week really would put him and Docherty inside. And he himself would have to tread warily if it became known the part he'd played in getting Mellors opposite Terry Jones. Because if Docherty went down he'd want retribution, there was no doubt about that.

'You'll make a good new life for yourself, Tony,' he said, 'and you'll have the woman you love.'

At the central police station all went smoothly. Instead of being dealt with as a common criminal, Mellors was handled almost as a VIP. Terry Jones clearly couldn't believe his luck. Treating Mellors with great courtesy he took him personally to an interview room, arranged for coffee, and made sure he knew he'd be in the hands of a 'good' cop.

He left him with Ted Benson, a DS, and came back to see Crane. 'I can't begin to thank you for this, Frank. It's looking to be one of the biggest deals we've ever had. I can still hardly believe it. Docherty and his people, we could have them all inside by this time next year.'

'It's not really down to me, Terry. Mellors has been living with attacks of conscience for a very long time.'

'But if he'd tried to do anything on his own he'd have blown it. He needed you, a trained cop, to get him here today safe and alive. Not to mention all that tear-arsing you did over the North York Moor. Well, this week everything else just about goes on the back burner while we let him get it all off his chest. We're going to take it nice and steady and give him all the time he needs.'

'You'll find him more than co-operative. He'd not be able to go on living with himself if he didn't make amends.'

'Christ, Frank, I wish you were back.'

They were words Jones had used several times in the past, since Crane had had to leave the force under a cloud, and they never failed to cheer him up. When he'd been a DS in the CID Terry Jones had been his boss and it had been Terry who'd pulled strings to help get him established as a private man.

'I'll wish you good hunting, Terry. Just by the way, this business of Mellors's wife, Josie. *Is* she at home?'

'Ted drove over there when you rang. She is at home and we've got a pair of DCs keeping an eye on the place, people we can't really spare. Why couldn't she stay with Mellors's PA in a house none of them knew about?'

'Because she's a stroppy bitch, always has to have her own way.'

'Doesn't she understand the danger she's in? She *must* be frightened living alone.'

'She doesn't know what fear is, Terry. Believe me, I was glad to have a woman like her at my side when we were in North Yorkshire.'

'Well, we've got the house covered till we can decide the best way to handle her. The boys tell me there was a bloke round there last night but he looked to be a boyfriend. We put his number through the wringer but he came out clean.'

'There'll be a steady supply of gentlemen friends. Our Josie likes a lot. She'll sit on anyone's knee just to see what pops up.'

Jones grinned. 'Like that, is it. Reminds me of the old joke; when this bloke was asked what kind of woman he'd like to marry he says, ideally a nympho whose father owns a pub. . . .'

Crane decided his involvement in the Mellors's case could be regarded as being over. The things that had happened over the weekend had put him behind with his routine work and the week passed quickly. He received numerous calls on his mobile from Josie. He'd not answered them but eventually, knowing she'd not give in, he'd relented.

'It couldn't be much harder getting through to the prime minister,' she said petulantly.

'What do you want, Josie?'

'You must *know* what I want. We had such a lovely time on Friday night. I can't get it out of my mind. I need you, Frankie.'

'I'm a very busy man. You'll have to make do with your boyfriends.'

'What boyfriends?'

'Those who come to call on a nightly basis.'

'What makes you think I'm keeping open house?'

'Because your house is being guarded, by CID men.'

She was silent for a short time. 'All right, there have been a couple of old friends round. That was to stop me moping about *you.*'

'You should *not* have left Heather's house. It's tying up a couple of DCs to ensure your safety. You don't deserve the care we're all taking of you.'

'Are these DCs the nice young men I keep seeing parked across the road? I'll have to invite them in for a drink.'

He sighed. 'Have you any idea of the danger you're in, insisting on living at home? As we speak, Tony is telling the police everything about Docherty's set-up. If it wasn't for those nice young men in an unmarked car it's almost certain that sooner or later you'd have been taken hostage.'

'Sounds fun.'

'It wouldn't be. I know from personal experience the injuries people can be given who've co-operated with the police. They call it grassing. And grassers' wives are at the same risk, they can be knocked about so their man will decide grassing isn't a good idea.'

'Oh, why does Tony have to *do* this, Frankie? All he had to do was keep schtum and it would have blown over and we'd be able to get back to a normal life.'

He knew he might as well have talked to a brick wall for all the sense he was getting out of her. A 'normal' life, where Mellors went on with his half-world activities and brought home the usual wads of cash.

'What time are you coming over, Frankie?'

'I'm not coming over, now or ever.'

'Oh, *please*, Frankie. I'm sitting here just in one of Tony's shirts, nothing else. That's how you like me, isn't it? I could tell that day you came to the house. I can always tell.'

There was nothing she didn't know about what men liked. He had to admit that Josie dressed in just a man's shirt on a hot summer's day was an image that plagued his memory on a regular basis. And now there was that other memory to cope with, of her incredible expertise in bed, the culmination of that dedicated training in a skill she'd devoted her life to.

'Don't ring me any more, Josie. And for God's sake try and get it into your head the risk you'll be taking if you don't do exactly what the police tell you to do.'

'Please come and take care of me, Frankie, please.' Her little-girl voice had rarely sounded more wheedling. 'If I'm going to be in danger and Tony's going in the slammer. I'll do anything to make you happy if I could just have you at my side, holding me in bed at night in your big strong arms.'

His mind boggling, he closed his mobile.

They sat over the breakfast things in silence. It was one of those English summer days of heavy cloud, heat and humidity, when you felt vaguely out of sorts and gloomy. Or in Melanie's case, even gloomier than usual. Could it have been such a short time ago they'd spent their leisure together chatting so cheerfully about a life that couldn't have seemed more full of promise?

'I think you slept a little better, Demmy.'

Their eyes met across the table. 'If you know that it rather looks as if you didn't sleep too well yourself.'

She shrugged, gave a wan smile. Sleeping had been in her gift, it had come within minutes of her head touching a pillow. She wondered if those days would ever return. 'I'm dreading it,' she said, 'a long weekend on the coast.'

'Tell me about it,' he said in a low voice. 'But I think the reason I slept better than usual is that I've made a decision.'

She waited in a questioning silence. They were both in their dressing gowns, as if barely able to find the motivation to put their clothes on. But at least he was managing to eat a banana and some toast instead of just the inevitable mugs of coffee.

'I've decided I've got to get him alone and have it out with him. When we're at Whitby I'll try and get him to go for a walk with me. We can't go on like this, Mel.'

'You'll . . . tell him you know?'

'I'll tell him he has two options. Either he goes to the police or I tell everyone what's he's been up to: Mum, Mollie, the relations, and then I'll walk out and never go back.'

'Oh, Demmy, won't that be dangerous? We know what he's capable of.'

'What's he going to do to me, what *can* he do? I'm his own flesh and blood, for God's sake.'

'I couldn't bear for anything to happen to you.'

'What's the alternative? We just carry on indefinitely playing happy families?'

'It'll be such a shock for Mollie and your mum.'

'I'd do anything to protect them from having to know the truth. But I couldn't live with the possibility of another young kid having her looks destroyed.'

She nodded sadly. 'Yes, that has to come before anything else.'

'Look, Mel, when we're in Whitby, on the Saturday, can you suggest that Mum and Mollie go with you to look at the shops?'

'Yes, I'll do that. What about Peter?'

'I'll think of something. But it's essential I get Dad alone, to be able to say the things I'm going to say.'

He was looking better for a decent night's sleep and there was a determination in his tone she'd not heard since she'd told him what Cilla had told her.

'Is this anything to do with what Frank Crane said?'

He shook his head. 'He thought it best to carry on as we were doing, as if everything was normal, but I think he'd understand if I felt I couldn't do that. Frank's a really decent bloke and I trust him, but going by what he says it could take several years before the police could tackle Dad's set-up. It wouldn't be fair to either of us to go on living like this.'

She didn't want to think about the possible consequences of Damien's having it out with Brendon, but she could sense his conviction and he was certainly looking better for having made his decision, the hardest decision he'd had to take in his entire life. And she had to admit to a sense of relief that, after this frightful time they'd had, any action, however dangerous and complicated the outcome, was surely better than none.

He glanced at his watch. 'Whatever happens, Mel, I'm not going back home to live. There's a flat advertised in Cunliffe. Are you happy if I take it? And when we're in we'll make a new start, simply live on what we can make between us. I couldn't bring myself to take another penny of his dirty money.'

She began to smile. His change in attitude was catching. 'Then you'll become what I thought you were when we first met. A bloke who could hardly scrape enough loose change together for a couple of halves of lager like the rest of us.'

Crane rang Inspector Jones towards the middle of the week. 'How's it going, Terry?'

'We've struck gold, Frank, pure gold. The things he's come up with. Exactly how they bring in the illegals and fix them up with security numbers, all that. He's told us all the different ways they get the drugs through, how the toms are organized, how they lay their hands on the thousands of fags they buy for coppers, how the housing scams operate. Docherty gets a rake-off on every deal that's pulled because no one can set up the scams like he can and if one of his people tries to conceal a deal he's going to have trouble walking for the next six months.'

'He must be worth millions.'

'The only tax he pays is on the legitimate business. The rest of the loot's spread among the no-questions-asked banks around the world. Mellors knows how everything works because Docherty was giving him more and more to do due to the bean-counter brain he has on him. And the man's memory is phenomenal; everything that went in stayed in.'

'And with looking like the man who takes the plate round at nine o' clock Mass. . . .'

'Incredible. The last man in the world you'd think would be side-kicking for an arsehole like Docherty.'

'When are you aiming to get Docherty in?'

'A couple of weeks, the way things are going.'

'It'll be a hell of a shock for the family.'

'Mellors is positive none of them know what he's really up to to live the life he did.'

'Oddly enough his son came to see me on Monday. He'd found out what his dad was by coincidence. He couldn't bring himself to believe it and wanted me to look into the way he lived his life and bring back news that none of it was true. What I had to tell him only confirmed what he was forcing himself not to accept.'

He went on to give Jones an outline of the discussion with Damien, the way he'd reacted and the state he was in. 'He was very agitated about what could be done. I said nothing, of course, about Mellors putting the boot in on Docherty even as we talked, just told him the police would get round to his dad when the time was right.'

Jones sighed. 'Well for him, poor devil, it's going to be bad news and terrible news. You and me know, Frank, that ninety per cent of villains' families *know* the old man's a bad lot. They may not like it but they accept it and live with it. But Docherty's family will be going to hell and back and there's nothing we'll be able to do about it.'

'We get case-hardened, Terry, the work we do. But the lad was so broken up, so desperately unhappy I'd have done anything to be able to spare him the misery. We had dads we could look up to and take as examples. Well, that's what Damien *thought* he had.'

'How could anyone do that to their family?'

'I suppose, to be scrupulously fair, he thought they'd never know.'

'I've got an appointment due, Frank, so we'll have to leave it. I'll get back to you. One last thing. We've got a raft of statements for Mellors to sign. He says he'll sign everything but before he does he wants to be taken to his house to see his wife. He's aiming to divorce her but feels he has to discuss it with her face to face.'

'Can't you get her to come to him?'

'He says there's no way she'd come to a police station. In any case, he wants to talk it through with her in familiar surroundings. We've agreed to that. Ted'll take him along and we'll have back-up in a following car just in case Docherty tries to pull anything. But the men watching the house say everything's been quiet so far, apart from the steady stream of boyfriends.'

'I reckon Docherty's biding his time. He'll certainly have a good idea what's going on. He'll be working out a strategy the way he's worked out everything else in that misbegotten life of his.'

When she flung open the door her eyes, for part of a second, were bright with expectation, as if it would be one of her boyfriends out there. She'd once looked at him like that back in the early days. But now her face fell as she saw him standing there with the CID men who'd brought him.

'Oh, it's you,' she said flatly.

'We need to talk, Jo.'

'I'd have thought you'd done enough talking down at the cop shop.'

She turned irritably away, leaving the door half-open and went across the hall. Mellors glanced at his escorts and they all went in.

'Look, Tony,' DS Benson said, as they stood in the hall, 'ideally we should be in the room with you when you talk to your wife, but you need your privacy and we trust you. We'll be out here till you're ready to go back.'

'Thanks, Ted, I appreciate it. I could rustle up some coffee—'

'No, not to worry. You go and sort things out.'

Josie had gone into the kitchen and Mellors joined her It was a spacious, airy room, expertly laid out, with ornate fitted cupboards and granite surfaces, state-of-the-art equipment and a marble-tiled floor. He looked round, affected by the slight unfamiliarity rooms seemed to have when you'd been away from them for any length of time. He could remember to the penny the vast amount of money all this had cost, could remember also how rapidly she'd taken it for granted and wanted something else that would cost even more.

The remnants of a take-away meal lay on a plate on the breakfast table and a glass a quarter full of red wine. She picked up the grass and drank from it. A bottle of vintage Bordeaux, half empty, stood nearby. Josie had best-year wines delivered by the case and he could remember the size of the bills that came with them. Well, there'd not be any more, though she'd continue drinking it until the temperature-controlled cabinet was empty, as she had never looked ahead, had always lived within the hour, if not the minute.

'Do you want a drink?' she said, a little more warmly.

'I'm not supposed to drink.'

'Who's to know? The flat-foots are out there.'

'We need to talk, Jo, I haven't much time.'

'You are a dozy bastard, Tony,' she said resentfully. 'We had a bloody good life and you've thrown it all away.'

'We had a good life because I was a crook.'

'Oh, for Christ's *sake*, a few dodgy deals. Nobody knew and nobody cared. And then you have to start blabbing to the police. And what's going to happen to poor Brendon?'

'Jo, the whole point of all this is to put Docherty behind bars.'

'That means we'll never go to that beautiful house again and those marvellous parties. Oh, Tony, you've ruined everything!'

'Can't you get it through your head that behind that facade he's the most dangerous man in town apart from being the top criminal? I could hardly believe you'd crept out of Heather's and come back here. You've got a twenty-four seven guard on this house because of what Docherty might do to you because I've talked to the police.'

'Brendon wouldn't do *anything* to hurt me. He fancies me rotten. God, she hit the rollover jackpot when she nailed him, that jammy Tessa.'

'She'll not think she's so lucky when he goes inside, poor woman.'

'All these lives messed up because of your silly nonsense.'

She wore an embroidered blouse in ivory with a scalloped edge and linen straight-leg trousers in stone. The sort of rackety life she lived hadn't affected her looks at all and nor, so far, had the amount of booze she put away. She was still almost as pretty as the day they'd met and it wasn't difficult to understand the obsession she'd aroused in him, even if it was now completely gone. There was a dimension missing in Jo. Despite all the warm, outgoing signals she gave to any attractive male who crossed her radar the only person who'd ever counted in her life had been herself. It was a self that demanded there was always something to look forward to: the next bottle of wine, the next party, the next dinner at the Ritz, the next Caribbean holiday.

He sighed. There'd never been any point in appealing to her sense of right and wrong; she'd been born without one. It was why Heather had begun to mean so much to him. She really cared.

He looked sadly at the woman he'd once not been able to get out of his mind. He fully accepted the guilt for the corrupt life he'd lived these past years, but he knew that but for her endless wheedling demands and his total infatuation with her he'd not be where he was now.

'Look, Jo, we're two very different people. I don't need to tell you that. Well, I'm here to sort it out.'

'How long will you be going inside for?'

'They think it will be a fairly short sentence because of my co-operation.'

'What happens to me?'

'They'll arrange to house you somewhere where you'll not be known.'

'They can stuff that. I'm staying here.'

'You can't stay here. The police can't guard it indefinitely and, anyway, the house will have to be sold off as well as the holiday house. The state will estimate a sum of money that came from the illegal activities and impound it.'

'Where will you live then, when you come out of prison?'

'Rent a flat, I suppose, in some other town.'

'There's no way I'll live in some grotty dump in Barnsley.'

'It won't affect you, what I'll do when I come out of prison.'

'Of *course* it will, you'll still be my idiot of a husband.'

She poured herself more wine. Mellors watched her in silence, thinking as so often before how little they had in common for all the years they'd spent together and the good times they'd had. And there *had* been good times along the way, despite the nagging guilt he'd lived with. Josie could make things happen and get people laughing round a dinner table at the droll things she could come out with. And when she was there staff always came running to give them priority treatment. She was a good-time girl and she'd given a lot of colour to this marriage. 'There's no easy way to say this, Jo, but I'm going to divorce you. When I come out of prison we'll be leading separate lives.'

'Oh, for pity's sake!' she cried. 'You've done it now, gabbing to the police. It's annoying, bloody annoying, but there's no need to start talking about divorce. A few years, right, and we make a new start as different people in a different town. I'm getting pissed off with Bingley anyway. It could be fun. I think I'll call myself Laura. Always fancied being a Laura. It has a virginal ring to it that'll turn the blokes on. What will your new surname be? How about Tremayne? Laura Tremayne, yes I like it.'

Her eyes became unfocused as she began to imagine herself in the new persona. She'd always winkled out the fun angle of everything she'd ever done and now she was beginning to see the positive aspects of a brand new life in a different town with a new set of boyfriends. He waited till she gradually emerged from a world that was already beginning to define itself as a sort of Shangri-La. 'The reason I want a divorce,' he said, 'is that I want to marry someone else.'

This got her full attention at last and her expression snapped from misty to stony in part of a second. 'Pull the other one. Who'd have a bloke who's just going in the slammer?'

'Heather would.'

'*Heather!*' she screamed. 'You've got to be *joking!*'

187

'It's no joke. She's the sort of woman I should have married in the first place.'

'*Heather*? How long has *this* been going on?'

'About a year.'

'You must be out of your *tree*. Heather? She's *plain*. She's the most boring woman I've ever *met*.'

'There are things about her that suit the plain and boring man I suppose I am.'

'There was once a woman called Heather, who'd only have sex in warm weather,' she began in a jeering tone, 'and when it got chilly—'

'Stop that! Stop that right now!' he shouted. He'd rarely been more angry but nothing could stop her when she was in this derisive mood.

'Does she have sex at *all*?' she taunted. 'Does she know what her fanny's for apart from having a pee?'

'I'll start proceedings once the trial's over,' he said.

'No, you bloody won't. It takes two to tango and I'll not agree to any divorce.'

'Then I'll just have to wait till I can get a divorce the long way.'

'You know what we agreed. Have any woman you like, including the one who looks like your Auntie Violet, but we stay married. Those are the rules.'

'Your rules.'

'Oh, come on, Tony. Get this prison business out of the way and we'll start a great new life. You're clever, you'll be able to get a well-paying job and . . . and—'

'And go to work with the local bad lots again, so I can bring home the sort of money you seem unable to do without.'

'Well, if you just stick with things like the property deals. . . . I know I'll have to scale down. I'll have plenty of practice while you're inside.'

'You just don't get it, Jo, do you? You never have. I'm just a boring, ordinary man and Heather's just right for me. You'll make do without me perfectly well.'

'Tony, the deal was we played the field but didn't go off with anyone permanently. Well, I'm sticking to that, even though you're going inside, and so are you.'

There was a serious collected note in her voice that he'd heard only rarely before. Half the problem with the marriage had been that she didn't do serious. She lived a lighthearted life based on instincts that made sense to her if not to anyone else.

'You can't make me *do* anything, Jo, you know that. The reason the police let me see you today was so that we could sort things out and you'd have plenty of time to adjust. I'll do the very best I can for you. I don't know how I'm going to be placed financially but I'll make sure you have enough to tide you over till you can get a job.'

She poured more wine into her glass. 'Let's have no more talk of divorce, Tony. You'll get over the typist when you're inside and thinking over the good times we've had.'

The cool tone was still there. He watched her in silence. He supposed that in the end he was all she'd really got. There were other men, always would be, but all they wanted from her was what she was only too ready to give them. When it was over they went home to the wife and kids.

'I'm sorry, Jo, I want the divorce to be as amicable as possible but I'm not going to change my mind.'

She got up from the table and crossed to the work surface that adjoined the sink. 'Is that your last word,' she said, 'you're willing to give me up for a tea-maker?'

'She's like me,' he said simply. 'You never were. I want to live the rest of my life with someone I genuinely love and respect.'

'Big mistake, Tony, big, big mistake.'

She turned round. She was clasping a chopping knife from the stand that held kitchen equipment. She often did this when they were having a disagreement, seize an implement and wave it around to emphasize her words. He was quite relaxed as she watched him in silence, as if sizing him up. Then she plunged the knife into his chest. He was so taken aback, so incredulous, that

189

he didn't even cry out. It was only as the knife went into his chest again and again that he managed to get out a single, strangled scream, just before he lost consciousness and the blood bloomed on his shirt front like dark red roses. The kitchen door burst open and the policemen piled into the room. 'God almighty!' Benson cried. 'Stand back, you stupid bitch and put the knife *down!*'

'I told him,' she said calmly. 'I made it quite clear that no one walks out on me.'

'Well, he did,' Benson said, shaking with rage, 'for good.'

'The Cunliffe flat's available. We'll go down this morning and look it over. If we can live with it I'll sort out a deposit.'

'Will you be able to find the rent?'

'I've got my savings and my job will give me a decent salary.'

'It'll be a year before I can contribute, assuming I can actually find an opening in these difficult times.'

'I'm pretty well placed. Dad always gave me far more than I needed. I could always save at least half of it.'

They sat again over the breakfast table. They were still in Melanie's house but her parents would be home shortly. They were both now eating properly and last night Melanie had slept quite well. She'd read that people could cope with almost any upheaval in their lives apart from not knowing where they stood. Well now they knew where they stood.

'I'm trying to be realistic about money,' he told her. 'I've decided I can use any money he gave me before we found out how he made it but I'll not take any more. I'll tell the bank to return the transfers.'

'What will you say when he finds out?'

'I'll tell him tomorrow on that walk.'

'Oh, of course.' For a moment she'd forgotten that things would be settled tomorrow, one way or the other, and nothing would ever be the same again, for any of them.

'What time are we setting off?'

'Mid-afternoon. Dad wanted us all to go in the transporter but

I said we wanted to stay loose. We meet up for drinks in the suite about six.'

'I can't tell you how much I admire you, Demmy, for tackling him.'

'I'm dreading it, Mel, dreading it, but I know it's the only thing I can do.'

'One of the biggest cases we've ever handled,' Jones said morosely. He seemed almost to have aged, his powerful frame to have shrunk. The CID was inured to disappointment; you won some, you lost some and just hoped the credit side of the balance sheet came out ahead at the end of the year. But Mellors's fatal stabbing had to have handed Jones one of the worst days of his professional life.

'The papers are all ready for signing,' Ted Benson said bitterly, 'but he'd only sign after he'd seen her. He seemed to think if he signed them as they came through we might not let him go home. They're worthless now. We could have written the bloody things ourselves.'

Crane said, 'What will happen to her?'

'Crime of passion,' Jones sighed heavily. 'That's how she'll twig to play it. Not only had she just found out he was a criminal, but he was aiming to divorce her and go off with his PA. She'll play it all sad-eyed and full of remorse. They'll take a lenient view, particularly with her looks and that little voice she has on her. Crime of passion and she'll be out in no time.'

'She'll know she's born then,' Benson said grimly. 'No husband, no money, no fancy house and cars. She'll have to work for a living.'

'I'm not so sure, Ted,' Crane said. 'Women like Josie live a charmed life. She might be just about the dizziest bitch you've ever known but she gets top marks for cunning. She certainly pulled Mellors's strings for a long time. She's got a whole raft of blokes standing in line to give her one. I reckon she'll work on nailing the richest.'

191

'And whoever comes across performance-wise.'

'Oh, yes. He'll just have to take care he doesn't damage his John Thomas with excessive use.'

'And if she doesn't get quite enough satisfaction?'

'I'm sure she'll be able to locate a swimming pool somewhere full of naked rugby players to take up any shortfall.'

Jones sighed again. 'Why couldn't she do all that and let the poor sod live?'

Crane thought of the day he'd met Josie. So much had happened since then it seemed like a year ago. He'd asked her how she'd react if she found Mellors to be in a serious relationship. 'I'd kill him,' she'd said in that giggly way she said so many things. He'd heard the same words on the lips of very angry women. But the angry ones had simply been letting off steam, it had been the giggly one with the little-girl voice who'd meant it.

He wondered if the killing had been because she'd come to regard Mellors as almost her own creation. She'd coaxed him to the stage of being able to give her virtually everything she'd ever wanted; he'd even agreed to an open marriage. It was impossible to know how Josie's mind worked but maybe she'd not been prepared to let anyone else have the man she regarded as being all her own skilled work. Perhaps so much of the energy she vibrated with had gone into the perfecting of Mellors in place of any normal ambition. And maybe the man she considered she'd made of him, if she couldn't have him, no one could, especially a no-account like Heather who did his typing.

He said, 'What will you do about Docherty?'

'Sod all. We'll put this stuff in front of the CPS but without signatures and a dead star witness we're banjoed. The sort of budget we're running on now it's going to be at least two or three years before we can think of tackling Docherty's set-up the long way round and even then we'd not be sure of a result. And every month we don't do anything, Docherty gets more secure.'

Benson said, 'It's the young guy I feel sorry for, Damien is it?

I've been trying to think how *I'd* feel if I suddenly found out Dad wasn't the dad I'd thought he was but a scumbag like Docherty.'

'You're right,' Crane said, 'I can't get the boy off my mind. He's spent twenty years seeing his dad like we see ours. I doubt he'll ever really get over it. And in his shoes what do you do? What *can* you do?'

TWELVE

He drove along the well-remembered roads in a state of intense sadness. He and Mollie, as children, had spent such a lot of time in Whitby. 'Dad thought children born to a temperate climate preferred holidays in their own country, even if the weather was unreliable. Too hot for them in August in places like Spain or Italy. It was a bit of a sacrifice for Mum and Dad as they liked heat and blue skies. But he was right and we never got scratchy, Mollie and me, in places like Whitby and Scarborough and Brid – loved every minute of it.

'That was the thoughtful kind of guy he always was. He must have been bored out of his skull playing beach cricket and paddling and hurling frisbies but every minute we were on the go he was right there with us. We always stayed in one of the suites and Dad would get the hotel people to make special little meals for us while he and Mum had normal room service. In the evening they'd go downstairs for a drink in the bar but every half hour they'd take turns to come up and make sure we were asleep and OK.'

He smiled wryly. 'Ironically enough, he was only saying a few weeks ago that the way things are these days you daren't leave children alone in a hotel room for five minutes.'

As he drove on to the North York Moor, ablaze with heather, Melanie put a hand over his at the wheel. 'No one, Mel, no one could have done as much as he did to make absolutely sure we were healthy and cared for and enjoying life.'

'I know, Demmy, I know.'

They drove on in silence. There was nothing more to say. They'd said it all, over breakfast tables, during the walks they'd taken, in pubs over a drink. The situation was insoluble but she was sure now that Damien had it right, that Brendon had to know that they knew about the life he led. And that would be that, Damien would never again live at home or accept any more money or favours. She'd wondered again and again how Brendon was going to take it. Behind the easygoing charm he was an astute and ruthless man. Would he try to talk his way out of it or would he threaten Damien with violence if a word of it went any further? As Damien had said, what could he do to his own flesh and blood?

Well, she'd know by this time tomorrow how he'd reacted to those two choices Damien was going to give him: he either gave himself up to the police or Damien told the family exactly how he made all that money. The trouble was she couldn't see a man like Brendon accepting either choice and it worried her.

They crested the rise that gave a first view of the Abbey ruins against the sea on East Cliff. It was downhill all the way now from the high moorland, the village gradually piecing itself together: the red-pantiled cottages, the bridge, the harbour and its extensions, the many small craft moored further up the estuary. All bathed today in that lifting quality of sunlight you seemed only to get on the north-east coast.

'I wish we could put the clock back a year,' Melanie said quietly. They'd come together then for a few days, just the two of them. It was the first time she'd been as her own parents had always favoured Norfolk when she was a child. Damien had shown her Robin Hood's Bay and Staithes and Sandsend and taken her on walks to Ruswarp and Sneaton and Saltwick. She'd loved the old fishing village with its rugged cliffs and its powerful creaming tides and the way afternoon sunlight had given the houses across the harbour a slightly blurred and dreamy appearance, like an Impressionist print.

'It's Damien Docherty. Mr Brendon Docherty has taken a suite. I think he's probably checked in.'

The receptionist gave them a warm smile. 'Yes, he has, sir, He's dealt with the form so you can go straight up. It's suite one, first floor. Need any help with your bags?'

It was clear she'd been subjected to Docherty's enveloping charm and the impression he was expert at giving, that an attentive level of service would be amply rewarded.

'Ah, the gang's all here!' Docherty said, beaming. 'And my lovely daughter to be.' He put an arm round her and gave her a kiss on the cheek. She forced herself not to shudder.

'You certainly look in a holiday mood, Brendon,' she said lightly, moving away from him as casually as possible. He wore a short-sleeved shirt checked in red and green, chinos and sandals.

'Sure, 'tis a taster for when we go to the Riviera in September. Work is making Jack a dull boy and Tessa needs a change.'

Tessa stood at a little table set up for drinks and Mollie and Peter came over to greet them. 'What will it be?' Tessa asked, 'G&T? There's also sherry, vodka or Scotch.'

It had always given Melanie such a glow to feel this kind of warmth and affection, to be sucked into the party atmosphere that was so often present with the Dochertys. But the aperitif hour now seemed to be taking place behind a sheet of glass; she could see it but somehow not feel part of it. 'A G&T would be very welcome,' she said, kissing Tessa on the cheek with the genuine affection it had been impossible to summon up for Brendon, affection combined with a sudden wave of intense pity to realize that this was to be Tessa's last happy break with the family. She felt it must have shown in her face but Tessa, preoccupied as usual with ensuring everyone was supplied with drinks and nibbles, fortunately never noticed.

Mollie said, 'Daddy, this is the suite we used to have when we were kids, isn't it?'

' 'Tis for sure, darling, the very same. I always took this one for the view of East Cliff and the church to the side and the open sea to the front.'

They stood or sat, sipping their drinks in a spacious lounge with the Mozart that Docherty was so fond of playing softly in the background on a portable music centre. Everything seemed so timeless and fine in declining sunlight and Melanie felt she wanted to cry.

'Will you not give your two eyes a treat,' Docherty said, gazing out at the sea, calm and glittering and dotted here and there with yachts with coloured sails.

'I've never forgotten the view, Daddy,' Mollie said, slipping an arm through his. 'You know how certain incidents stick in your memory forever? Well I'll never forget coming in from the play room with Mummy and seeing you standing exactly as you are now, admiring the view with a drink in your hand and the Horn Concerto in the background. It must be what, fifteen years ago?'

Melanie wondered how she'd get through the weekend. The sunlight, the music, the drinks, everyone in a state of such anticipation for the enjoyment of the next two days. She caught a glimpse of Damien's face in a brief unguarded moment; it was totally expressionless. But the warm smile was clipped back on as he turned to chat to his sister, of whom he was very fond, while Tessa looked on at them both, almost moist-eyed at the picture her grown-up children presented after the long years and the many happy holidays they'd had here. The sense of expectancy in the atmosphere seemed almost as tangible as blown air but she simply couldn't share it and it only increased her dejection.

'Will you let me be getting you a refill, darling?' Docherty stood at her side looking relaxed and fit, an imposing figure with his broad shoulders and his powerful frame, strong features and dark, well-cut hair flecked with grey. She thought of how attractive she'd always found him, the flirty way they'd had with each other. But there were ghastly images she now couldn't get out of her mind.

'Yes, thanks, Brendon.'

'When are you going to let that son of mine come back home?' he said, smiling. 'The place isn't the same without him. Poor Tessa, she misses the both of them. Says it's not the same just having me to look after. Ah, Mel, I think we both sometimes wish we were back when they were youngsters and the house was full of noise.'

She nodded, forced a smile. A couple of weeks would have done her, but with things true to what they'd seemed. 'Demmy . . . he should be back with you next week. Mum and Dad are back over the weekend.'

He took her empty glass. She'd sipped the first drink quickly to calm her nerves. He said, 'Have you been able to get your eye in on any houses?'

'I think Demmy thinks it best to leave it till I finish my studies.'

'Have a look at Ilkley. Peter and Mollie love it. Tess and me, we're thinking Ilkley might well suit us eventually. I'd go now but the work keeps me in Bradford for the next year or two.'

He moved to the drinks table, leaving her pensive about how their future, hers and Damien's, would have to be so carefully thought out now that there'd be no house as a wedding present and they'd have all the problems of mortgages and down payments everyone else had. It was such a disappointment when they'd both become accustomed to being able to face a future free of financial distraction. But neither of them would have taken another penny from the man; it would simply have been a comfortable life based on endless, nagging guilt.

'Penny for them.' Docherty's ironic words cut into her thoughts. She'd not been aware he was back at her side. He was smiling but there was a slight edge to his tone as he gave her that searching glance she'd seen before, as if he could tell what was going on in her head and sensed she wasn't enjoying being here. She knew he'd picked up on the way she'd moved off a little too quickly from that earlier embrace. He had acute instincts. 'Sure, you seem not quite yourself this past week or so, love, nor Demmy, either.'

'Oh . . . I was just miles away, thinking how nice the suite is and how lucky Demmy and Mollie were to have had such nice holidays here. It was Norfolk for me and a B&B if we were lucky; a tent if not.'

He chuckled and the moment passed but she knew she'd have to be very careful to dissemble to be the carefree, chatty woman he'd known in the past. Both she and Damien were tested to the limit as the evening went on. They all had dinner in the great dining room with its pillars and chandeliers and ornate plaster mouldings. They'd been led to the best table and there'd been champagne with the fish and a velvety red wine for the main course. Melanie caught several wistful glances from other tables at the attention they got from serving staff. Damien joined in with the talk and the laughter but Melanie could sense the strain he was under to put on the act.

After the lengthy meal it was along to the ballroom, where a trio with a backing synthesizer played music to cater for the tastes of all age groups.

'Oh, look,' Mollie said, sitting down next to Melanie, 'they can't resist the old-time dances. They learnt them at the church rooms. There they go!'

As they watched, Docherty and Tessa began to swirl round the floor in a graceful St Bernard's Waltz. 'Don't they look happy,' Mollie went on. 'We were so lucky to have such loving parents. You know, Mel, I never take my good fortune for granted: a house as a wedding present; a loan to help Peter with his business. Poor darling, he was almost speechless. It's made it so much easier to get his little firm going.'

Melanie could hardly bring herself to look at her. She wondered dismally how Mollie would face up to the sudden ending of handouts when her father was exposed as the criminal he was. 'Menswear, isn't it?' she said.

'He spotted a niche in the market for good quality handmade goods, mail order. He's worked very hard and the business is taking off. But I told him Daddy would only have bought us a house and advanced him money if he could tell he was going to put his back into it.'

'I was talking to your dad before dinner. He thought Ilkley might be a nice place to live, near you and Peter. He even thinks he and your mum might settle there one day.'

'I know.' She put a hand on Melanie's. 'Oh, Mel, wouldn't it be marvellous all to be together. We get on so well, don't we, you and I. We'd have a great time and when the babies come along we'd never be short of sitters.'

For a time, Melanie found it impossible to maintain the animated mood she'd forced herself to display during the long evening. How thrilled she'd have been to live near Mollie and Peter and the Dochertys. The parties, the walks on the moor with children, the joint holidays on the coast. And now it looked as if there'd be nothing for any of them except the sad years that would begin tomorrow. 'It sounds wonderful, Mollie,' she said, barely able to keep the forlorn longing out of her voice. 'I can't wait.'

The dance music changed from old-time to ballroom to disco and the two women began to dance with Peter and Damien while the coloured lights flashed and the mist was blown and the music grew steadily louder. But later, when Melanie and Damien were taking a break and sitting together she couldn't throw off that isolated feeling that she was seeing things that she wasn't really part of. It was like watching a film in which the actors were playing characters who were cheerful and optimistic but which you knew would end tragically.

The dancing ended at midnight and back in the suite Tessa asked if anyone wanted a last drink. 'I think we'll push off to bed, Mum,' Damien said, 'We're both pretty tired.'

It seemed as if Damien was in the grip of an impulse he couldn't control as he embraced his mother and gave her a warm and tender kiss before he and Melanie went to their room. 'I don't think I've seen her looking happier than she looks tonight,' he said bitterly. 'All of us together in a place that has such pleasant memories for her.'

Melanie sat on the bed, totally exhausted with the sheer strain of acting, for so many hours, a self who no longer existed, a self who'd once found every part of her life enjoyable, stimulating and filled with hope.

'Do you think you'll sleep, Demmy?'

'I'm taking a tablet.'

'I do wish I could share it with you, the walk.'

'It has to be just me and him, Mel; you've already had too much involvement in this rotten business.'

The tablet worked rapidly and within minutes his breathing was deep and regular, as his mind and body were given the rest that she hoped would somehow help him to find some sort of solution to the monumental task he'd set himself for tomorrow.

'Sure, Demmy, you can be giving yourself a cooked breakfast when you're on holiday. Will you look at the state of Peter's plate.'

Peter, who was working his way through a plateful of bacon, eggs, mushrooms, beans and tomatoes, said, 'One great British breakfast a week at home and the rest of the week it's a mug of tea and a kick at the table leg. But holidays don't count, as you say, Brendon.'

They all chuckled. They were sitting once more at the big circular table in the lofty dining room, but Melanie knew the effort it was costing Damien even to face a little cereal and a slice of toast and marmalade. 'I'm . . . a bit off fried food at the moment,' he said. 'Doesn't seem to agree with me, for some reason.'

'I do hope you're not developing an ulcer, dear,' Tessa said in a concerned voice. 'My friend Peggy's husband had one and he couldn't cope with fry-ups either.'

'Don't worry, Mum, I'm sure it's just a phase.'

Docherty glanced at his watch. 'Well, what's the form for today, folks?'

French windows stood open to the foot of the long room; it was another day of clear sun.

'I'd like to go fishing from one of the piers,' Peter said, pushing away his cleared plate and reaching for toast and honey. 'But I don't suppose anyone else does, including Mollie.'

'You're spot on there, sunshine,' Mollie said briskly. 'I'm sure I never gave an impression that fishing was my favourite hobby next to watching paint dry. You haven't done your honey joke, by the way.'

'You're right.' He held up his miniscule individual pot of honey. 'Ah, I see the hotel keeps a bee!'

There was more laughter but Melanie could only force a smile as she concentrated on giving the right casual tone to the words she had to say. 'We could have a look at the shops this morning, the distaff side, that is.'

Tessa said, 'Well, it should take us all of ten minutes to do Flowergate and Baxtergate.'

'I wouldn't mind, Mum,' Mollie said, 'the shops often have things you don't see at home.'

'We could save the beach for after lunch,' Melanie added, the very slight tremor in her voice only detected by Damien.

'How about you and me taking a stroll on East Cliff, Dad, like we used to, if Peter wants to go fishing?' Damien said, his tone as casual as Melanie's had been. 'Up the steps and past Saltwick. If we make it to Robin Hood's Bay we could have a bite of lunch there and come back on the bus.'

'Sounds good, son,' Docherty said, nodding. 'If the ladies don't mind trying to cope without us till this afternoon A lot to ask, I must admit.'

'I'm sure we'll occupy ourselves perfectly well, Brendon,' Tessa said airily. 'And there might even be a new T-shirt in it for you.'

'Conscience money for the shoes and the dress you're going to treat yourself to,' he said, grinning.

So it was decided: Peter to fish, the women to shop, Damien and his father to walk the cliff tops. They all separated outside the hotel's entrance, Melanie's eyes meeting Damien's in a final glance that told him how much her thoughts and hopes would be with him.

The two men, in chinos and lightweight jerkins, walked along the little road called Khyber Pass that led down from West Cliff to the harbour side. 'Sure, 'tis a fine day for it, Demmy,' Docherty said, 'and the exercise will do me good. We walked such a lot when you and Mollie were growing up, the four of us: Heaton Woods, North Cliff Woods and the footpath alongside the golf links.'

'We used to do one of the walks almost every Sunday afternoon in summer.'

'Would you be recalling the miniature railway in North Cliff? Grown men, grown *men*, dressed like railwaymen and blowing whistles and waving flags for a dozen kids sat in open carriages about as high as your knee.'

'I actually went on it once, Dad. Didn't see anything odd at the time in men pretending to be engine drivers.'

'Sure, didn't I fancy driving the little train meself, when I saw them stoking the boiler with bits of coal the size of sugar lumps and shovels no bigger than a tablespoon.'

He chuckled, gazing about him and revelling in the clear morning light as it struck the red-tiled roofs of the cottages over at the foot of East Cliff and the activity in the harbour, as yachts with partially furled sails edged towards the open sea. Trippers passed with excited children and they could hear from one of the amusement arcades some cheerful piano music that Damien could instantly identify as *Poor People of Paris*, and which he remembered as if it had been yesterday when he'd first heard it and not a dozen years ago.

They were walking now along past what had been the fish quays. 'I can't think what the state of the fishing is now,' Docherty said. 'When I was a boy the fishing boats were parked two abreast along this side of the harbour. I suppose they've had to diversify and the tourism must help, though it's a very short season in this area.

He drew to a halt. 'You'll have forgotten, maybe, but we once saw a catch of lobsters being handled. The men were shaking each of the lobsters and it made a sound like a castanet and then they packed them in wooden boxes. You were fascinated. One of the men told you they shook them to daze them so they could pack them more easily. You were very cross and told them it was cruel putting them all together in a box. He just grinned and told you they hadn't enough money to put every lobster in its own little box.'

'I remember the lobsters very well and the way their claws clicked. Don't remember telling them off, though.'

They walked on to the bridge that would take them across the estuary to Church Street. 'And those little alleys that run between the buildings to the harbour,' Docherty went on, 'they're called ghauts, pronounced like goats the animal. That didn't amuse you, either. "Why do they call an alley a goat?" you used to say. "That's just silly." '

Damien was unable to control the tears pricking his eyelids. There had been so many walks taken with his father, filled with little tales like this, taking him back to a childhood that must have been one of the happiest anyone could possibly have had. He brushed his eyes surreptitiously with the back of a hand and they continued up Church Street to the foot of the hundred and ninety-nine steps that wound up to St Mary's and the ruins of the Abbey.

'And these *steps*,' Docherty said, 'the times you and Mollie counted them going up and you could *never* get the total to be a hundred and ninety-nine.'

Damien dismally recalled those times, too, as they began to tackle the steps now. It was hard going now and had been, even as children, and Docherty fell silent, to Damien's intense relief. They stopped once at a short level area which could be used as a resting place and stood for a time, drawing their breath and looking down on the village, peaceful in near-vertical sunlight. Beyond the piers the sea creamed in on a flow tide and the River Esk was like a band of silver as it stretched inland, the many small craft moored on it beyond the bridge swaying gently.

'Sure, it makes you glad to be alive, son, on a glorious day like this.'

Damien wondered bitterly if the day would ever come now when he'd be positively glad to be alive. Then his father said, 'I've got something to tell you while we're away from the others. I'm thinking of buying a cruiser.'

'A .. cruiser?'

'Family-sized. Decent sleeping and living accommodation. It'll need to be moored in the south, somewhere like Torquay. Easier down there to hire crew. I've gone into it.'

'A crew?'

'Sounds a bit grand but I'm only talking two or three pros to sail her and someone to cook and clean.' He grinned. 'But I can see your mum wanting to pack dusters and a tin of Mansion polish and her little book of recipes. Anyway, these people will sail the boat and we can lend a hand with the simple stuff. I'm thinking Greek islands next year, all six of us. We'll have total flexibility, you see, go anywhere, dock anywhere. It's something your mum's always wanted to do, not be tied to a cruise liner's schedule. Well, when I've sorted out the purchase details I'll take your mum out to a nice restaurant and tell her over dinner.'

'Won't it be very expensive?'

Docherty put a hand on his arm. 'It will indeed, though the boat's not new. But, well, I've got a bit of money in the bank and I might as well use some of it.'

'It .. it sounds tremendous, Dad.'

'Should give us all a lot of pleasure over the years.'

They continued their trudge up the rest of the steps. Damien knew his father was wealthy but had never guessed he could lay his hands on the sort of money that would buy cruisers that needed crewing.

They finally reached the top and took the path that led past the church and the Abbey ruins and on to East Cliff, with Docherty still musing about the old times. Damien forced himself to respond as his father chatted on but he was very preoccupied, now the time was almost upon him, with trying to decide just how to open the dreaded confrontation. His hands shook and he was conscious of the heavy pounding of his heart. A few other people drifted along the track but they turned off at Saltwick Bay and from then on they were completely alone, the sea surging to their left many feet below and grazing land to their right, the animals contained by electrified fencing.

'Demmy, you seem a bit withdrawn. Have done this past week or so. Would you be having something on your mind? It's not like you to be quiet.'

'We .. we need to talk, Dad.'

The other turned to him, with a look of concern. 'Well, son, if we need to talk there's no better time or place. What would we need to be talking about?'

Damien watched him for some time in silence. 'Just . . . just how you make these vast amounts of money.'

Docherty also took his time in speaking. Damien had been expecting some sort of perplexed reaction, however slight, but his father's eyes rested on his with an expression that was totally neutral. 'What exactly do you need to know about how I make my living, Demmy?' he said, so softly that the words were almost carried away in a thin breeze.

'I don't really need to be told at all,' Damien broke out. 'I know how you make it. You make it from organized crime.'

Docherty went on watching him with a face in which nothing moved. 'And what makes you think that?' he said in the same soft tone. 'Who've you been talking to? Who's handed you this rubbish?'

'I'm not going to say but . . . but it's a source I completely trust.

I know everything, Dad,' he said, his voice harsh but uneven, 'the dodgy property deals, the illegal immigrants and the benefit frauds, the drugs you bring in, the young prostitutes you control and the acid you arrange to have thrown in their faces if they step out of line.'

For all his lengthy pursuit of iron control of voice and features, Docherty was unable to cope with the shock of these last angry words. 'Lies!' he cried. 'It's all *lies*! I didn't know I had the sort of enemies who'd feed you this kind of garbage. I just run an import-export business. I move goods and services, as I've told you before.'

'Oh, I know what you import. When's your next lorry-load of knock-off cigarettes coming in?'

'Demmy—'

'You're a criminal, Dad. You're the top criminal in this town. Public enemy number one. The police would nail you tomorrow if they could find the money and the staff to investigate your set-up.'

'Demmy, it's just not *true*.'

'Don't lie, Dad. I know I'm right and it's got to be sorted.'

'What do you mean, it's got to be sorted?' The calmness had been blasted aside by an anger that was beyond him to control but Damien felt he also caught a guarded note.

'I mean,' he said more evenly, 'that you have to turn yourself in to the police.'

'But there's nothing I have to go to the police *about*.'

'You've got two choices, Dad. Either you turn yourself in or I tell the entire family what sort of man you are and then I leave home, and as far as I'm concerned you become a non-person.'

They'd stopped walking some time ago and were facing each other across the footpath. A silence fell between them again, Docherty giving an impression he was thinking hard. Damien had never known a mix of such powerful emotions: love and affection for this fine-looking man with his hair blowing in the breeze who had been there since childhood as a father to base his own life on and an intense hatred that had developed in him for the dreadful creature he'd found him to be.

Suddenly Docherty smiled, in the warm embracing way he had. 'Demmy, Demmy, let's talk this thing through like sensible adults.'

'There's nothing to talk through,' he said, in a low, breaking voice. 'How can there be?'

'Perhaps there is, son,' he said, back to his former calm self. 'I should at least have the chance to put my side forward.'

'Are . . . are you trying to say there can be anything, anything at all, that justifies you being a criminal?'

'There were eight of us,' Docherty told him. 'You only knew uncle Sean and the two aunties, Carmel and Joan. The other four cleared off and never kept in touch, could be anywhere, we neither know nor care.'

Damien stared at him. This really was a surprise – four missing aunts and uncles.

'Being Catholics, Granny and Grandpa Docherty kept on having kids. We were as poor as tramps on the street: bread and scrape, hand-me-downs, shoes in holes, you name it. Grandpa Docherty might have seemed a nice, mild old man but back in those days apart from being a great one for having kids he managed to drink away a good deal of what money there was. And the government wasn't as generous with taxpayers' money as it is today. We weren't kids who got on, couldn't stand the sight of each other, most of us. I reckon it happens in a lot of families where you're on free school dinners.

'Free school dinners,' he repeated in a reflective tone. 'When the other kids knew you got one and they could see your shirt-tail through a hole in your pants and you were on the small side like me you were given a thorough kicking on a daily basis.'

Damien stood in a state of shock. He'd never heard any of this, not even heard it hinted at, apart from Mum occasionally telling him that Dad had come from a poor but decent Catholic family.

'I fought back,' Docherty went on, 'but it got me nowhere when

208

the others were bigger. I should just have taken it. If you don't retaliate they just get bored and go and kick someone else. But I fought back and lying in a crowded bedroom at night I swore that one day, one day, it would be me in control.'

'These . . . these things that happened to you,' Damien cut in before he could go on speaking, 'you can't think they can give you the right to manipulate people. Christ, Dad, you could have got just as far without being a crook, a clever man like you. That's what I always thought you *were*, someone who'd got on through hard work, brains and luck.'

'What did *you* leave school with?' Docherty said bitterly. 'Starred As. What did I leave with, at sixteen? Sod all. There was no job I could get that wasn't rubbish. So I had to sort it all out for myself.'

'By bribery and cheating the public and forcing young women into prostitution.'

'We're talking *underclass*, Demmy. You know what the underclass is, you read the broadsheets. Families where no one has worked for three generations. Where the kids destroy their bodies with alcohol and drugs, where teenage girls have babies by different men so the state will feed and house them. That's the underclass. I know it very well because I used to be underclass myself till I walked away from it.'

'And these are the ones you manipulate now.'

'I sort out the ones where I can see a trace of the young bloke I was. I give them some point to their lives. I pay them well and all they have to do is exactly what they're told. They're only punished if they ever try to think for themselves.'

'Oh, Dad . . . Dad.' Damien gave a half-sob. 'I admired you, respected you for all the hours you put in and the life you gave us. Can't you begin to understand what it's done to me to find you're a common criminal who likes to have first go with the call girls? Apart from anything else, how could you do that to Mum?'

For the first time since it had all begun, isolated up on the cliffs between the whispering sea and the farmland where cattle placidly grazed, Docherty's eyes fell from Damien's. He sighed. 'Oh, Demmy, the women, once the kids come along, they often lose interest in sex. It might happen to you one day and you'll be seeking out someone to have sex with. Just sex, nothing else.'

'No, it'll never happen to me,' Damien said, to his father's averted face, 'because I love and respect Melanie and always will. Nothing will ever tempt me to go near a call girl.'

After another lengthy silence, Docherty raised his eyes to him again. 'You don't get it, Demmy, do you? Why do you think I always kept it under wraps, the way I make a lot of my money? Because one day I'd be out of it and living on investments. The very last thing I ever wanted was a criminal family like those in London's East End. And the money I made was all for the family, for you, especially. I was so pleased you wanted to go into politics as I knew I could use the money and the pull to help you into a seat. With your brains and drive I could see you in the Cabinet one day.'

'Don't go on,' Damien said bluntly. 'I'll be going nowhere in politics, not now. There's no way the Party will be finding a place for a man whose father's either in the slammer or on the way to it.'

'Oh, come *on*. John F. Kennedy's father virtually bought him the presidency. And where did that money come from? Bootlegging during Prohibition. But John himself was straight as a stick. I can help you go a long, long way, Demmy, and you can stay as clean as a whistle. I *want* you to.'

'I could only have the chance of a political future if your background was swept under the carpet. And I'm going to make sure it isn't.'

Docherty's gaze seemed to hold a hint of derision. 'Let me run one or two things past you. The expensive clothes in your wardrobe, the sports car, the house I'm going to buy you, the generous allowance I transfer to your bank account. Well, how do you think you'll cope if the tap turns off?'

'I'll find it very difficult, no question about it. But I'll get up.

I've already cancelled the allowance transfers, told the bank to return them. Next week I'll sell the car and send the cheque to you. And you can forget the house; me and Mel have taken a flat and we'll buy a house when we can afford it. I'll never live under the same roof with you again.'

It threw Docherty another shock he couldn't conceal. 'There was no need to do that, son. Surely we can . . . can come to some arrangement. It would be such an awful upset for your mum . . . and Mollie. . . .'

'You should have thought of that a long time ago.'

'Look, let's give ourselves a breathing space. Let's have this little break and we'll talk it all through next week. What if I wound everything down and retired?'

'But you'd not have *paid* for anything, Dad. All the crooked things you've done, all the people you've brought into crime, all the dreadful punishments you've handed out as if this were a third-world country. I could never come to any kind of arrangement with you. Christ, I don't even want you as a father.'

Docherty stood in silence again, watching him. He looked to be in the grip of a profound sadness. Then he said, in a low, almost hoarse voice. 'I'll not be going to the police, not now or ever. You'd better accept that and decide how you're going to relate to me exactly as I am.'

'I shan't be relating to you at all, not when I've told Mum and Mollie the sort of man you are.'

'Do you think they'll believe a word of it?' His voice had taken on a rasping note. 'Have you ever *seen* me do any of the things you're accusing me of? It's every bit circumstantial and you know it is. I'd just deny it and that would be that. They'd take my word because they always have.'

Damien was caught by a sudden frustration. He was right, it *was* all circumstantial. His father had conducted his affairs behind a wall of secrecy so impregnable that nothing had ever shown. It would be just the same if the police ever did get round to investigating his set-up. Unless an insider could be persuaded to inform on him he'd be virtually untouchable. And which insider would ever do that when they were paid so well and the consequences too grievous to think about. His father had won.

Docherty's strong features took on a stricken look, then, almost as if he wished he hadn't won. 'Let's . . . let's put it all behind us,' he said in a voice Damien could only just hear. 'I'll pack it in next week, wash my hands of the entire carry-on. I'll take your mother on long holidays; she loves to travel. Whatever you think of me, and I know it's not much, let's turn over a new leaf and move on.'

'I can't do that, Dad, no matter what I've felt for you in the past. You've done too many unlawful things, the sort of things I react against because of the way you and Mum have brought me up. Ironic, isn't it?'

Docherty's broad shoulders sagged; Damien had never before seen his face twisted in such wretchedness. He could barely stop himself from stepping across the path and hugging him as he'd always hugged him when getting home from university for the holidays. Yet he knew his father's intense unhappiness was due to the abrupt shattering of the bond between them and that there was nothing there of the contrition he should have felt for the life he'd led.

Docherty turned away, moved to the cliff edge and stood gazing over the wide expanse of sea as if trying to draw solace from the heaving waves, the endless pattern of the tides and the way sea met sky almost seamlessly on a fine summer's day when the earth's curve could just be defined.

Damien stepped across the track, directed by a force it was beyond him to control. He raised his right leg and thrust it with all his force into the small of his father's back. Docherty pitched cleanly over the cliff edge and down the sheer drop, soundlessly, as if total shock had robbed him of even a terrified scream.

THIRTEEN

Damien, down from the cliff, had been picked up in a police car in Church Street and taken to a mortuary where he'd confirmed the body to be his father. He'd then been driven back to the hotel. Two uniformed police, one a woman, had later been brought to the suite by the hotel's under-manager.

'I'm PC Debbie Andrews,' the woman had told them, 'and this is PC Tim Drake. I'm afraid we shall need to ask these questions so we can make a full report on the accident, Mr. . . ?'

'Docherty. Damien Docherty. He was my father.'

'I'm very, very sorry, sir. This has been a dreadful shock for you.' It was clear PC Andrews had been sent along because of her sympathetic manner.

'Why was your father so close to the edge, sir?' PC Drake asked.

'He . . . he was just admiring the view. The ground was uneven. He just . . . just seemed to lose his footing. I'm sorry I can't explain it better, it happened so suddenly.'

'Was your father on any medication?' the woman asked. 'Did he have blood pressure problems or anything similar?'

'You'd have to ask my mother.'

Tessa, crouched over in an armchair, her face red and swollen from the weeping, moaned every few seconds like a wounded animal. Mollie sat on the arm of the chair with a protective arm round her, her own face drenched in tears.

'Mum,' Damien said gently, 'did Dad take any medication?'

She gave him a dazed look from bloodshot eyes, as if she'd registered the voice but couldn't grasp the words.

'I think he did have blood pressure tablets,' Mollie answered for her in a thin mewing tone, wiping her eyes with the back of a hand. 'I could check his toilet bag.'

'That would be very helpful, madam. He may possibly have had a stroke or a heart attack. Did you go up to East Cliff by the steps, sir?'

He nodded. 'He found it pretty hard going.'

'That could have been the trigger,' she said, 'climbing all those steps when he wasn't perhaps really in trim. The medical people will be able to pin it down.'

They waited for Mollie to return from the main bedroom's en suite, the PCs talking quietly to each other and the woman making notes. Melanie stood near a window, occasionally looking back at Damien. She, too, was in a state of shock but he knew it wasn't possible for her to weep as the others wept. His brain was still everywhere, unable to hold down a thought for more than a few seconds. He could still scarcely believe what he'd done, was still unable to cope with the memory of that sudden uncontrollable impulse that had made him kick the man who'd been his father over the cliff edge.

In that same trance-like state he'd rung the emergency services on his mobile. Within minutes a helicopter was circling above. He'd been told to stand exactly where he was and to wave so that the pilot could get a fix on where his father, or what would almost certainly be his father's body, was located. A motor boat had sped out almost as rapidly from Whitby and the body was picked up and secured to a stretcher, then winched to the helicopter and borne off. Damien was then told, through a loud-hailer, to make his way down to Church Street where a police car would pick him up.

Mollie came back with containers of pills. 'He ... he was taking something called Atenolol and something called

Simvastatins,' she told them, her cheeks still glistening with tears.

PC Andrews looked in a section of her notebook. 'Atenolol is a beta blocker for the control of raised blood pressure and Simvastatins are to lower cholestoral.' She wrote down the milligram details. 'Your father may have had a stroke, sir, or even just a dizzy spell with the effort of climbing the steps.' She spoke in the comforting tone she did so well, as if sensing that eventually they might feel a little better if the death could be considered due to natural causes rather than an appalling accident through losing his footing.

'Were there any witnesses apart from yourself, sir?' PC Drake asked.

'There seemed to be no one around at all. There'd been a few people on the earlier part of the walk but they'd turned off to go to Saltwick.'

The PCs nodded and the woman said. 'I think we have all the information we need, sir. If you'd let me have your mobile number I'll keep in touch when you return home about the formalities and when Mr Docherty's body can be released. May I say again how very sorry we both are about this sad event.'

Tessa gave a muted scream of anguish as Damien showed the officers out. Then they sat or stood in silence, apart from Tessa and Mollie's endless sobbing. The lounge door was suddenly opened and a cheery voice said, 'I'm back, folks. Not a solitary bite from the blessed fish. I'd have been better going for a walk with Brendon and Demmy. . . .' It was Peter, back from his fishing and ignorant of the tragedy. His mouth fell open as he saw the wet faces and became aware of the atmosphere.

Damien strode across the room, grabbed Peter by the arm and led him back into the hall. 'Something dreadful's happened, Pete. Dad fell off the cliff top. He either stumbled or had a dizzy spell. He's dead.'

The healthy colour drained from Peter's face. 'Good God!'

'Mum and Mollie, they're in a terrible state, that's why I

brought you out here.'

Peter gave a dazed nod. He was having trouble breathing. 'I . . . I can't get this together, Demmy.'

'None of us can, Pete. The police have been. There was a young woman PC, who seemed to know about these things. A very decent type. She thinks Dad may have had a stroke or a heart attack with the strain of climbing all those bloody steps. I'd not have let him tackle them if I'd known he was on medication for blood pressure.'

Peter looked stunned. He'd regarded Brendon with great affection. He, too, was broad and stocky with a head of thick black curly hair. Damien had read that some women tended to favour men who reminded them of their fathers and Peter and Docherty had had things in common: they were both hard-working, resourceful, ambitious, good with people. But Peter wasn't a criminal, of course.

'Can I sit down, Demmy? I'm shattered.'

Damien took him in to the dining room, where he seemed almost to collapse on to a hardback chair. He wasn't as obviously distressed as the women had been, but Damien knew he was just as floored. 'He was my idol, Demmy,' he said in a low voice, still breathing heavily. 'I've . . I've never known anyone like him.'

Damien clasped his arm. 'I know, Pete, I know. He was one on his own.'

'He bought us a *house*, Demmy! He made me have money to get my business off the ground.'

'He was a very generous man.'

'It . . . it wasn't just the money; he was so generous with his time. He spent such a lot of it on me.' He began to speak vaguely, with an unfocused gaze, as if to himself. 'Get your debtors to pay on the nail and pay your creditors as late as you possibly can, your cash-flow is crucial, that's what he was always telling me. He sent his accountant round to show me how to pay the smallest amount of tax on my return. I owe him so much, Demmy, I owe him everything. He was such a good man. Look at

216

the money he gave the church. Father Pat told me how he'd helped the poor families in the parish, buying furniture, sending them groceries. He was such a good man. . . .'

Later, Melanie and Damien went to their room to pack their bags for the journey home. Melanie carefully closed the door and said quietly, 'Had you talked to him about. . . ?'

He nodded. 'It all came out, everything.' He spent the next twenty minutes giving her the details of the lengthy exchange he'd had with his father. She listened in silence, her eyes widening now and then. When he'd finished she said, 'And . . . and he wanted to go on as things were?'

'He said he'd pack it all in, live on the money he'd made. I'd never seen him look so . . . so defenceless. I think it was losing the respect I'd always had for him.'

'You don't think . . . falling off the cliff . . . you don't think he was so cut up that . . . that—'

'Suicide? I really can't be sure. It seemed like a genuine accident but . . .' he shrugged. 'Maybe he wanted it to *seem* like an accident.'

They looked at each other. Her eyes were questioning, she was clearly expecting him to say more. He sensed she suspected there was more to tell. He longed to tell her the truth but he wasn't going to. She'd had enough, a lot more than enough of Brendon Docherty this past two weeks.

She stood at the window, gazing out. The old fishing village seemed so peaceful in the afternoon light: the harbour and the little cottages in Henrietta Street and the bones of the Abbey. But it had now become a place of ghastly tragedy and she felt she never wanted to see it again.

She turned back to the room. Damien stood motionless by the bed, holding shirts that needed to be packed as if not quite sure what to do with them. She was certain he was holding something back. She thought again about that fall. Was it likely a man of Brendon's capability would have lost his footing? Could he really have had a sudden stroke? He might have been on medication but so were a lot of middle-aged men who didn't exercise enough or ate a little too well. The pills were simply a safeguard, things doctors handed out like Smarties so that their patients wouldn't *have* strokes.

It didn't leave much else. She really couldn't sell herself the idea that the Brendon she'd known would have committed suicide. Not if he wouldn't go to the police and was talking of retiring to live on the money he'd made. Then she remembered that Damien had once said that he'd have done anything to spare his mother the truth of what his father really was. And then she was suddenly glad that he was sparing *her* the truth of what exactly had happened on East Cliff. Whatever had happened, Brendon Docherty was no longer around to have acid thrown in the faces of young women.

'Demmy,' she said, 'I think it's better your mum and Mollie should mourn him for his sudden death than find out the truth about him in the end if he'd gone on living. Dying this way means the truth will probably never come out.'

His body seemed to slacken with relief. He could tell she'd devined what had really happened. He would never tell her and he knew she'd never ask, but they'd carry the unspoken secret between them and the pain and guilt of it all would be shared. He nodded. 'He'll always be the man they loved as the man he seemed to be. And the police, well they'll simply regard it as a case that solved itself.'

'I thought you'd be dreadfully cut up. Even though he was—'

He began to pack the shirts he still held. He glanced at her. 'Everything finally changed for me this morning, Mel, about how I felt about him. Even when we were having it all out I knew that if he'd been able to face the police and show genuine remorse I would still care about him as I always had. But he couldn't bring himself to do that.'

He fell silent again and the room became so quiet that she became aware of street sounds, the distant cries of seagulls and the chiming of St Mary's clock. 'He couldn't do it and I knew that, in the end, I was looking at a common criminal and that the man I'd always somehow thought he was, right up to this morning, had just been an illusion. I just couldn't feel anything for him any more. But I'm glad the others will keep their illusions intact.'

Melanie turned back to the window. 'I wish we could keep our illusions intact, Demmy.'

'Sit down, Damien. How are things?'

'Thanks for sparing me a little of your time, Frank. It's about my father. I don't think you'll have heard yet. He . . . he died on Saturday.'

'*Damien!*'

'We . . . we were walking together, me and him, on East Cliff at Whitby. He went too near the edge, lost his footing and fell.'

'Damien, I'm so *sorry*. It must have been a dreadful shock for you all.'

The young man was pale-faced, even now, with what had to have been the shock of it and wasn't finding it easy to get the words out.

'Mum . . . and my sister and my brother-in-law are inconsolable.'

'I can imagine.'

But not Damien and his fiancée, Crane guessed, knowing, as they did, the truth about Docherty. Yet Damien seemed very tense. Crane wondered why, as his father falling off a cliff must have solved a lot of problems.

'It was me who got him to go for the walk,' Damien told him. 'I'd made up my mind to have it out with him about his criminal activities.'

'I see.'

Damien began to tell him what had come out on the cliff walk. 'I tried to get him to turn himself in but he wouldn't. He said he'd get out of crime and retire but that was all.'

Crane nodded. 'I'm afraid criminals of his calibre don't do giving themselves up, not in my experience, anyway.'

'If he could have done that, Frank, it would have made all the difference to the way I felt about him. There'd still have been something there of the man I'd once admired. I just despised this dreadful man who'd replaced the father I'd cared about so much.'

'Perhaps this accident,' Crane said, in a consoling tone, 'perhaps it means that everyone who'd no idea of his double life will keep good memories of him. Had he lived there's a fair chance he'd eventually have been exposed.'

'That's how Melanie and I see it. He'll be leaving an awful lot of money. Do you think the police will want details?'

Crane shook his head. 'Had he stood trial and been convicted the police would arrange to have an estimate made of the money deemed to have been made illegally and that would go to the state. A lot of horse trading goes on, as you can imagine. But as it is, in the eyes of the law he's an innocent man who had a successful business. The police won't want to know. And your father would have had the big money salted away in off-shores – the NQAs, in the jargon – no questions asked.'

'I just hope there's enough straight money to tide Mum over.'

'Your father did have a legitimate business as a cover. I gather that that was very profitable, too. If he made a will that would be part of the estate left to the family. The details of the NQA money may have died with him.'

Damien nodded slowly. Crane had a strong impression he still had something on his mind. The tension hadn't left him and he sat on the edge of his chair, hands clasped. He wondered just why he'd come here; today the death would be public knowledge and Damien wasn't really wanting him to do anything. He thought of the first time the young man had sat on the other side of his desk. The unconvincing request had been that he should try and find out how his father made his living. The hidden agenda had been that he really wanted him to bring back information that he made it legally.

And now here he was again, giving him the same feeling, that the things he was saying were a displacement of what was really on his mind. Crane said, 'Up on East Cliff how did your father lose his footing?'

Damien watched him for several seconds in silence, then said in a low voice, 'He was standing on the edge. There was nothing else we could say to each other – it had all been said. He just stood there looking down at the sea. The ground was uneven and when he finally turned back he lost his footing. The police think there's a possibility he had a stroke – he was on medication for blood pressure and so forth.'

'The medical people will be able to confirm that, even though he's dead. And no one else saw the fall?'

'No one. There were several yachts in sight but they were a long way out.'

'From memory, parts of East Cliff are sheer rock face. No ledges jutting out to break his fall.'

'It's . . . it's a straight drop.'

Crane said softly, 'Damien, I don't suppose you had anything to do with him losing his footing?'

Damien sat back in his chair, the tension seeming almost visibly to leave him. 'I . . . I kicked him over. It was just something I felt compelled to do, couldn't stop myself. Are you going to tell the police?'

Crane got up, crossed to the window and stood with his back to it. 'If anyone's going to the police, Damien, it would have to be you.'

'What do you think?'

'Well, no one saw it happen and the Whitby police seem satisfied with your explanation. Look, I'm an old CID man and I live by the law. And the law says you should be punished. But I also believe some things are outside the law. Your father brought a lot of pain and unhappiness to a lot of people for all the love and kindness he gave to the family. You've done society a good turn and I don't think you should be punished any more than you've punished yourself. And it would send your mother into a total decline if she were to find out her son had killed her husband. I'd try to put it out of your mind, if possible, and get on with your life with Melanie. I don't suppose she knows?'

'No, but I'm sure she's guessed. We're very close. But neither of us wants to put it into words.'

'I can understand that.'

'You're .. you're the only one I've told. I just needed to talk about it. I felt I couldn't carry it around with me without *anyone* knowing. I've never stopped thinking about what I did, that . . . that utter compulsion. I suppose it was due to all the things that had never stopped going through my mind: not wanting Mum to know the truth, not wanting any other young woman to have acid thrown in her face, loathing this man who stood in front of me for robbing me of a father I'd always loved.' He broke off for several seconds and then added, 'But when I kicked him off the cliff, Frank, I wasn't thinking at all, it was just blind impulse.

'Well,' he said, almost in a whisper, 'that's really why I came here this morning. I knew you'd be able to advise me. If you'd said I should go to the police and tell them the truth I'd have gone. I trust you. I believe with you what you see is what you get. I wish I'd had someone like you for a father, someone with. genuine qualities to respect.'

Crane had seen it many times before when he'd been in the force. Young men who'd failed to report a hit and run or injured someone badly in a drunken brawl or robbed an old lady. They'd not been bad people, simply men who, like Damien, had had an impulse they'd been unable to control. But also, like Damien, they'd been prepared to put their hand up and take the punishment, and had gained some kind of mental peace by talking about it.

He moved away from the window and put a hand on Damien's shoulder. 'Well,' he said, 'I'm just an ordinary kind of bloke but it's nice of you to say that. If I'd married and had a son I'd have been very pleased if he'd turned out like you. I know it won't be easy but try to put it behind you. Above all, don't torment yourself with endless guilt. Your father's best out of it, whichever way he got to *be* out. Go off and work hard, I've found work's the best answer to most of my own troubles. And when you and Melanie have kids, give them the sort of father they'll always remember for the right reasons. . . .

'Life,' Terry Jones said, 'is a tale told by an idiot.'

'Glad to see you're back in Macbeth mode, Terry,' Crane said, smiling.

'Well, isn't it? That sex-mad trollop knifes Tony, to give me one of the worst days of my working life, and then Docherty goes over a cliff. Talk about bad news-good news, Frank. What were they doing on a cliff anyway?'

'They'd gone for a walk. Damien was determined to have it out with his father about his criminal activities. Well, they talked it all out and Docherty was so pissed off he stood brooding at the cliff edge. And then, when he turned back, he lost his footing and took a dive.'

'You don't think he topped himself?'

'Damien couldn't be sure but men like Docherty, sitting on millions, aren't normally candidates for the big sleep.'

'Too right.'

'No, Damien thinks it was a genuine accident. There's a possibility he might have had a stroke or a dizzy turn. He was on medication and not long before he'd clambered up the hundred and ninety-nine steps.'

'Not wise if you're over fifty. Frank, it couldn't have gone better. With Mellors gone we might never have managed to nail that bugger. Tackling him head on would have set us back a million, no problem. And with his loot he'd have hired the best defence in the country.'

Crane had rarely seen Jones looking so buoyant. 'What about the rest of the gang, Terry?'

'Piece of piss. He had them all so shit scared they daren't pick a pocket at the races without his say so. They'll not be able to think for themselves. Docherty kept total control through two or three older blokes he paid well. We know who they are and we'll be watching them. Sooner or later they'll try to get the old scams going again but they'll not have Docherty's organizing skills, so we'll have them. The foot soldiers, the street types, aren't worth spit. A few raids and half a dozen banged up and it'll all go very quiet, you watch.'

As so often before, Crane wished he was back. It would be fun dismantling Docherty's set-up.

'Yes, he did us all one big favour, falling off a cliff,' Jones said gleefully. 'A really thoughtful career move, saving the taxpayers all that money and us a shed-load of time and trouble.' He began to chuckle. 'You know, Frank, if I'd been on East Cliff with my dad and found out what an arsehole he'd turned out to be I'd have God's own job not to *push* him over the edge.'

The words trembled on Crane's lips but were not spoken. 'Funny you should say that. . . .'